THE PRINCESS
AFFAIR

Visit us at www.boldstrokesbooks.com

By the Author

By Nell Stark

Running With the Wind

Homecoming

The Princess Affair

The everafter series by Nell Stark and Trinity Tam

everafter

nevermore

nightrise

sunfall

THE PRINCESS AFFAIR

by
Nell Stark

2013

THE PRINCESS AFFAIR

ISBN 10: 1-60282-858-X
ISBN 13: 978-1-60282-858-2

This Trade Paperback Original Is Published By
Bold Strokes Books, Inc.
P.O. Box 249
Valley Falls, NY 12185

First Edition: March 2013

Credits
Editor: Cindy Cresap
Production Design: Susan Ramundo
Cover Design By Sheri (graphicartist2020@hotmail.com)

Acknowledgments

The seed of this book was planted in the autumn of 2000, when I had the opportunity to study at St. Catherine's College at Oxford University, and I am grateful to everyone who made that term of study one of my most rewarding educational experiences. As I "returned" to the United Kingdom in my imagination while working on this project, two books proved especially useful for research purposes: *William and Kate, the Love Story* (Robert Jobson) and *William and Harry* (Katie Nicholl).

Writing is a solitary task, but it was made less lonely by several important people. My partner (and sometime co-author) Trinity Tam is my sounding board as well as my Muse, and I thank her deeply for her support, encouragement, and patience throughout my writing process. Brighton Bennett was an invaluable beta reader who also served as my fashion consultant, rescuing me from a panic when I realized I had no idea how to clothe a contemporary princess. Eileen Fitzgerald provided me with important information about the Irish American community in Pearl River, NY. Many thanks also to Cynthia for her feedback and encouragement.

As always, Cindy Cresap's editorial wisdom and advice—coupled with her wit and humor—have honed both the style and substance of this book, and I am very grateful for her input. I also remain indebted to Radclyffe for giving me the opportunity to publish with Bold Strokes Books, and I would like to thank all of the wonderful, hardworking, and selfless people at BSB—Sandy, Connie, Lori, Lee, Jennifer, Paula, Sheri, and others—for helping to market and release quality product year after year. The members of Team BSB, including our many fellow authors, continue to inspire us, and we count you all in our extended family.

Finally, thank you to the many readers who have been so generous with their support and feedback over many years. This book is for you!

Dedication

For Jane, who dared to disturb the universe.

CHAPTER ONE

Her Royal Highness Princess Alexandra Victoria Jane—better known to her subjects as "Sasha"—pretended indecision. As she scrutinized the blond model who had provocatively posed herself to flaunt her barely-there bikini, the crowd held its breath. Even the two other judges sat in tense anticipation. The entire club was hanging on Sasha's pronouncement. She had been teasing the animals adeptly all night, and now she held them in the palm of her hand. The power tasted even sweeter than her chocolate martini.

"Ten." She spoke the word coolly as she raised the proper sign with a flourish.

The room erupted into screams and cheers. Sasha sat back in her chair and sipped at her glass, watching the host try to settle the masses. As their roaring subsided, he thanked the judges and congratulated the new "Miss Royal Flush." Haloed in the center stage spotlight, the winning model met Sasha's eyes and moistened her lips with the very tip of her tongue.

The man seated to Sasha's left leaned over to brush his shoulder against hers. "What do you say, Sash? You, me, her, and a suite at the Four Seasons?"

Marcus "Finch" Finchley, star professional footballer for Manchester City, had been making crude sexual overtures to her for years—ever since his skill on the pitch had granted him occasional access to her social circles. His come-ons had only grown worse over time, and Sasha didn't dignify him with a response. She drained her glass and rose from the chair, then allowed her protection officer to help her down from the stage.

"I'm going back to the VIP area, Ian."

At times like these, she wished she'd been born a Tudor or a Stuart, who would have been well within their rights to order Finch decapitated. Then again, had she been born a Tudor or a Stuart, she likely would have already died some gruesome death herself.

Shouts of "Sasha!" greeted her passage through the throng, and she forced herself to suppress her irritation at Finch's impropriety. It wouldn't do to be caught grimacing on camera—especially when it only took seconds to upload an unflattering shot onto the Web. With a smile and a wave, she acknowledged her people while the paparazzi's cameras zoomed and whirred around her.

As she approached the staircase, a bouncer held aside the chain. She ascended quickly, eager to escape the grasping hands of the crowd. The air grew cooler the higher she climbed, until she finally emerged onto the spacious balcony overlooking the dance floor.

"Are you all right, Your Highness?" Ian offered her a bottle of water, and she took it gratefully.

"Fine. Thank you."

But she wasn't. By all rights, this event should have been entertaining. Royal Flush, one of the leading online poker companies, had spared no expense on their annual bash. When they had asked her to judge the swimsuit competition, Sasha had readily agreed. And then, her older brother, Arthur, had received his deployment orders. This was his last day in London until Christmas, and she wished she could have spent at least some of it in his company. The only reason she hadn't decided to blow off this engagement was because Arthur was likely focused on soaking up every remaining second with Ashleigh, his fiancée.

"Sasha! There you are!"

She turned to the sight of her best friend and business partner, Miranda, who was tottering toward her in a zebra-stripe dress and matching four-inch stilettos. Miri clutched a brimming martini glass in each hand and proffered one as she approached.

"Hi, Miri."

"Did you really prefer that blonde? Her face was too angular and that hair was just too severe. I liked the leggy brunette better. You know the one I mean, right? The third one?"

Miranda's shrill chatter summoned delicate tendrils of pain that, if unacknowledged, would quickly put down roots in Sasha's temples and flower into a full-blown headache.

"Are we talking about women or horses?"

Miranda's plump lips rounded into a small "o" of dismay, and Sasha immediately regretted lashing out. She touched Miri's thin arm with two fingers. "I didn't mean that. I'm sorry."

Miranda peered at her suspiciously from under artificially-enhanced lashes. "You're so cruel sometimes. Even to me. Your best friend. Why?"

A consummate socialite, Miranda was adept at navigating the complex political undercurrents of high society. Her priorities might be superficial, but she had a keen sense of loyalty and powerful influence within their social circle. Surrounded by people who either wanted something from her or wanted to bring her down, Sasha needed a person like Miranda who could help to sculpt her public image and draw prospective clients to her fledgling party-planning business.

She tucked a tendril of hair behind Miranda's left ear. "Finch was being an ass earlier, and he's put me in a pissy mood. I shouldn't have lashed out."

Miranda sniffed, but her rigid body language began to thaw. "What did he say?"

"Just some misogynistic prattle. We should plot our revenge."

The use of "our" had been a calculated move, and it worked exactly as planned. Miri immediately launched into a laundry list of possible tactics, and Sasha was able to nod and smile while focusing most of her attention elsewhere. It would not do to be melancholy, and so she searched the crowd for a distraction. Preferably a tall, androgynous one. Sadly, most of the VIP section was filled with slick-haired men in expensive suits and emaciated women who clung to their arms.

Then the crowd shifted, and Sasha's gaze was arrested by the sight of a spiky-haired brunette in a sports coat and jeans, a tie looped insouciantly around her neck. She stood conversing with David Sterling, the CEO of Royal Flush, and when she laughed at something he said, the spinning disco ball made her eyes flash.

Miranda had trailed off. "What are you—oh."

"Do you know who she is?"

"One of those online poker players. I met her earlier, while you were judging, but I don't remember her name."

Thrilling to the hunt, Sasha took a long sip of her drink before beckoning to Ian. "I require a private room. Make the arrangements, please."

"Certainly." Without a moment's hesitation, he raised his arm and spoke quietly into his wrist mic.

Miranda was crestfallen. "Already? But the night has barely even started! Let's dance. You might find someone you fancy even more."

"I'm not in the mood to dance at the moment."

"So you're just going to abandon me?"

"You know plenty of people here. You'll have a delightful time." Ignoring her crestfallen expression, Sasha pulled her into a quick hug. "Find Finch and exact our revenge. Tell me the whole sordid affair in the morning. Shall we meet at that new café in Piccadilly you like so much?"

The offer of breakfast seemed to mollify Miri. "Ten o'clock?"

"Perfect." Sasha leaned in for a swift kiss on the cheek before setting off across the room toward Sterling and the poker player. Her approach did not go unnoticed—it never did—and the pair lapsed into silence as she approached. Sterling executed the brief bow from the neck traditionally used to greet members of the royal family.

"Good evening, Your Royal Highness." In his designer jacket, collared shirt, and jeans, Sterling was a poster boy for casual chic. "Are you enjoying yourself, I hope?"

"Very much. Excellent party, David." She angled her body toward his companion, detecting the faintest hint of a spicy cologne. "And you are?"

"Please allow me to introduce Nova, ma'am. The best online poker player in the world at the moment."

Nova seemed nonplussed at the prospect of meeting her. Clearly, she had no idea of the proper protocols, and Sasha enjoyed the uncertainty that flashed across her handsome face. She liked having the upper hand.

"Dispense with the 'ma'am,' David. It makes me feel ancient." She stuck out her hand and was gratified to feel a twinge of desire low in her stomach as Nova's warm palm slid across her own. "Sasha. It's a pleasure."

"Likewise." Their brief contact seemed to embolden Nova. "Do you play at all?"

"Poker?" Sasha gave Nova the briefest of once-overs, making it clear that she might be up for other kinds of games as well.

"Yes." The syllable hitched ever so slightly.

"On occasion. My brother taught my sister and me when we were children. We would play for chocolate coins, much to the chagrin of our nanny who thought it wasn't ladylike."

Nova's answering smile revealed two dimples in her cheeks that Sasha found irresistible. Thankfully, at that moment, the CEO of Smirnoff approached and engaged Sterling in conversation, leaving the two of them to themselves.

"It's rather crowded, isn't it?" Sasha said softly, careful to keep their bodies separated by a solid foot of air.

"Getting stuffy, yes," Nova agreed.

When she licked her lips and visibly swallowed, Sasha laughed. "If your poker tells are that obvious, you should take care never to sit down at a table."

The bloom of red across Nova's cheeks was endearing. "Why do you think I play online?"

Sasha laughed, enjoying the easy banter. "That seems wise." She drained what was left of her martini. When Nova's eyes widened in clear appreciation, she smiled. But just as she was about to suggest that they move their conversation to a more private place, the cheerful chords of "Yellow Submarine" began to emanate from her purse.

"My brother," she said apologetically as she reached for her phone. "Hi, Artie."

"Don't call me that." The reply was automatic. "What are you doing right now?"

"I've just finished judging swimsuits and am currently chatting with a delightful poker champion. Why?"

"Forget all that. Come to Ashleigh's flat. I'm having an impromptu send-off."

"At this very moment?" She was torn. On the one hand, she wanted very much to finish what she'd just started. Nova's refreshing lack of pretension likely meant she would be a very pleasant experience, indeed. But on the other hand, she would never pass up the chance to attend a farewell soiree for Arthur, especially since she'd only have limited contact with him for the next several months.

"Yes, right now. No excuses."

Sasha disconnected the call and turned to Nova, allowing her regret to show. "I was hoping we could continue our chat elsewhere, but I'm afraid that won't be possible now."

"Is it rude to admit I'm disappointed?"

"Not at all. Perhaps we'll run into each other some other time."

"I hope so."

Forcing herself to turn away, Sasha sought out Ian, where he waited near the balcony railing. "Change of plans. I'll be going directly to Ashleigh Dunning's flat. Will you inform the driver?"

"Certainly."

After making her excuses to Sterling, Sasha followed Ian out a side entrance and slid into the cool leather seats of the black Bentley. As it pulled away from the curb, Ian angled his body to face her.

"Will you be staying the night at Ms. Dunning's, ma'am?"

"No. I'll likely not stay more than a few hours."

"Very well."

Sasha relaxed into the embrace of the seat and tilted her head just enough to examine her reflection in the window. The early September night was warm and its mugginess had deepened the natural wave of her hair. The near-curls lent her a more sensual air somehow. Even had Nova been inclined to resist, she never would have stood a chance.

Looking past her reflection, she watched London slide by, lights smearing together in a washed out blur. By day, the capital was orderly and proper—a resplendent, well-oiled machine whose heartbeat set the pace of English culture. Sasha knew how to navigate its gears and cogs, but she never stopped feeling like an outsider. By night, London's veneer of civility slipped, revealing sharp edges beneath the glamour. Ironically, the darkness made her feel seen.

Her driver pulled up to the curb just outside the entrance to Ashleigh's building, and Ian jumped out to hold her door, offering her a steadying hand as she stepped out onto the curb. When she smiled at him in thanks, his lips curled ever so slightly in return. When he'd first become her bodyguard almost two years ago, he had refused to show even a hint of emotion. Never able to resist a challenge, Sasha had thrown herself at him for months, intent on crumbling his stoic façade and gaining the upper hand. Finally, after a particularly egregious seduction attempt, Ian had grasped her by both naked shoulders and fixed her with a firm stare.

"You're a charming and beautiful woman, Sasha," he had said. "You don't need to behave this way. But since you seem to need the reassurance, I'm sure I would have broken down long before now if you were my type."

It had taken several seconds before she'd comprehended what he was trying to tell her. Relaxing in his grip, she'd thrown her head back and laughed.

"To be honest? You're not really my type, either."

At that, he had smiled at her for the very first time. "I know."

Ever since that day, they'd had an unspoken agreement. Sasha stopped making Ian's life a living hell, and Ian did everything in his power to protect her—not only from physical harm, but also from the prying eyes of the paparazzi. They weren't friends, exactly. Ian's sense of professionalism would never allow for that. But they understood each other.

Their mutual trust allowed him to wait in one of the armchairs in the building's atrium rather than being forced to stand in the hallway outside Ashleigh's flat. As the elevator sped toward the thirtieth floor, Sasha wondered who would be in attendance tonight. Arthur's innate charisma won him friends wherever he went, but his inner circle was actually quite small. She hoped he'd invited only his closest confidantes.

When she rang the bell, he answered. Tall and broad-shouldered, he took up most of the doorway and immediately enveloped her into a bear hug. She ruffled his shock of hair to make him let go. As he stepped back, he had to push an errant lock out of his warm brown eyes, and she wondered how he would look when the Royal Air Force made him get a buzz cut upon reporting for duty tomorrow.

"Thanks for being here," he said as they walked down the short hallway that opened into Ashleigh's sitting room.

"You didn't exactly give me a choice." But she nudged him with her elbow to take any sting out of her words.

Arthur turned into the kitchen, where Ashleigh was pouring champagne into several flutes on a silver tray. Long, blond hair flowed down the back of her white blouse, nearly touching the fabric of her shimmery black pencil skirt. She turned with a smile and embraced Sasha as though they hadn't just seen each other a few days prior at a family dinner in Buckingham. But that was Ashleigh. She had a way of making each person feel like the most important one in the room. At first, Sasha had been suspicious of her cordiality, but after years of seeing her at Arthur's side, she had come to recognize that Ashleigh Dunning was one of those rare, genuinely compassionate individuals.

"Sash, hi! You look stunning. New frock?" Ashleigh held her at arm's length and rubbed the material of one strap between her fingertips. "Velvet. Beautiful."

"It's an Alexander McQueen. Quite comfortable. I'll have one sent over for you tomorrow."

As Ashleigh protested, Arthur reached over her shoulder for the tray.

"You may as well just say thank you," he said, leaning in to kiss her cheek. "Once Sasha's mind is made up, she becomes the immovable object."

"It's true." Sasha let Ashleigh precede her back into the hallway. "My stubborn streak is the stuff of legends."

As they entered the sitting room, Sasha realized she wasn't the first guest to arrive. Devon Oldham, son of the prime minister and Arthur's closest friend from Eton, was sitting on the loveseat near the fireplace. His new girlfriend perched beside him, looking a bit nervous, or perhaps just star struck. Sasha's lips tightened. This changed things. She couldn't exactly be herself in the presence of someone she barely knew. She trusted Arthur, Ashleigh, and Devon. Along with Miranda and Sasha's younger sister, Lizzie, those three were the only ones who knew her secrets—and even they didn't know everything.

"Sasha! You look smashing." Devon rose to kiss her on the cheek. "You remember Charlotte?"

"Of course. Wonderful to see you." She embraced Charlotte lightly before reaching for one of the champagne flutes. "Shall we have a toast?"

Once everyone had a drink in hand, she looked across their small circle to Arthur, who was grinning happily with his free arm looped around Ashleigh's waist. He seemed genuinely excited about this tour with the RAF, and no wonder. Arthur had grown to become a man of action, like their father. He wanted to be in the midst of important matters—to have a hand in making a difference among the people. Thankfully, he hadn't also adopted their father's temper and judgmental attitude.

"To Arthur." She raised her glass. "You great lug. Don't break anything expensive, and come home in one piece."

Once the laughter had subsided, Sasha chose the comfortable armchair closest to the fireplace. She sipped her champagne lightly as the conversation turned to the topic of the not-for-profit Ashleigh had launched a few months ago—a micro-financing company that worked to provide start-up capital to women in Third World countries who hoped to open their own small businesses.

When Charlotte asked her a question about the living conditions of her clients, Ashleigh reached for a book on the coffee table.

"In a few weeks, I'll be traveling to East Africa to see for myself. I just finished reading this memoir of a man whose life's work has been to build schools in the region. It's very well written and paints a disturbing, though hopeful, picture of what daily life is like."

She passed the book around as the conversation continued. When it came to Sasha, she flipped it open and did her best to feign interest in the jumble of words. Her focus was particularly bad tonight, and once she'd handed the text over to Charlotte, she drank more deeply of the champagne, hoping it would relax her.

"While I'm there, I'll also be supervising the filming of a documentary," Ashleigh was saying. She turned in Sasha's direction. "Which reminds me, I want to throw a party in London for the film's premiere. Would you be willing to organize it? This wouldn't be until sometime late next year, but I know your services are in high demand."

Sasha just barely stopped herself from betraying her surprise. While certainly popular amongst London socialites, her year-old party planning company had yet to be patronized by anyone within the inner royal circle—probably because her father hadn't hid his displeasure at her choice of career. Now Ashleigh Dunning, who would one day be Queen and was already the darling of both the people and the media, had enlisted her services.

"I'll be happy to," she said. "I'm already meeting Miranda for brunch tomorrow. Would you like to come along so we can talk preliminaries?"

"Perfect."

As Sasha was explaining the café's location, Arthur's cell phone rang. "It's the King himself," he said before moving to the far side of the room to take the call. Even as she continued to pay attention to Ashleigh, Sasha kept her ears open to the sound of Arthur's conversation.

"Hi, Father. Doing well, thanks. At Ashleigh's, yes. Just a small gathering. At 0800, that's right. Yes, I'm looking forward to it. Sasha? She's here. Yes, all right." He returned to the sitting area and held out his phone. "Father would like to speak with you."

His expression was sympathetic, and Sasha worked hard not to noticeably grit her teeth as she took the phone and walked back toward the kitchen. She couldn't remember the last time she'd had a conversation with her father that didn't somehow take a turn for the uncomfortable.

"Hello, Father."

"Hello, Alexandra." He used her full name—always had and always would.

"How are you?"

"Fine. I can't speak for long right now, but I wanted to remind you of the reception at New College in Oxford on Wednesday evening—the one your brother was originally supposed to attend."

Resentment soured the taste of champagne that lingered on Sasha's tongue. He could never resist an opportunity to put her in her place. Always a bridesmaid and never a bride.

"Yes, I remember."

"I expect you to be punctual and professional. Please don't do anything to embarrass this family to the Rhodes Trust or to Oxford, Alexandra."

Sasha gripped the kitchen counter until her knuckles turned white. "Good night, Father."

She turned to find Arthur leaning against the wall. Without a word, she pressed the phone into his palm.

"I take it he was an ass?"

"Isn't he always?" She crossed her arms beneath her breasts and exhaled slowly, as if by doing so she could deprive her anger of its fuel. "I know you'll be off doing the right thing, and that it makes you happy. But selfishly, I wish you weren't deploying. Without you here, I have no buffer."

"Sash. I'll be doing Search and Rescue in Scotland, not MI6 in Afghanistan. I'm not going far. You'll be fine. Lizzie will help." The buzzer rang, and he smiled. "Speak of the devil. That must be her."

Delight suddenly trumped Sasha's frustration. "Lizzie came down from Cambridge? Just now?"

"Left a pub crawl with her mates and hopped on a train, just for me." Arthur flashed the megawatt smile that always charmed the media.

As they waited for Lizzie at the door, Sasha resolved to tamp down the remnants of her anger. This was the last night in many months when she'd be able to share the company of her siblings and their closest friends. For the next few hours, she could put aside her frustrations and celebrate her brother's accomplishments among people who truly *saw* her—who loved her for who she was, not who they wanted her to be.

The trick was believing she deserved it.

CHAPTER TWO

M ist shrouded the city streets, lending a ghostly touch to the orderly lines of the neo-Georgian façades lining Grosvenor Square. As she stood in the loose crowd of her peers that had gathered beneath the hotel awning, Kerry Donovan watched the fog curl its tendrils around stone balustrades and Corinthian columns, claiming the buildings for some ethereal, spiritual realm. Smiling at her flight of fancy, she sipped from the steaming coffee cup that warmed her palms.

"How on earth can you be happy at this ungodly hour of the morning?" Harrison Whistler was clutching his own, larger cup as though it could hold him upright. A mop of shaggy dark hair curled around his ears to brush the sheepskin collar of his coat, and his bloodshot eyes testified as to how he had spent his night.

Like him, Kerry had begun the previous evening at a reception for the incoming class of Rhodes scholars sponsored by the American embassy, where she'd had the chance to meet the American ambassador to England and several other high-ranking consulate officials. The event had been her cohort's official sendoff; having completed their initial orientation in the capital, they would continue on to Oxford. There, they would be greeted by members of the Rhodes Trust who would help them to settle in to their respective colleges before the start of the academic term.

Kerry patted the muscular shoulder of her new friend in a show of sympathy. "I called it quits after dinner. Where did you end up?"

Harris flipped his hand over to reveal a club's imprimatur just below his knuckles, and Kerry felt a twinge of regret that she had chosen to miss the group's festivities. Friendships and allegiances were being formed without her, and while she didn't want to become embroiled in the group's burgeoning politics, neither did she want to be pegged as a loner. Not the easiest of balancing acts.

"The Lightbox, apparently." Harris grimaced. "Don't ask me where it is or what it looks like. Though do tell me if you have a surefire hangover remedy."

"You're not going to like it."

"Try me."

"Sweat. An hour on a stationary bike, though I imagine an erg machine would work just as well."

He let out an explosive sigh. "You're making me queasy."

Kerry shrugged, grinning. "Told you."

"Masochist. That's what I get for asking the goody-two-shoes."

Her smile evaporated, ephemeral as the mist. Harris was joking, but even so, the moniker stung. Since arriving in London almost a week ago, she had kept herself firmly in check. While most of her peers had made a favorable first impression, she still barely knew them. Even Harris, who had pulled her into an embrace and called her "sister" at their very first reception in New York, was still too much of an unknown for her to risk letting down her guard.

She was no goody-two-shoes. The restlessness felt like mercury rising, like cumulonimbus clouds building in her brain. She needed a night like the one her peers had just experienced, but first she needed to be settled. Secure.

Kerry inhaled the mist into her lungs, willing it to soothe her nerves. Soon. Tonight, she would fall asleep in her room at Balliol, the college that would be her home for the next three years. In the morning, she would meet members of the university's architecture program. She would buy the right books and get a pass to the library. She would learn the lay of the land. Then, she could relax.

A charter bus pulled up to the curb, "Oxford" emblazoned on its marquee. After handing her bags to the driver, Kerry climbed up the steep steps. The odor of exhaust mingled with the tired smell of the upholstery inside, and the collage of scents catapulted her back in time to high school. Sophomore year—the last year she had taken the bus before inheriting her grandmother's long-nosed Buick. For a moment, the world shifted sideways and she became that girl again: the tall, broad-shouldered girl who could only find grace on the soccer field. The intense, studious girl ridiculed by teammates for her large vocabulary. The model child who habitually bewildered her family by excelling at everything.

On the bus rides to school, she'd made a habit of going over her notes from the previous day's classes. On the bus rides home, she had gotten an early start on her reading assignments. Every once in a while, she had allowed herself to look out the window at the rolling hills and daydream about what it would feel like to go away to college. Her parents had stopped their own schooling after high school. Her sister had done a year at the local community college before getting married. Her brothers had forgone higher education altogether to join their father in his roofing business. Kerry couldn't explain her ambitions, and they made her feel like a changeling. But she could as easily stop dreaming as she could keep herself from breathing.

Really, she'd been about as perfect as it was possible for a daughter to be. There had been no boyfriends for her mother to fawn over, but between school and soccer, Kerry hadn't had the time to date even if she'd wanted to. She had worked hard, played hard, and earned a spot on both Princeton's campus and its women's soccer team. Loans, financial aid, work-study, and several outside scholarships had made it possible for her to attend.

At Princeton, she found Gothic spires and acclaimed faculty and new teammates. She also found Virginia. Virginia, who had taken the seat next to hers on the first day of their humanities class—who had admired the doodles in her notebook as their professor droned on about Plato's allegory of the cave. Virginia, with her spiky, pink-tipped hair and outrageous T-shirts and infectious laugh. Virginia, who had kissed her under the budding cherry tree outside the School of Architecture on the first day of spring. Virginia had endured life in Kerry's closet for almost two years before finally walking away. And who could blame her? She deserved someone who would hold her hand in public and invite her home for Thanksgiving.

Virginia's absence accomplished what her presence never could. The loss of the only person who had truly seen her—and loved what she'd seen—shook Kerry to the core. Her closet was no shelter from the storm; it was Plato's cave, full of shackles and shadows.

Finally, she found the inspiration to confess herself to her Irish Catholic family. In the time it took to speak four simple words, she fell from grace. Her mother quoted Romans. Her father quoted the Pope. Her sister proclaimed her "disgusting." Only in her two brothers did she find some measure of compassion.

But at least she was free.

Kerry slid into the seat next to Harris, who groaned as he pressed his forehead to the cool window. The cascade of memories had set her own head to pounding and she leaned back, closing her eyes. She was not that uncertain, frightened girl—not anymore. She had faced her fear. She had lost Virginia, but won the Rhodes. She had purpose. She had loftier goals now, along with the means to fulfill them. Life stretched before her, a corridor of open doors extending past the horizon. So what if she was lonely?

She opened her eyes when Harris stirred beside her. As the bus pulled away from the curb, he swallowed down the dregs of his coffee in a series of noisy gulps, and she had to smile. Built like a bear but gentle as a kitten, he reminded her in many ways of her brothers. Had he suffered when he'd finally come out? Had his fellow rowers ostracized him or joined ranks around him?

Only when he blinked his red eyes and said, "Do I look that bad?" did Kerry realize she was staring.

"You're fine."

"Liar." Harris massaged his temples. "I'd better pull it together by tonight. We're meeting Princess Sasha, remember?"

Kerry nudged him with her elbow. "I think you're supposed to address her as 'Her Royal Highness Princess Alexandra.'"

"I like Sasha better. Sassy Sasha. Try saying that ten times fast."

"You're incorrigible."

Harris laced his hands behind his head. "Actually, by all accounts *she's* incorrigible. The gossip rags claim she's bi."

"The gossip rags also claim the Rapture is happening next week. For real this time."

He rolled his eyes. "Does that mean you're not going to let me try to fix you up?"

Kerry had to laugh. "Me? With a British princess? You're delusional."

"Why not?"

"For one thing, I'm utterly plebian. A commoner. Besides, isn't there some kind of prohibition against the royals carrying on with Roman Catholics? Even lapsed ones?"

"They got rid of that. And so what if you're not a Rockefeller?" He cocked his head, squinting. "Who could resist those cerulean eyes and fiery hair? Or that chiseled jaw? Or your tight—"

"Enough!" Laughing, Kerry covered his mouth to stop his rhapsodizing. At his baleful stare, she pulled her hand away. "Like I said. Delusional."

"You need to learn to take a compliment."

His dark eyes held a serious expression, and she looked away. Harris, she was learning, could be like a dog with a bone when he sensed a touchy subject. She scrambled for a way to distract him.

"Forget Princess Sasha. Yesterday, I overheard Anna and Kieran debating which of our group is most likely to become president."

He immediately warmed to the topic. "Good one. Don't tell me. I want to guess…"

Two hours later, the bus pulled in front of the Rhodes House, an impressive colonial structure that had been built in the early twentieth century in memory of Cecil Rhodes. Kerry took in the sight eagerly: the portico's tall Ionic columns, the rotunda topped by a copper dome, the slate roof peeking up behind several wide parapets. As they entered the building, she looked around eagerly. The rotunda was bedecked by royal blue banners emblazoned with the university's motto: *Dominus Illuminatio Mea.*

"Can you read Latin?" Harris had evidently noticed the direction of her gaze. "What does it mean?"

"God is my light."

"Are you still a believer?"

Kerry crossed her arms beneath her breasts in a protective gesture as automatic as it was unnecessary. Harris's eyes held no hint of judgment, only curiosity. She didn't have to put up shields against him. He was on her side.

"My head is agnostic. But my heart…" She gave him a half-smile and shrugged. These days, that was all the answer she could offer. "You?"

Before he could reply, the group was called together by a lean, dark-haired man wearing a crisp white collared shirt and gray slacks. His tie was several shades darker than the blue of the banners, and a pair of round glasses drew attention to the freckles that liberally sprinkled his nose. He introduced himself as Brent, their primary liaison with the Rhodes Trust.

Anna stood on her toes and leaned into Kerry's space, hands fluttering. "He looks like Harry Potter!"

Harris gave her an incredulous look. "He's much more attractive than Harry Potter."

Apparently, that was a heretical thing to say, because she huffed off to report her epiphany to a more receptive audience. Kerry shot Harris a bemused glance before falling in behind Brent for a tour of the House. As he led them past the large hall where Einstein had once delivered a lecture series, the extensive library dedicated to Commonwealth and African Studies, and the spacious dining room, he answered questions about the facility and explained their privileges. Kerry could hardly wait to take advantage of them and make this incredible space her own.

The tour concluded in one of the reading rooms. A middle-aged woman dressed in a dark gray wool suit, her hair pulled back severely into a bun, awaited them behind the podium. Brent joined her as the remainder of the group filtered inside.

"I'm very pleased to introduce you all to Mary Spencer, Secretary of the Rhodes Trust," he said before stepping aside.

"Good afternoon, and welcome to Oxford University." Speaking in a rather nasal tone, Spencer over-enunciated each syllable. "On behalf of the Trust, we are delighted to welcome you, the newest class of scholars. For the past several months you have celebrated your success, but now it is time to rise to the challenges that await you. You are all not only representatives of the Trust, but of the United States of America. As you embark upon your studies, remember to acquit yourselves in a manner becoming your status."

"Cheery, isn't she?" Harris muttered as she paused to look around the room, and Kerry struggled to keep a straight face as Spencer's gaze swept over them.

"Good luck and God speed," she concluded, relinquishing the podium once again to Brent. Within minutes, he explained, they would be joined by Rhodes scholars in their second or third years who had agreed to mentor the incoming class. Free of Spencer's iron grip on the crowd, Kerry barely registered his words; she was enjoying the atmosphere of the room, which boasted several clusters of high-backed leather chairs between walls lined with bookshelves.

A table nearby held several platters of sandwiches and pitchers of iced tea. As they mingled and ate, Brent made the rounds. Kerry was amused to notice that Harris immediately stopped shoveling sandwiches into his mouth at Brent's approach.

He extended his hand to her first. "Brent Franklin. It's a pleasure."

"Kerry Donovan. And this is Harris Whistler."

Brent's eyes narrowed in concentration as he regarded her. "Kerry. Out of Princeton. Studying sustainable architecture. Soccer player." He flashed a perfect smile. "Welcome."

"That's impressive," Kerry said as Brent turned his attention to Harris.

"And you led the U.S. eight-man boat to a silver medal in last year's Olympics."

Harris blinked. "I suppose I did."

"Fantastic race. I was never good enough to make it out of the C-boat back in college, but I still follow the sport."

Kerry excused herself and made her way to the periphery of the room. Harris's attraction was readily apparent, and she wanted to give him some space. She was also curious about the books. From what she could make out from their spines, they were all about Oxford in some respect; histories of the town and university, biographies of presidents and famous professors emeritus, proceedings from conferences held on the grounds. She was thumbing through a history of the city during the Roman period, when she heard a soft, "Excuse me," and turned to the sight of a Latina woman dressed in skinny jeans and a pale yellow blouse. Gold teardrop earrings matched the necklace at her throat.

"Kerry, right? I'm Julia. Your peer mentor, or whatever it is they're calling us."

"Hi." Kerry slid her book back onto the shelf, smiling at the mild self-deprecation in Julia's tone. Her palm was smooth, her smile open and expressive.

"Did you enjoy London?"

"It was a whirlwind. When I wasn't in the meetings, I was sightseeing."

Julia nodded. "I can empathize. I went overboard at the theater during my orientation week."

"Is that what you're studying? Drama?"

"The oversimplified answer is yes." Julia laughed quietly. "I can give you all the gory intellectual details later."

Kerry felt herself warming to Julia's easygoing manner. "How long have you been here?"

"This is my third year." Julia angled her body toward the door. "Like you, I'm in residence at Balliol. Whenever you're ready, I can show you Holywell Manor, where we graduate students live."

Kerry smiled in relief. "That sounds perfect. I'm more than ready to be done living out of suitcases."

She collected her roller bag and sketched a wave in the air to Harris, then followed Julia out the front door of the House. They paused on the steps.

"Would you like to go the long way or the short way? The Manor is only a five-minute walk from here, but I can take you on a longer loop past Balliol, if you'd like."

"Let's do the long way. My legs are still stiff from the bus, and I'd love to see Balliol."

The early September day had turned warm and humid, and Kerry quickly stripped off her raincoat. As they walked, she took note of street signs and landmarks. Rhodes House was situated in an area dominated by academic buildings and other colleges, but as they turned toward the south, more restaurants and trendy clothing shops began to appear. As they turned onto Broad Street, Julia pointed across the street.

"There's the Bodleian. You'll be calling it 'the Bod' within a week. And behind this wall to our left is Balliol. You'll be able to see it best from the gate, in just a moment."

A rush of exultation skittered beneath Kerry's skin as her gaze shifted between the checkered courtyard of one of the world's most famous libraries, and the high stone wall that enclosed her new alma mater. There was so much to explore, and she almost suggested that Julia leave her at this crossroads. But that was silly; she had her suitcase in hand and needed to settle in before she did anything else. The term didn't officially begin for another week. She had time.

Julia must have noticed her dragging steps. "Did you want to stop by the college now?"

"I do, but I also want to get rid of these bags. Let's keep going."

She peered eagerly through the rails of the fence surrounding the Bodleian as they passed it. Across the courtyard, she had a perfect view of the library's main entrance, the Tower of the Five Orders. Designed to be an architectural chimera, the tower had been built by using each of the five classical modes. She couldn't wait to see it up close.

"So," said Julia as they crossed the next street, "In your London sightseeing, did you make it to the Tower of London? Are the ravens still there?"

Kerry flashed back to the gleaming black birds that had somehow managed to look regal despite being earthbound. "Still there, wings clipped. The monarchy is safe."

"I'm glad to hear it, especially given the guest of honor at tonight's reception. Did you hear?"

"Oh, I heard. Princess Alexandra. Everyone's been abuzz."

"I'm glad they're excited. Some of the people in my year have gotten awfully pretentious about the whole thing."

"How so?"

Julia's mouth puckered as though she had eaten something sour. "Sasha—you know that's what they call her, right?—is not exactly the brain trust of the monarchy. A few of my peers would have preferred someone more...academic."

Kerry considered how to reply without offending either Julia or her friends. "I'm not much for pretension," she finally said.

"I agree. Who cares about her IQ? It'll be exciting to meet her."

Kerry considered what she knew about the British monarchy. In preparation for this trip, she had done some reading about the current royal family, the Carlisles. King Andrew prided himself on being both an intellectual monarch deeply interested in the affairs of the nations for whom he acted as head of state. He had a doctorate in political science and took as active a role in policy-making as Parliament would allow. His oldest child, Arthur, appeared to be following in his footsteps; he had just completed a master's degree in public policy and was about to begin a stint in the Royal Air Force. The King's youngest daughter, Elizabeth, was also rumored to be quite bright. But Sasha, the middle child, had cultivated a reputation as a hellion since she was very young. After barely making it out of Oxford, she had gone into the party planning business. The tabloids loved her.

"Here's The Turf," Julia was saying as she gestured down an alley to her right. "One of my favorite pubs in town. They say it's been around since the thirteenth century."

"Really?" Kerry peered down the narrow lane, marveling at the existence of a tavern that was three times as old as her homeland. "I'll have to check it out."

As they continued on, they discussed the usual topics. Julia hailed from California and had attended Stanford. She'd been an all-American swimmer but had switched to water polo since her arrival in Oxford.

"Have you heard anything about a Balliol women's soccer team? The website looked promising, but I don't know how up-to-date it is."

Julia raised her sculpted eyebrows. "This is England. Soccer, or should I say, 'football,' is life. I'm sure our women's club will be thrilled to have you." She gestured to the large park across the street. "Speaking of which, those are the college's athletic fields. Very convenient for us, because here we are."

They halted before a sprawling stone house framed by twin gables. A matching wall extended from both sides, enclosing a large yard and several outbuildings. The front door was made of dark-stained wood, and as Julia produced a key, Kerry trailed her fingertips over the small placard that read, "Holywell Manor."

As the door opened, Kerry realized that her new home was much larger than she had originally expected. The Manor wasn't one large building, but four separate wings in the Queen Anne style, enclosing a grassy courtyard crisscrossed by gravel paths. Immediately to her right, an arrow pointed toward the office. Once she had received her own key, Julia led her down a corridor to the middle common room.

"My favorite place to read," she said, preceding Kerry into a rectangular chamber whose windows looked out onto the gardens. Oil portraits hung on the walls and deep couches upholstered in navy velvet surrounded a wooden coffee table. The scent of the air—a combination of wood polish and book bindings—reminded Kerry of her own favorite study spot in Princeton's library. She tested out the nearest couch and smiled. Even more comfortable than it looked.

"I love it."

Julia perched on the table. "Do you want to just drop off your suitcase and grab a bite to eat? Or would you prefer to spend some time settling in?"

"I'd like to get squared away in my room, I think. But can I buy you lunch tomorrow? I really appreciate everything you've done."

"We'll go Dutch. Let's figure out the details at the reception tonight."

After exchanging phone numbers with Julia and receiving directions about how to find her room, Kerry made her way down the corridor and turned into the north wing of the Manor. Too impatient to hunt down the elevator, she dragged her bag up the stairs to the second floor and scanned the doors until she found the one that now belonged to her.

When she opened it, she was bedazzled. Early afternoon sunlight streamed through windowpanes that looked out onto the garden, creating flickering golden patterns on her bed's blue coverlet. The room was small but cheery: the bed was pressed up under the windows, and a large desk filled the opposite corner. A few shelves had been built into the wall just above it. The bathroom was barely large enough to turn around in, but she'd manage.

Kerry left her bag in the middle of the room and flopped down onto the bed. Her bed. For the next three years. She stared up at the plaster ceiling, gaze following a hairline crack that ran diagonally into the far corner. And then she closed her eyes, allowing her other senses free rein. The aroma of clean linens mingled with the sharp scent of pine outside her window. A sudden trill of birdsong grew louder, then faded. The soft feather pillow cradled her neck.

The stillness of the air pervaded her body, and she sank into the mattress's embrace. For now, she could allow herself to enjoy this. To rest. Soon enough, life would resume the frenetic pace to which she was accustomed, but for now, there was nothing wrong with savoring the peace of the moment.

CHAPTER THREE

The monotonous ticking of the grandfather clock had long since burrowed into Sasha's head, making her want to murder someone. Preferably her father's insufferable secretary, who resembled an emperor penguin in both physiology and dress, and who shot her a dirty look every time her phone buzzed with an incoming text message. As Miranda's name popped up once again on the screen, she almost stuck out her tongue at the man, whose name she could never remember. Clearly, he didn't approve of her. Surprise, surprise.

Still waiting?

Sasha rolled her eyes as she typed out her affirmative response. Almost one hour after she'd been abruptly summoned to her father's office in Buckingham, she still sat in the anteroom. Apparently, the Speaker of the House of Lords was in with him, but she suspected they were having a nice chat about the most recent cricket results while she sat stewing. King Andrew was adept at playing people off one another in order to get what he wanted. In this case, Sasha suspected that he wanted to remind her of who was in charge. As if she could ever forget.

Finally, the door swung open to reveal two men, both dressed in expensive suits. The first, pale with close-cropped, salt-and-pepper hair, was rather stout with jowls that hung over his starched blue shirt. The King followed close behind, and the physical differences between them were striking. Sasha had often heard the media describe her father as "leonine," and it was an appropriate adjective. Tall and tan, he boasted a mane of honey-colored hair long enough to brush the deep gray collar of his jacket. Deep-set, piercing blue eyes looked out from under thick brows in a face most referred to as "striking" rather than "handsome."

"Alexandra." The Lord Speaker had a rather thin, nasal voice. "How lovely to see you."

"My Lord Cranmer."

Sasha rose and extended a hand as he approached, preparing herself for the inevitable. When he brought her fingers up to his lips, she decided to be thankful that he wasn't one of the old letches who liked to slip a bit of tongue into the so-called chivalric gesture. As far as she was concerned, chivalry was long dead—if it had ever even existed in the first place.

After a few platitudes, Cranmer left. Immediately, the tone in the room shifted. Her father beckoned for her to join him in his office, forcing her to trail in his wake. No matter what time of day she visited him, the room always felt constricting. Paneled in dark oak and lit by lamps hanging on chains from the ceiling, it fairly reeked of chauvinism.

Once she had closed the door behind her, he gestured to one of the chairs directly in front of his desk. They were pretty to look at—old and probably famous in some way—but incredibly uncomfortable. Worse, they were fairly low to the ground, so that when she sat in one and her father took his place behind the desk, he was looking down at her. Crossing one leg over the other, she tried to fight down her rising tide of frustration by letting out a slow breath.

Her father tapped a folder on his desk, then slid it over. When Sasha flipped it open, she found a calendar on the left side and several pages of text on the right. Immediately, the words began to blur together, and she blinked rapidly in an effort to dispel the effect. If she could only stay calm, it would be easier to focus.

"This is your itinerary until Christmas. As you can see, you will be representing the family at several events for which your brother was originally scheduled. When possible, I've asked Elizabeth to fill in, but for the most part, she needs to concentrate on her studies."

Sasha closed the folder and set it back on the desk. "And I need to concentrate on running my business."

He sketched a wave in the air. "Let one of your associates handle that. You have a duty to your family, Alexandra. To your people. To this country."

"I also have a duty to the company I founded. Which is doing quite well, no thanks to you."

He leaned forward, clearly aggravated. "Did I just hear you compare your inconsequential hobby to your royal responsibilities?"

"My royal responsibilities?" Sasha gripped the wooden armrests of her chair. "To do what? Dress nicely, behave properly, and parade around in the public eye like a glorified show dog? Your entire office is inconsequential, Father. You're the only one who doesn't seem to grasp that."

"Enough!" When his fist slammed down on the wooden surface, she felt a surge of satisfaction at having rattled him. "You will do as you're told, or I'll freeze the assets of your precious 'business.' Are we clear?"

Sasha's grip tightened until her knuckles began to ache. He could and would make good on that threat, and he wouldn't even feel an ounce of remorse. Raising her chin, she met his steely gaze without flinching.

"I hope you're happy with the results you get by bullying others. If Mum could see you right now, what would she say?"

A shutter closed behind his eyes, leeching all emotion from his face. "She would say that I am doing what's best for our family— which, I might remind you, remains ensconced in this happy position at the whim of the public you seem so eager to disregard. Tomorrow morning, before the car arrives to take you to Oxford, you will see Reginald to go over your remarks for the reception. I expect you to meet with him on a daily basis from now on."

Reginald Bloom was the secretary appointed by her father to facilitate his children's official appearances. He was most accustomed to working with Arthur, and Sasha had no doubt that he was dreading his new assignment even more than she was. Perpetually overworked, Reginald was a skinny, frazzled man with a nervous tick above his left eye. She had only to smile in order to reduce him to stammers. At least he should prove malleable.

"Did you hear me? Every morning."

"I'm dyslexic, Father, not deaf."

When he winced at the word, Sasha felt herself rapidly approaching her boiling point. The grating scrape of her chair legs against the wooden floor was wholly in tune with her mood, and she couldn't help herself from calling him out as she got to her feet.

"Winston Churchill was too. And he's a bloody hero."

She spun on one heel and headed for the door. One way or another, Buckingham always gave her claustrophobia, and today was no different. She needed to tell Miranda about her father's threat to their company. She needed to find someone who could take her mind off his tyrannical micromanaging, if only for a few hours. Mostly, she needed an exceedingly strong dirty vodka martini.

"Churchill knew his duty. See to yours, Alexandra."

His words followed her out the door. She could feel the condescending glare of his secretary and the curious stares of the other people now waiting in the anteroom, but she didn't slacken her pace until she stood before the elevator flanked by two members of the Royal Guard. When both inclined their heads and bid her a good afternoon, she bit back a caustic reply and managed to return the sentiment.

Only when she was alone in the elevator did she finally let down her guard. Releasing her hair from the bun in which she'd wrapped it before entering the palace, she stared at her flushed reflection and silently vowed not to let him get the best of her.

"You have all of the virtues I dislike, Father," she quoted as the car reached the bottom floor, and freedom. "And none of the vices I admire."

Kerry woke suddenly to the sight of unfamiliar surroundings. A strong sense of disorientation washed over her, and for one panicked moment, she had no idea where she was. Scrambling into a sitting position, she pressed the heel of her palm over her chest. Her heart was pounding as though it wanted to escape, and as her rational brain kicked into gear, she willed her body to relax. Oxford. She was in her new room at Holywell Manor, where she had accidentally fallen asleep. After checking her watch, she exhaled in relief. She'd slept for less than an hour. It was just past one o'clock, and their dinner wasn't scheduled until six. Plenty of time.

She padded into the bathroom and braced both arms on the sink to stare at herself in the mirror. Her mop of hair was tousled with sleep, and she wet her fingers to comb it back into place. In general, she found it difficult to drift off—even at night—and the impromptu nap surprised her. Perhaps she was more worn out from all the recent excitement than she'd thought.

After splashing some cold water on her face, Kerry wolfed down an energy bar and set about unpacking her suitcase. Within minutes, she had arranged her belongings neatly in the chest of drawers and small closet. Last, she positioned two photographs on the desk—one a picture of her senior-year soccer team after winning the Ivy Championship, and the other a snapshot of her extended family at graduation.

A moment later, she stuffed that one back into her bag. There was no need to torture herself with the insincere smiles and taut postures of most of the Donovan clan on what should have been a celebratory occasion. Not only did her family not approve of her sexuality, but they also had taken issue with her plan to do graduate work in England. Her hometown of Pearl River was still the top American destination for Irish immigrants, as it had been for well over a century. Every year, its St. Patrick's Day parade rivaled the one in Manhattan, and every year, plenty of citizens marched waving the "Get England out of Ireland" flag. Anti-English sentiment still ran high, especially in the older generations. While the dyed-in-the-wool Irish nationalists were proud of Kerry for her academic accomplishments, they were innately suspicious of where she was studying. It was a good thing she hadn't told anyone back home about the guest of honor at tonight's event. They probably would have wanted her to hand-deliver a list of grievances to Princess Alexandra.

Once she was pleased with the state of her room, Kerry sank back onto the bed and considered her options. She needed to purchase a few things to make her space truly habitable—a coffee maker, some fruit, and a bottle of good single malt, for starters—but she wasn't in the mood to do errands right now. In the wake of her nap, she felt restless. Suddenly decisive, she returned to the dresser and pulled out a pair of running shorts and a tank top. After briefly consulting a map of Oxford on the Internet, she pulled on her sneakers and began to stretch.

Despite never having traveled to this city—not to mention this side of the Atlantic—she didn't need to worry about getting lost. Thanks to the uncanny sense of direction she'd inherited from her father, she could point out the cardinal directions automatically and had only to glance at a map in order to learn the lay of the land. According to her Intro to Psychology professor, she had a highly evolved spatial intelligence. Kerry often found herself grateful for her natural aptitude—not only because of her chosen career, but also because she'd never had to request directions to anything. Unlike navigation, asking for help with anything did not come naturally.

A light breeze had risen during her time indoors, and Kerry smiled at the scent of freshly cut grass mingled with lilacs. After slipping out the Manor door, she immediately turned to her left and broke into a jog. If she ran toward the river, she would pass several more of the university's colleges. Then, she could cut through town by a different road than the one she and Julia had walked, and if she still felt like continuing on, she could investigate some of the parks and residential areas to the north.

Almost immediately, the road began to slope downward, curving into a long hill framed by stone walls. On a whim, she brushed one wall with her fingertips, wondering how old it was and marveling at the layers of history she could see with each bend in the road. A Roman tower. A Gothic spire. A Tudor façade. Like the rings in a tree trunk, Oxford's architecture told the story of its long and complex past.

By the time she reached the bottom of the hill, the slow burn of lactic acid had taken up residence in her quads. She welcomed the minor discomfort, relishing the slap of her sneakers on pavement. While in London, she'd opted to work out in the hotel gym, and it felt so good to run outside again.

A tour bus lumbered slowly through the intersection in front of her, forcing Kerry to jog in place for a moment. She would never have wanted to see Oxford from a bus, unless she were somehow infirm. And maybe not even then. The passengers peered out the windows, faces pressed to the glass, completely at the whim of the driver. She, on the other hand, could run wherever she liked for as long as she wanted, seeing exactly what she pleased. There was simply no contest.

She slowed as she passed the gates of Magdalen College, peering through the metal rungs to take in the well-manicured lawns and paths of its central quad. Harris was in residence there, and she wondered whether he was settling in, or off somewhere with Brent. Kerry was glad they weren't living on opposite sides of town. He would be easy to visit. What's more, she had read that Magdalen boasted a very fine chapel choir. Perhaps one day, she could convince him to brave a worship service with her.

After turning onto High Street, she found herself running directly into the heart of town. Buildings marked with the Oxford University seal were interspersed with restaurants, barbershops, bookstores, and high-end boutiques. As she wove between pedestrians, around ornate lampposts, and beneath store awnings, Kerry felt herself transition into her running zone. When the endorphins kicked in, her mind finally quieted. The individual details of the city became sharper— the curved claws of a gargoyle on a parapet overhead, the scent of cinnamon and vanilla wafting from a nearby bakery—even as her lingering anxiety eased. Relaxing into the rhythm of her pace, Kerry pulled Oxford into her lungs and made it a part of her. In medieval times, she remembered having read, the act of walking the borders of a piece of land had been part of several important legal and religious ceremonies. Centuries later, she was following suit—staking her own claim on Oxford by running its periphery. Her lips curved ever so slightly as she imagined what some of her more cantankerous professors would have thought of that romanticized notion.

When High Street narrowed, she turned to the right. Up ahead, she noticed a placard of a large eagle clutching a swaddled baby, and the unexpected sight made her stumble even as her smile broke free. The Turf may have been the oldest drinking establishment in the city, but this pub—The Eagle and Child—was probably the most famous. C.S. Lewis, J.R.R. Tolkien, and their colleagues had met there each week to discuss their works-in-progress over a few pints. Kerry, who had devoured every book in her family's home by the time she was eight, couldn't remember a time when she hadn't been enthralled with Narnia and Middle Earth. Silently, she vowed to return soon and pay it a proper pilgrimage.

Several minutes later, as she waited for a traffic light to change, a black limousine caught her attention. It was idling in front of a nearby coffee shop, and for one crazy moment she entertained stopping inside just to see if she would recognize the VIP. But that was ludicrous; according to her teammates during senior year, she was living in a cultural black hole. Whenever they had discussed actors or musicians, Kerry's prevailing expression had been one of blankness. While her music tastes were diverse, she couldn't seem to keep up with the latest trends. And while she loved movies as much as the next person, she found it much easier to remember the names of characters than the real people who played them.

After one last glance over her shoulder at the limo, she turned to enter the large park to the north of town. Within moments, she felt wholly removed from the cityscape. The gravel path was lined with trees just beginning to change hues, and she took delight in the panoply of color visible from every angle. When the trail forked, she couldn't resist taking the small spur, despite the fact that it led farther up and not back toward the Manor. After a few twists and turns, the path began to skirt a pond, and Kerry smiled at the antics of the ducks and swans as they squabbled over their territory. A small child stood on the far shore manipulating a remote-control sailboat, and the entire pastoral scene inspired a sudden and rare sense of contentment that spread through her chest like a balm.

When the path branched again, she reluctantly chose the fork that would lead her back. It was time to take a shower and run those errands—to prepare not only for the exciting evening ahead, but also for the beginning of whole new chapter in her life. The waiting was over. Finally, after months of meetings, paperwork, and orientations, she was exactly where she was supposed to be.

With the surge of anticipation came a welcome rush of adrenaline, and as Kerry turned toward her new home, she picked up her pace.

CHAPTER FOUR

Sasha slouched in the red vinyl booth farthest from the door, doing her best to casually shield her face from the other patrons who streamed in and out of the coffee shop. It was her favorite in Oxford, and her unofficial endorsement had helped to make it a tourist destination.

Today, she had dressed in her incognito attire: chunky Doc Martens, olive cargo pants, a black tank top, and black arm warmers. A matching beanie sat low on her forehead over her blond wig. Sasha was always gratified by the results whenever she went with this look. Since she had walked into the shop ten minutes ago, she had been checked out by three different women, none of whom recognized her from Eve.

The clickity-clack of Miranda's heels heralded her approach, and Sasha looked up to the sight of her best friend, dressed in a deep blue silk dress with a plunging neckline and carrying two steaming paper cups. She deposited one in front of Sasha before gracefully sinking into the opposite booth.

"You're a saint," Sasha said as she popped the lid off to reveal coffee the color of midnight, swirling with just a splash of skim and a dash of cocoa powder. Perfection.

"How was your meeting with the weasel this morning?" Miri had bestowed the rather uncharitable nickname on Reginald Bloom during their adolescence, and it had stuck.

She shrugged. "Long and boring."

In fact, the first of her preparatory sessions had been long and humiliating, but Sasha wasn't about to admit that to anyone. Bloom had handed her a printed copy of the officially sanctioned remarks for the evening's event. Then, he had made her read it out loud at least a dozen times, until he was satisfied that she had committed enough of it to memory not to flub her performance. The entire time, she'd felt like schoolgirl in remediation.

At several points, she had tried to convince him to let her deliver her remarks off the cuff, but he had rejected the idea out of hand. She didn't need a script. Whenever she stood before a crowd, she could sense its prevailing desire. If they wanted her, she flirted with them. If they required persuasion, she summoned a clever anecdote that would help to prove her point. If they craved reassurance, she channeled the memory of her mother and comforted them. Pulling their energy into herself, she magnified it and reflected it back.

Reading in public, on the other hand, was a nightmare. Letters unhinged from their proper order and rearranged themselves willy-nilly. The page blurred and swirled like a river, engendering nausea and headaches. At such times, the expectation of the crowd didn't serve to inspire her confidence, but to destroy it. Sasha couldn't escape the feeling that despite having practiced her bland speech repeatedly this morning, she would still trip up when she delivered it. That meant more humiliation, this time in front of a crowd of intellectuals and their new, snobby protégés.

If only she could convince Bloom of where her true talent lay. She was brilliant at extemporaneous public speaking in a way her siblings weren't, and yet she was rarely called upon to do it in any official capacity. Part of that was her own fault, of course—having embarrassed her father several times, she had lost his trust. But had he been more tolerant of her as a child, she wouldn't have wanted to act out. A vicious circle.

Miri reached for her purse. "I have some news that might cheer you up."

"Oh?"

"The bloke who owns The Box is opening a club here as well." She passed a gold-embossed postcard across the table. "It's called Summa, and we're on the guest list."

Sasha turned the card over in her hands and perused it carefully. The words shivered once and then were still. The club's grand opening involved a reception catered by one of the most exclusive restaurants in London, a private concert by the hottest new boy band, and an open bar all night long. For the first time since she'd woken this morning, Sasha felt a rush of anticipation. A night of dancing was the perfect remedy for the funk she'd been in since leaving Clarence House yesterday.

"You're more than a saint, Miri, you're a goddess. I'll leave the bloody event as soon as I possibly can."

When Miranda cocked her head, the delicate sharpness of her features gave her a birdlike appearance. Gold teardrop earrings tipped with diamonds framed her jawline, winking in the dusky light of the shop. She had that mischievous, almost predatory look about her that always signaled trouble.

"Why not just skip it? Tell them you're ill."

"This thought just occurred to you now?"

"No, it occurred to me last night when you called. But you seemed so rattled that I didn't think you would be sympathetic."

"Are you trying to taunt me into doing this?"

"Taunt you?" Miri squeezed her forearm lightly. "Of course not. I'm just trying to help you get out of a situation that's clearly making you unhappy."

Sasha leaned back against the vinyl, enjoying its coolness against her shoulders as she took another sip of coffee. Miranda's attempts to manipulate her were always so obvious.

"And you don't want to go alone."

Her lower lip jutted into a pout. "Fine, yes. And that."

As her internal debate waged, Sasha closed her eyes. She knew exactly what would happen if she kept her promise to her father: she would make some kind of blunder while regurgitating the canned lines she'd been spoon-fed. Outwardly, her audience would remain polite, but later she would hear them murmuring. They would look at her slightly askance, with that nauseating blend of pity and condescension perfected by academics. Word would get back to King Andrew, and he would chastise her for not taking her responsibilities seriously.

Well, fuck it. She wasn't going to be controlled by anyone. She would either call her father's bluff, or force his hand in making good on his threat to her company. And if he dared to do the latter, she might be able to spin the story to her advantage. The tabloids were shallow in their interests and fickle in their loyalty, but at least they always listened.

❖

The Great Hall at New College was everything Kerry had anticipated from one of the university's most venerable institutions. Founded in the late fourteenth century, the college's oldest buildings exemplified the Perpendicular Gothic mode, with their high ceilings, tall windows, and narrow arches. The space gave the impression of an ornate cage, but she didn't feel trapped. As she occasionally contributed to the conversation that ebbed and flowed around her, a part of Kerry's mind remained detached and observant, marveling at the intricacies of the ornate vaults high above her head.

Elaborate chandeliers hung down between the arches, and their light cast dancing shadows along the stone floor. The room was nearly filled to capacity with several long rows of tables covered with deep blue cloths, each of which boasted a tall, sweet-smelling candle as thick as the circumference of her biceps. The high table was set perpendicular to the rest and elevated on the stage. Glancing up from her cup of tea, she realized it was beginning to clear.

Kerry wondered where Princess Alexandra was. She'd assumed the princess would be dining with the warden of the college and the members of the Rhodes Trust, but perhaps she would only be joining them for the reception. Harris's fascination seemed to be rubbing off on her, if only a little. She supposed it was natural. Most Americans couldn't help but be curious about the vestiges of the system that had prompted the very foundation of their country.

When the butler of New College stopped at the head of their table to ask them to follow, Kerry pushed her chair back, stood, and immediately winced at the soreness in her legs.

"What's wrong?" Harris asked.

She waved off his solicitousness. "Just a little stiff. I meant to run five miles today. Ended up being closer to ten."

He gestured for her to precede him as they filed toward the door. "While I took a nap this afternoon, you accidentally went on a ten-mile run? What are you training for, the Premier League?"

Kerry laughed. "No, I just wanted to see the city. It was a good way to take myself on a tour."

He clapped one hand on her shoulder. "They have buses for that, you know."

"How on earth did you win silver in the Olympics with your lazy attitude?"

"I'm an entirely different person when there's a coxswain in my life who will chew me out and get my butt into gear."

Kerry glanced back at him, incredulous. "I'm not touching that sentence with a ten-foot pole."

A devilish grin spread across his face, and she only narrowly dodged his attempt to ruffle her hair. When they were forced to wait at the door, she turned warily to face him.

He held up his hands. "Truce. And if you ever want a running buddy, let me know."

"You can come with me whenever you like. But here's the catch: I prefer to run early in the morning."

Harris groaned. "Never mind."

As they filed outside, Kerry buttoned her suit jacket. The temperature had fallen significantly during dinner, and a light rain began to fall as the butler led them across the immaculate quad. When she turned her face into the wind, the spatter of cold drops against her cheeks mingled with the scent of damp autumnal foliage to stir up a tide of nostalgia in her blood. Soccer weather. This was the first September in memory when she hadn't been in training, and her insteps ached with longing for the pitch like the pain of a phantom limb.

A wave of homesickness crashed over her as she thought of her teammates, now dispersed to the four corners of the globe. One of them, their star forward, was training with the national team. The others were either employed or had moved on to graduate school. She missed their easy camaraderie—the way they'd protected each other and teased each other and finished each other's sentences. She even missed her nickname, though she never would have admitted that to them.

But freshman year wasn't so long ago that she couldn't remember how it took time to settle in with an unfamiliar group of people. She had a new cohort now, and though they weren't joined by anything like the ties of shared purpose that bound a team together, some wonderful friendships would surely grow out of their shared experience. She just had to be patient.

"The name may have predisposed you against it, but I didn't think the spotted dick was *that* bad." Harris's teasing whisper sliced through her reverie.

She jostled him lightly in the ribs. "I liked it quite a bit, actually."

"So why the long face?"

"Just thinking."

Up ahead, the butler was explaining to one of her compatriots that the warden of New College had wanted to host this reception in his garden, but that the inclement weather had interfered. As they paused at the entrance marked "Warden's Lodgings," Kerry turned to admire the picturesque view of the quad and its surrounding buildings, most of which were at least two full centuries older than anything on Princeton's campus.

Harris flung one arm around her shoulders. "The only thing you should be thinking about right now is how you're going to behave in the presence of royalty."

"You're the one obsessed with Princess Alexandra. I'm going to leave her alone, and I'm sure she'll afford me the same courtesy."

"Oh, bollocks," he said, and Kerry couldn't help but smile at how easily he'd appropriated the expression. "Where's your sense of romance? We're not talking about the daughter of some media kingpin or dot-com-bubble entrepreneur. This is the British crown!"

Before he could launch into a rapturous ode about "this royal throne of kings, this scepter'd isle," they emerged into a rectangular, mahogany-paneled room that smelled of pipe smoke with a faint undercurrent of wood conditioner. Firelight flickered in the far corner, and Kerry moved instinctively toward the flames. When a waiter appeared before them with a tray of champagne flutes, Harris deftly plucked two and handed one to her with a chivalrous flourish.

"Good evening, distinguished guests." Space cleared around the warden as he spoke. "On behalf of the university, I am immensely pleased to welcome the newest Rhodes scholars to Oxford. I shan't bore you with a long speech, and I look forward to conversing with each of you individually. I have only one announcement: Her Royal Highness Princess Alexandra sends her regrets with the news that she is ill, and will therefore be unable to attend our soiree this evening." Harris's face fell even as the warden raised his own glass high. "Now, for a toast: may your time with us be at once challenging and illuminating, and may you bear that light with you when you finally travel hence. Cheers."

Slipping her arm around Harris's waist, Kerry lightly clinked her glass with his. "I'm sorry. I know you were looking forward to basking in her presence."

As she watched, his disappointment gave way to determination. "We're here for two years at the very least. Plenty of time to have a royal encounter."

"That's the spirit. Oh, look—there's Julia. Let me go introduce you."

For the next hour, Kerry made a methodical effort to say all the proper things to all the proper people. Burying her melancholy, she slowly circuited the room, moving from group to group like a honeybee gathering nectar. This performance was one she'd delivered successfully many times before, and it came easily now. She sipped only lightly from her flute as she exchanged pleasantries with her peers, with the warden, with members of the Rhodes Trust. The approval of her superiors washed over her like a drug, blunting her lingering homesickness. She belonged here. She could do this. Already, the pieces were falling into place.

As the reception drew to a close, Brent mustered them near the fireplace. "We're very sorry that Princess Alexandra was unable to be present," he said. "But I have some good news. Thanks to one of our trustees, your names have been added to the guest list at Summa, a brand new nightclub in town. If you're interested in continuing tonight's celebration, please stop by. Otherwise, I'll see you at our morning breakfast."

The excited hum began as soon as she walked away. Summa was Latin for "highest." Kerry knew that much. But her peers had far more specific information. Anna informed them that it was owned by the same person behind one of the most exclusive clubs in London. Tonight was the grand opening, and she'd heard that someone famous was giving a private concert. The event was nearly impossible to get into, and yet they'd all just been given a free pass.

"This is so exciting!" Harris linked his arm through hers as they reemerged into the misty night.

Kerry didn't answer right away. She'd never been inside a club of Summa's caliber, and part of her wanted very badly to witness the dazzling spectacle. The rest of her was fatigued and needed to do some recharging, far away from crowds and noise. Harris must have sensed her hesitation, because he stopped and grasped her shoulders.

"You're coming with us. No excuses."

"But—"

His eyes reflected the wet lamplight. "Once classes have started, Kerry Donovan, I'll let you sequester yourself all you like. But not tonight. Not when we have the chance to pretend we're VIPs already." The serious set of his jaw gave way to a smile. "Besides, what if I need a wingman?"

Kerry threw up her hands in surrender. Harris was right. Tomorrow would come soon enough. She had done well at the reception. She was on the right track. She could indulge just a little, and enjoy this unexpected perk. After all, how often did the name of a blue-collar kid from Pearl River appear on an exclusive guest list anywhere?

"All right. I'll come along."

Twenty minutes later, she was riding an elevator up to the penthouse level of a sixteenth century tower near the southwest corner of the city. This building had likely once served as a guard post of some kind, perhaps during the English civil wars. Now it served the desire of the elite socialites for a gathering place where the rabble couldn't interrupt them. She wondered what Cromwell would have thought.

Kerry followed Harris into the club, which fused the original early-modern stone architecture with translucent partitions and a transparent ceiling. She wished fleetingly that the stars were out, before her attention was drawn to the stone bar topped with frosted glass. Colored lights embedded into the ceiling playing across its surface in shimmering, almost psychedelic patterns.

"Epic!" Harris shouted over the throb of the DJ's electronic beat. "Let's get a drink."

Kerry followed him to the bar and ordered a Sazerac. Her college friends had poked fun at her for her love of what they called "old man" drinks, but the bartender seemed excited to mix something that required a bit of skill. As they waited, Kerry angled her body to get a good view of the dance floor. Some of her new friends were already out there, grinding against both strangers and each other. Idly, she wondered if their group had missed the band, or whether it would be performing later.

And then the crowd parted to reveal a woman in a shimmering, open-back silver dress, her wavy dark hair brushing against her delicate collarbone as she swayed in time to the music's rhythm. She was surrounded by a ring of admirers, but she had made the beat her own. She danced with none of them for more than a few moments before turning, always turning, in search of her own space. Kerry's breath caught at the sway of her hips and the light sheen of sweat at her temples and the brilliant emerald color of eyes that were suddenly locked on hers.

Harris cursed beneath his breath and gripped Kerry's arm hard enough to bruise. She wanted to ask if he knew the identity of the woman, but the words stuck in her throat. Fortunately, he had become adept at reading her mind.

"*That* is Princess Alexandra. And she's checking you out."

The princess turned away. A light tap on Kerry's shoulder heralded the arrival of their drinks, and she closed her hand tightly around the glass as though it might be able to anchor her to reality. She took a deep breath followed by a long sip, and finally, logic kicked in.

"She was not checking me out. She just glanced this way."

Harris's drink remained untouched on the bar, his attention riveted to the crowd.

"Oh, really? Because she just 'glanced this way' again."

Steeling herself, Kerry looked back to the dance floor. "What are you talking about? I don't even see her now."

"To my right. Near that cluster of tables."

Princess Alexandra had retreated to the periphery and was engaged in a tête-à-tête with a blond woman who was wearing high heels so tall it was a wonder she didn't topple over onto her face. Kerry was struck by the disparity between the two women. On the surface, they were similar. Both wore sleek, form-fitting dresses that probably cost at least ten times more than Kerry had ever had in her bank account. But while the blonde was elaborately coiffed and made-up, the princess seemed wild around the edges. More unrestrained. Kerry couldn't tell exactly why she got that impression—her hair, perhaps, or maybe her posture—only that it was very strong. The more she looked at Princess Alexandra, the faster her heart raced.

"You and the rest of the world," she murmured.

"What?" asked Harris.

"I guess she lost interest." Kerry made her tone light. "You're crazy, you know that?"

He shook his head as he reached for his drink. "Believe me, Ker. She was checking you out. I know attraction when I see it." He leaned in closer. "And you seemed pretty gobsmacked, too."

Kerry could feel the flush crawling up her neck, but she refused to act flustered.

"Of course I was. She's beautiful."

"Who is?"

Kerry didn't have to turn around to know whose lilting, soprano voice had spoken the words; Harris's expression betrayed all. His back went ramrod straight, his thick eyebrows shot into his hairline, and his hand visibly trembled as he set down his glass. He opened his mouth, but no sound emerged.

The sudden roar that filled Kerry's ears made her feel a little dizzy, and she kept one hand on the bar as she turned. Alexandra looked even more striking now than she had from a distance. Her full lips held the hint of a knowing smile, and Kerry did the only thing she could think of. She confessed.

"You, Your Royal Highness."

The bridge of her nose crinkled adorably as her smile broke free. "Please. It's Sasha. And you are?"

"Kerry Donovan." Kerry wasn't at all sure about whether commoners were encouraged—or even permitted—to shake the hands of princesses. Fortunately, Sasha solved her dilemma by reaching for her hand and squeezing briefly as she grazed her thumb across Kerry's knuckles.

"Hello, Kerry."

As Sasha introduced her friend, Miranda Howard, Kerry focused on taking slow, steady breaths. She had just told a British princess that she was beautiful, and now they were chatting. Subtly, she dug the fingernails of her free hand into her thigh. She wasn't dreaming.

"And this is Harris Whistler." Kerry didn't know how she was managing to keep from stammering.

"We missed seeing you at the reception earlier this evening," Harris blurted.

In the ensuing awkward silence, Kerry fought not to smack his beefy shoulder. For someone so bright, he could be incredibly dense. Why had he called attention to her absence? Clearly, her illness had been a convenient excuse. Could he think of nothing better to say?

Sasha's eyes narrowed. "You're both Rhodes scholars, then?"

Kerry hurried to speak before Harris could shove his other foot into his mouth. "We are." She flashed what she hoped was a charming grin. "I'm smarter, obviously."

Sasha laughed—a hearty sound that wasn't at all what Kerry would have expected from a princess. Endearing and infectious, it lightened the mood considerably.

"And what are you studying?"

"Sustainable architecture," Kerry said, thankful that by now she could explain her chosen profession without even having to think. "Specifically, I'm interested in developing techniques for modifying historical buildings in order to make them more environmentally conscious."

"That's fascinating. I hope it goes well for you."

She seemed genuinely interested, but Kerry had no doubts that Princess Alexandra was adept at bluffing. As Harris chimed in about his focus on colonial history, Kerry snuck another glance at Sasha. This close, she could appreciate the finer details of her beauty—the curl of her long lashes, the light flush dusting her cheekbones, the elegant curve of her lips. For several surreal minutes, they chatted about superficial topics—where Kerry and Harris were from and how they were liking Oxford. And then the DJ put on a new, popular song that roused a cheer from the crowd.

"Let's dance." Sasha slipped her hand back into Kerry's grip. Her fingers were warm and smooth, and as they entwined with Kerry's, a spark kindled low in her belly.

Before she could reply, she was being led out onto the dance floor. When Sasha let go and began to move with the beat, Kerry felt the strangest mixture of relief and regret. In an effort to calm her racing mind, she tried to focus on finding and maintaining some sort of rhythm instead of simply flailing about.

At first, Sasha danced several feet away across their small circle, leaving Kerry with enough space to admire the sensual grace of her movements. As Sasha raised her slender arms above her head, Kerry was drawn to the elegant lines of her collarbone and the lone diamond that rested against her throat, winking in the light of the strobe. It was smaller than she would have expected from a member of the royal family, and she wondered if the delicate necklace had some kind of sentimental value. Then Sasha spun in a tight circle, and Kerry found herself mesmerized by the slide of silver fabric up and down her firm thighs.

Blindsided by a rush of desire, Kerry struggled to catch her breath. She felt as though she'd suddenly been plunged into an entirely different world where she didn't know the rules—a world in which a stranger had the power to so completely ensnare her attention. She suddenly wanted to believe in sorcery. What other way was there to explain these feelings?

The crowd grew larger around them, forcing their small circle to collapse. Sasha's arm brushed against Kerry's, sending a bolt of electricity through her. When she sucked in a sharp breath, Sasha's lips curled. She tipped her head to the side.

"Let's get another drink."

The crowd parted before Sasha like the Red Sea and Kerry trailed in her wake, helpless to resist her magnetism even if she'd wanted to. She didn't glance back at Harris, afraid of breaking the spell. Once they reached the bar, a space opened up for them immediately. Sasha ordered champagne. The drinks arrived within moments, and she raised her flute, clearly on the cusp of proposing a toast. The swirling lights created rainbows in the bubbling glass and glinted off a gold ring inlaid with tiny emeralds on the index finger of her left hand. The sight of her elegant fingers, tipped by short, well-manicured nails painted the same shade as her eyes, made Kerry's mouth go dry.

"To new beginnings," Sasha said, leaning her glass forward.

Feeling herself blush, Kerry tore her gaze away from Sasha's hands and clinked their flutes together. Silence fell between them then, and Kerry frantically wracked her brain for a new topic of discussion. What was one supposed to chat about with a member of the royal family? Sasha was a party planner by profession, but before tonight, Kerry had never been to the kind of lavish event that drove the princess's business. Sasha had enjoyed high-profile trips to southern Africa and Australia in recent years, but before two weeks ago, Kerry had never even traveled outside the eastern seaboard of the United States. She didn't know anything about trends in high fashion or the charities Sasha had chosen to patronize. What on earth could they talk about?

As her panic escalated, Kerry finally decided to be honest. "How does it feel to know that everyone in the room is looking at you?"

Sasha's eyes widened slightly, and then she laughed. "I'm accustomed to it. But I think you're wrong. At least half of them are looking at you."

Kerry didn't particularly want to think about that, and she kept her eyes firmly trained on Sasha's face. Not that that was a hardship. "Only because I'm fortunate enough to be sharing a drink and conversation with the Princess Royal."

"Wrong again." A mischievous smile played around the corners of Sasha's lips. "I haven't been able to stop looking at you since you arrived."

The confession momentarily robbed Kerry of her breath. "That's...well, that's very flattering."

Sasha polished off the contents of her glass and returned it to the bar, never once breaking their gaze. "I want you to wait right here for a few minutes." The words were soft, but they held an edge of command that made Kerry's heart pound even faster. "Can you do that for me?"

"Absolutely."

Kerry stood rooted to the floor as Sasha set off across the room. Her eyes feasted on the elegant contours of Sasha's shoulder blades, the strong curve of her calf muscles, the tantalizing hint of a tattoo on her right side. She was exquisite. No other word came to mind.

Sasha paused at one of the tables set against the wall to confer with a tall man dressed flamboyantly in a white tuxedo and fiery red shirt. After kissing her on both cheeks, he inclined his head and listened as she spoke, then nodded. A moment later, she turned away and promptly disappeared into the crowd. Kerry blinked and peered fiercely through the hazy air, but to no avail. She was gone.

Was that it, then—the end of her royal encounter? Sasha had told her to wait, but what if that had been a ploy to escape? By being honest, had Kerry made the wrong decision? Their chemistry had been undeniable, or so she had thought. But perhaps she'd been utterly wrong. As she stood sipping her drink, she focused on bringing her heart rate back down to normal. Even if Sasha didn't return, this would go down as one of the crazier days in her life.

"Kerry?"

At the light pressure on her shoulder, she turned to see the tall, waif-thin woman Sasha had introduced as Miranda standing behind her. "Hello," she said, hearing the uncertainty in her own voice. What did this woman want with her?

"Follow me, please," she said with a knowing smile, and set off in the same direction Sasha had gone without looking back to see if she would obey.

Kerry's legs propelled her forward even as her mind erupted in tumult. Was Miranda leading her to an assignation? There was no other explanation for the secrecy, was there? Should she turn around and leave, or keep going? If she found herself alone with Sasha, what would happen? She hadn't so much as kissed anyone since Virginia. Was she really considering some kind of tryst with a member of the royal family?

Then again, perhaps she was being too hasty. Maybe Sasha just wanted to talk without so many eavesdroppers nearby. Just because she had a reputation didn't mean it was true. And even if she did want something…physical…that didn't mean Kerry had to say yes. Once she learned Sasha's intentions, she would make the smart decision.

Miranda led her to a door marked "Staff Only" and produced a key. It opened onto a narrow corridor, and she paused at the first door on the right. After knocking four times, she turned around and headed back the way they had come.

"Have fun." The words trailed behind her along with the scent of her perfume.

Seconds later, Sasha appeared in the threshold. "I'm glad you came," she said, beckoning Kerry inside.

"I don't really know what I'm doing here."

As the door closed behind them, Kerry caught a glimpse of a glass-topped desk and leather chair before Sasha filled her field of vision, eclipsing everything else. When those sparkling green eyes bored into hers, Kerry was helpless to look away.

"Don't you?"

"I—I might be starting to get an idea." Kerry heard her voice crack, and felt an answering snap in the steel cord of her resolve. "Is this really wise?"

Sasha bridged the gap between them and pressed one finger to Kerry's lips. The touch burned like a shot of whiskey, spreading tendrils of heat throughout her limbs. "Don't think. Just feel." She took one step forward, then another, until their bodies were flush. The sensation of her breasts pressing against Kerry's ribcage was dizzying.

"You feel incredible."

"You make me wish I'd attended that reception." Sasha twined her arms around Kerry's neck as she spoke. "But believe me when I say my absence was for the best."

Kerry licked her lips, willing her voice to work. "Oh? For whom?"

"For everyone."

"I'm not sure I can believe that, actually."

"You're smooth."

When Sasha began to toy with the short strands of hair on the nape of Kerry's neck, Kerry finally dared to cup her waist. The fabric of the dress was sleek and warm, and when she trailed her fingertips along the twin curves of Sasha's hips, a light shiver greeted her touch. Not only beautiful, not only alluring, but also responsive.

Desperately, Kerry grasped for the thread of their conversation. "No. Just honest."

"In that case," Sasha whispered, "tell me honestly: do you want to kiss me?"

The wanting was a riptide, pulling Kerry under. Drowning out the alarm bells.

"More than I want to take my next breath."

Sasha raised herself up onto her toes and tightened her grip on Kerry's neck. Her glistening lips were mere inches away.

"Then do it."

Slowly, Kerry bridged the gap between them to brush her mouth across Sasha's. The touch was fleeting—as light as butterfly wings against flower petals—and immediately, she craved more. Again, she indulged in the skimming touch, and then again, until she felt a sharp tug at her neck. Exultant, she dipped her head to catch and hold Sasha's lips with her own. Within moments, she was lost in incomparable heat and sweetness and softness.

When Kerry dug her fingers into the soft skin above Sasha's hips, Sasha groaned into her mouth. Galvanized, Kerry skimmed her tongue along lips that parted instantly, granting her access. Sasha sucked lightly on her tongue, and Kerry shivered. Heat flared between them as the kiss intensified, until their tongues tangled and their teeth clashed. Surrendering to her own need, Kerry slid her hands down to pull Sasha tightly against her thigh, wringing a tortured moan from her throat. Sasha's hips jerked and Kerry drove her hand down, down until she encountered smooth skin, then up under the hem of her dress—

The door opened.

Kerry leapt backward as Sasha spun away, but after the initial surge of adrenaline, her loss felt worse than the fear of discovery. Squaring her shoulders, she stepped into the path of the interloper, vowing not to be a coward. A lean man stood just inside the door, wearing a suit that matched the color of his dark hair. Perhaps she could distract him.

"What's the matter, Ian?" Sasha sounded breathless but not upset. Her words halted Kerry in her tracks. She knew him?

"Your Royal Highness, an impromptu business meeting will be conducted soon in the office down the hall," he said, all trace of censure absent from his tone. "To be safe, you'd best leave now."

Sasha shot her a rueful look. "Go ahead, Kerry. I'll meet you back on the dance floor."

Kerry nodded. Heart pounding against her rib cage, she turned toward the door. As she walked past the man—Ian—he didn't so much as meet her eyes. Forcing herself not to cast a backward look, she focused on taking one step after another. Disbelief warred with the shattered remnants of her desire. Upon reentering Summa, she was immediately engulfed by a wall of sound that echoed the roar in her fevered brain. The club carried on as though mere moments before, she hadn't been locked in a passionate embrace with the woman second in line to the British throne.

No one had noticed. But if Ian hadn't interrupted them, they might have been caught. The realization doused her ardor more effectively than a bucket of cold water. Suddenly, she wanted to slam her fist against the wall—to punish herself for her own stupidity. Instead, she hustled toward the exit, intent on being long gone before Sasha could notice. What was she doing? Why had she let herself be trapped by the intricate web of Sasha's charisma? She could easily have been a tabloid headline—a disgrace to the Rhodes Trust before she had even begun her course of study.

Kerry took the stairs instead of the elevator, pounding out her frustration against the concrete. The cool, misty air was a relief after the heat of the club, and she turned her face up to the clouds to catch the moisture, hoping it could somehow wash away her lingering arousal. She'd been such a fool. An undeservedly fortunate fool. But as she turned back toward Holywell Manor, one comforting thought pierced through her self-recriminations.

At least she would never see Princess Alexandra again.

CHAPTER FIVE

Sasha was finishing her first cup of coffee in front of the morning news when Miranda emerged from the suite's second bedroom wearing only a terrycloth robe monogrammed with the hotel's insignia. Sasha downed the dregs of her mug in an attempt to mask her disappointment. She'd been hoping to slip out before Miri could notice.

Miranda blinked at her, clearly surprised. "You're awake. And dressed."

"I'm going out."

"If you give me twenty minutes, I'll go with you."

Seeing as it usually took Miranda nothing short of an hour to prepare herself, twenty minutes was quite the concession. Still, Sasha firmly shook her head.

"Don't bother. I'm going to drop by a breakfast for the Rhodes scholars. Hopefully, that will placate the trustees. And my father."

Miranda's eyes narrowed. "Bollocks. You just want to see her again."

Sasha's mind's eye focused on the memory of Kerry as she'd looked just before they'd kissed: her sunset hair, her tropical eyes, her parted lips. The mental image made her heart skitter in her chest. Miranda's accusation was spot on. Her desire to see Kerry again had been strong enough to drive her out of bed before ten o'clock—an exceedingly rare event—but she wasn't about to admit it.

"Believe what you like." Sasha rose, smoothed the front of her dress, and headed for the hall closet.

"Why are you being so cagey?"

Biting back a quick retort, Sasha took a deep breath as she shrugged into her pea coat. It wasn't Miri's fault that she hadn't slept well and was in a sour mood. Still, a line needed to be drawn.

"When I want to explain myself to you, I will. For now, I'm leaving. I'll be back by noon."

Before she had to witness Miranda's pout, Sasha stepped into the hallway. Ian was waiting outside, and after bidding him a good morning, she fell silent again. Thankfully, he didn't say anything beyond returning the sentiment, and she made a note to get him something extra nice for Christmas this year.

As he preceded her through the revolving door, she turned up her collar against the morning chill. Last night's rain had washed the streets and purged the humidity from the sky. Breathing in the crisp air, she smiled at the first taste of autumn. Ian moved toward the car idling at the curb, but she reached out to stop him.

"Would you mind if we walked?"

He looked up and down the street, and she could practically hear his internal debate. The sidewalks were busy but not overly crowded, and she was making an unscheduled trip only a few blocks away. Her request didn't pose much risk. Finally, he nodded.

"Very well, ma'am."

As they walked, Sasha indulged her own nostalgia, hearkening back to the pub crawls, the theme parties, the late nights spent "studying" that had devolved into prank-playing. Her years as a student here had been mostly happy ones, marred only by a few unpleasant conversations with her tutors and the administration about her less than stellar academic performance.

When she indulged in a sigh, Ian looked over in concern. She smiled, wanting to reassure him. At times like these, she wished she could treat him like a friend—to link their arms together and ask his advice on matters of fashion, or laugh at the social faux pas from the previous evening, or confess her latest crush.

Unbidden, the image of Kerry's face rose again to the forefront of her mind. Sasha shook her head, silently vowing not to think about her in those terms. They'd barely spoken, after all. They knew next to nothing about each other. What's more, Kerry had rejected her. Once

Sasha had returned to the dance floor, she had scoured the club to no avail. She'd tried not to be too obvious about it, but she felt like an idiot all the same. Kerry hadn't waited.

Worst of all, when Sasha finally threw in the towel and considered seeking out another potential conquest, she'd found no one who caught her eye. Eventually, she had returned to her empty hotel bed, restless and peeved. And now, after a poor night's sleep, she was pursuing the only woman who had ever walked away. At the thought, she very nearly stopped in her tracks and turned around. Why couldn't she just let Kerry bloody Donovan go and call the entire experience a wash?

"Because that was the best kiss of your life, that's why," she groused under her breath.

"I'm sorry, ma'am, I didn't catch that," Ian said.

She waved his question away, hoping he hadn't noticed the color she could feel rising in her cheeks. Maybe he would attribute her flush to the coolness of the air. Taking a deep breath, she willed herself to stop remembering the taut strength of Kerry's body pressed against hers and the warmth of her touch that had seeped through her dress to set her skin ablaze. An echo of the heat surged down her spine at the visceral memory of digging her fingers into the nape of Kerry's neck as their tongues dueled. Sasha wanted to scream, and she really couldn't. Ian would never let her go for a walk again.

Struggling to maintain her equilibrium, she took deep breaths and tried to distract herself by paying attention to the subtle ways in which the city had changed since her graduation over a year ago. But the smattering of new boutiques, restaurants, and novelty shops couldn't hold her attention. No matter what she did, her mind drifted back in time, diabolically picturing what might have happened had she and Kerry not been interrupted.

Thankfully, the daydream shattered when she rounded a corner to find herself facing the imposing façade of Rhodes House. After chatting briefly with the porter, Ian ushered her inside the tall, wrought-iron fence. Sasha glanced at her watch as they passed through the tall columns guarding the entrance. Half past nine o'clock. Right on cue for a fashionably late entrance.

The Secretary of the Rhodes Trust—a willowy woman whose layered chestnut hair was streaked with gray—was waiting just inside the rotunda. She inclined her head deferentially as Sasha approached.

"What an unexpected pleasure, Your Royal Highness. My name is Mary Spencer."

Sasha offered her hand. "Good morning, Ms. Spencer. I apologize that I couldn't be in attendance last night."

"Quite all right, of course. Lovely of you to make the time this morning."

She turned and led them into the dining hall, chattering all the while about how what a magnificent job the Trust had done this year of selecting a diverse, intelligent, and ambitious group. Sasha forced herself not to roll her eyes. Had she honestly subjected herself to a cadre of academics, just because of one perfect kiss? What was her life turning into—some kind of modern day farce of a fairytale?

And then she caught sight of Kerry, who had chosen a seat at the farthest table near one of the tall windows where she was deep in conversation with another woman. Sunlight streamed over her, rendering her curly hair a crown of flames. Dressed less formally than the night before in gray slacks, a white collared shirt, and a thin black sweater, she made Sasha's mouth water. There was no use in denying it.

The secretary cleared her throat. "Ladies and gentlemen, I have some wonderful news. Her Royal Highness Princess Alexandra has decided to break her fast with us this morning since she was unable to join us last night. Please welcome her."

As the applause began and every pair of eyes in the room focused on her, Sasha realized just how many people she was going to have to mollify before she could confront Kerry and demand an explanation. But at least she didn't have to read them that vapid speech concocted by Bloom. Squaring her shoulders, she smiled as though her mind wasn't in turmoil.

"Good morning. On behalf of the royal family, I'd like to welcome you to England. I wish you all the best in your academic endeavors, and I look forward to speaking with you over the next hour."

With that, she let the secretary direct her to her table. Usually, she spent events like these on autopilot, with a practiced smile on her lips and a banal quip on the tip of her tongue. Sometimes, she was even able to ascend into a sort of fugue state, gliding through her responsibilities while her imagination wandered. But today, she couldn't seem to lose herself in the familiar ritual of public appearance. Instead, she felt magnetized. As Mary Spencer introduced her to several other trustees, Sasha had to force herself not to angle her body so that she could keep an eye on Kerry. By the time she had been introduced to two tables' worth of students, her skin was tingling as though she'd absorbed some kind of electrical charge.

She felt a flash of panic when she came face-to-face with Kerry's friend Harris, but thankfully, he acted as though they'd never met. He did, however, make a point of stepping out of her field of vision just in time for her to see Kerry walking briskly toward the corridor leading out of the hall. Surely, she wouldn't leave before the event's conclusion. Perhaps she was seeking a temporary asylum?

"Ms. Spencer," Sasha asked quickly, trying not to sound desperate, "would you kindly direct me to the nearest WC?"

"This way, ma'am." She gestured the way Kerry had gone. "I'd be happy to escort you."

Sasha shook her head. "Thank you for the offer, but my protection officer will accompany me."

She spun away, Ian two steps behind, and struggled to maintain a dignified pace across the room. As soon as she rounded the corner, she lengthened her strides.

"Your Royal Highness—" Ian began.

Sasha cut him off. "Listen at the door if you must, but no one else enters."

His long-suffering sigh almost made her feel guilty. When they reached the door, she pulled it open and entered to find Kerry, arms braced against the sink, gazing intently at her own reflection. Wariness suffused her face as she turned to face Sasha.

"Your Royal Highness."

"Oh, stop that." Sasha wished she could take the words back as soon as they'd left her lips. Forcing herself to move slowly, she halted a few feet away from Kerry. This close, she could make out the smudges beneath her eyes that hadn't been there yesterday.

She raised her hand, wanting to touch the delicate skin, but then thought better of it. How long had it been since she'd felt uncertainty in the presence of an attractive woman? Not since her first adolescent kiss in the doorway of her room at boarding school.

"You look exhausted."

Kerry let go of her death grip on the sink. The stiffness of her posture was belied by the darkness of her eyes. Attraction.

"I didn't sleep very well last night."

Sasha took a slow step forward, and then another—approaching Kerry the same way she'd been taught to approach her easily-spooked polo pony.

"Me, neither. I wish you hadn't left."

"Oh?"

"We could have gone back to my hotel. You would have slept like a baby. Eventually."

Sasha watched Kerry's throat constrict in a swallow and saw the quick flash of pink as her tongue darted out to moisten her lips. Mesmerized, she belatedly noticed that apprehension had joined the arousal plain on Kerry's face. Was she being too forward?

"I never should have allowed anything to happen between us last night," Kerry said into the awkward silence. "I'm afraid you caught me at a weak moment. Please accept my apologies."

Sasha shook her head and took one more step. "I don't want your apologies. And 'weak' is not a word I would use to describe you at any moment."

"Please. Stop." Kerry held up one hand to ward her off. "I want you. I won't pretend otherwise. You…you're rather irresistible, and I got carried away. But you don't know me. All I'd be is a notch on your bedpost, and I don't want that."

The words felt like a slap to the face. "You truly believe that's all I'm after?"

Her tone was sharp, and Kerry seemed chagrined. "I didn't mean to insult you. But look at the facts. We met at a club, and barely half an hour later we were…"

"Snogging."

"Snogging?"

Sasha couldn't help but smile at Kerry's incredulous tone. "That's what we call it."

Kerry laughed quietly. "Apparently, I've learned something new already today." But as they continued to stare at each other across the tiled floor, her smile faded.

"So...friends?" Color suddenly bloomed in her cheeks, drowning out her freckles. "Not that you need any more of those, I imagine—"

"One can never have too many friends." Fighting to remain gracious, Sasha extended her hand across the gap between them. "I come to Oxford often. I'm certain I'll see you soon."

As their palms slid together, she heard Kerry's quiet intake of breath and had to force herself not to capitalize on the chemistry between them. If she pushed just the slightest bit harder, Kerry would surrender. The temptation was strong, but if she gave in, then she would be resorting to a kind of coercion. Sasha had to be manipulative enough in her dealings with her father and the public. She didn't want—or need—to coerce her lovers, too.

She forced the smile back onto her face as she rejoined Ian in the corridor. Whatever Kerry Donovan's hang-ups were, Sasha wasn't about to let them get to her. There were plenty of other attractive women out there with no compunctions whatsoever about falling into bed with her. Spending any more time dwelling on one rejection was just plain silly.

Kerry let out a long breath and felt her shoulders slump as the door clicked shut. The hollow sound seemed to echo in her chest, bouncing between her ribs. This entire morning had been completely derailed by Sasha's unexpected appearance at their breakfast. The Princess Alexandra introduced by the Secretary was a poised and elegant woman who bore only a superficial resemblance to the sensual whirlwind that had decimated Kerry's reason last night. She walked differently, talked differently, dressed differently, spoke differently. And yet, as soon as they were facing each other alone again, the sparks had leapt up between them.

It wasn't at all difficult to imagine what would have happened had she accepted Sasha's offer. In fact, she'd tossed and turned all night in an effort to shake her lingering regret at having fled Summa.

Now, Sasha's absence felt suffocating. Kerry shook her head in an effort to dispel the odd sense of claustrophobia. She had made the right decision. It only felt like the wrong one because she was lonely.

"And because you didn't have any self-control last night," she scolded her reflection.

The door banged open and she whirled to the sight of Harrison stalking toward her, his hair nearly brushing the low ceiling.

"Harris! This is the ladies' room!"

He crossed his arms over his muscular chest. "I'm not leaving, and neither are you, until you tell me why she came here this morning."

Kerry narrowed her eyes, but he showed no sign of relenting. Sometimes, he put her in mind of her brother Aidan's obstinate bulldog puppy. She sighed.

"Something happened last night."

He threw his hands into the air. "You told me nothing happened!"

"I lied."

"Never lie to me again."

"I won't." Guilt and confusion roiling in her stomach, she reached for his right hand. "Look, I'm sorry. I really am. I didn't know how to process it all, and—"

His scowl deepened. "You process it by talking it out with me!"

"Okay. I get it. I will from now on. Promise." She tried to grin but could feel it coming out lopsided. "Not that it's likely to happen again."

Harris pulled her into a quick hug, then grasped both her shoulders. "Start from the beginning."

"I'll tell you everything, but not here and not now. Can we just go try to survive the rest of this event? I'll answer any question you like, afterward. I swear it."

Thankfully, Harris relented. But as they walked slowly back toward the hall, he bumped his shoulder against hers.

"Just tell me one thing now."

After her lie, she owed him, and he knew it. The mercenary. "Fine."

"Was she good?"

Kerry grit her teeth. She should have seen that coming. "We made out a little," she muttered. "That's all."

Harris was smiling like the cat that had swallowed the canary. "And I repeat. Was she good?"

Suddenly blindsided by the memory of Sasha's hips surging against her thigh, Kerry found herself momentarily speechless. Her fingertips flashed hot, as though Sasha's smooth skin had invisibly branded them. How was it possible that the passion she'd experienced in those few short minutes rivaled the heights of what she'd found with Virginia? They'd been in love, and their relationship certainly hadn't been prudish. For one heated moment to compare in any way to that kind of history was ludicrous.

"Ker-ry." Harris drew out the syllables of her name as he snapped his fingers in front of her face. His grin was even wider now. "Where'd you go, hmm?"

Taking a deep breath, she stopped and turned to face him. "She was amazing. And that's all the detail you're getting."

She spun and walked resolutely back into the hall, struggling not to roll her eyes at the sound of his diabolical chuckling behind her. Almost immediately, she caught a glimpse of Sasha conversing with a trustee and a few of her peers. The princess was laughing at something, and her left hand rested lightly on Anna's forearm as she leaned in to make some sort of comment. Kerry looked away and pinched the bridge of her nose as her head began to pound. Had she actually felt a twinge of jealousy, minutes after firmly rejecting Sasha's invitation? That was beyond ludicrous. She wanted nothing more than to hit the "undo" button on the last twenty-four hours.

After scanning the rest of the room, she noticed Julia standing near the coffee station and began to make her way over. She had to pull herself together or she'd be a mess for her meeting with the architecture faculty. There would be no more thinking about Princess Alexandra today. Or ever again. Forgetting that the past day had ever happened was in the best interest of everyone.

But in the evening, as she sat at her desk poring over one of the books she'd been instructed to purchase, Kerry couldn't seem to escape her memories. She'd been trying to read the introduction for the past half hour, but her focus was in tatters. Each time she bent her head to the page, her brain conjured up a vision: the hungry gleam in Sasha's jade-colored eyes just before their kiss; the taste of expensive cognac lingering on Sasha's tongue; the fine shiver she'd felt when her fingers first encountered skin.

Kerry cursed and leaned back in her chair, staring at the ceiling. Immediately, her legs began to twitch. The restlessness was riding her hard tonight, exacerbated by the desire Sasha had ignited in every cell. Her body felt as though it was a firestorm, smoldering from the inside out. This seething sensation had plagued her off and on, ever since Virginia had called off their relationship. It felt like fire ants crawling under her skin, and try as she might, she'd never been able to resist its imperative. In the past, she had always given herself two options: exercise until she was too exhausted to keep her eyes open, or stay in, get drunk, and try to ease the ache by her own hand.

Tonight, neither appealed. Her tryst with Sasha had blown open the Pandora's Box of her desire. She needed to feel the press of a crowd, the burn of alcohol cascading down her throat, the heat of a woman's desirous gaze traveling down her body. Most of all, she needed touch.

After only a moment's indecision, Kerry quickly went to her dresser. She put on jeans and a black tank top, then shoved a few pound notes, one credit card, and her university ID into a front pocket. Before she could change her mind, she grabbed her black leather jacket and was out the door. The night was clear and cold, and she walked quickly toward the northern edge of town. There was a women's bar near the park she'd run in yesterday. At the very least, she could check it out. If it wasn't any fun, she could always go home.

The Coven's entrance was down an alley that opened out onto Broad Street just a block from the park. Inside, ambient music poured from speakers set into each wall corner. The walls were painted black and decorated with strange iridescent markings that looked vaguely pagan. High tables and chairs lined the wall opposite the bar, while the back of the establishment seemed to be open for dancing. Kerry claimed a bar stool next to a young, heavily pierced couple engaged in a languorous make-out session.

When the bartender came around, she ordered a shot of Ketel One and a Newcastle. She downed the shot immediately, finding a small measure of relief in the chill of the vodka as it sluiced into her empty stomach. Grabbing the beer, she swiveled on her stool to observe the denizens of the club. Despite the fact that it was a weeknight, most of the tables were populated. Two couples shared the dance floor with a ring of women who looked to be about Kerry's age, or maybe a bit older.

One of them, a thin blonde in a red dress, caught her looking and smiled. Kerry couldn't help but continue watching as she moved more provocatively, exaggerating the swing of her hips. She danced very well, but her motions were studied. She had none of the intrinsic wildness that had attracted Kerry to Sasha. Which was, she reminded herself as the woman broke off from her group and walked toward her, a good thing. Because she was here to forget all about the princess.

"Do I know you?" the woman asked.

Kerry forced herself not to wince at the hackneyed line. "I don't think so. I'm Kerry."

"Heather." As she extended her hand, gold bracelets jangled on one thin wrist.

"Can I buy you a drink?"

Heather smiled, and Kerry caught a flash of silver in her mouth. That, at least, was tantalizing.

"Just a shot. Then we should dance."

When Kerry offered the stool, Heather perched on it lightly and reached for Kerry's hand. "Share it with me."

Breasts pressed to Heather's back, Kerry flagged down the bartender with one hand while Heather guided the other onto the smooth skin of her thigh. Trying to relax, Kerry brushed feathery strokes back and forth above her knee. Heather's cologne tickled her nose, and she took shallow breaths.

"I haven't seen you here before," Heather said. "Are you new in town?"

"I am. I'm just about to begin graduate school."

"Where in America are you from?" As she spoke, Heather covered Kerry's hand with her own, urging her to move higher. Kerry's heart began to pound, but not from arousal. She had come here seeking closeness and touch, but this didn't feel right. At all.

"New York."

"New York. I've been once. Such a thrilling city."

Kerry decided not to explain that she didn't live in the city itself, but in a small suburb populated by the Irish cops and firemen who worked in Manhattan. She was just about to try to distract Heather by asking for more details about her trip to the States, when their shots arrived. They clinked glasses and drank, but the chill did nothing to dispel Kerry's growing sense of trepidation. This had been a bad idea.

After a few more minutes of idle chat, Heather turned, bent her head, and pressed a kiss to Kerry's right bicep. "I'm going to run to the WC." She brushed Kerry's jawline with her knuckles. "Then you should join me on the dance floor."

"Okay."

But as soon as Heather disappeared, Kerry threw a few bills on the bar and hustled out the door. She was being an ass, but she had to escape. This wasn't what she needed. Every second of her encounter with Heather had felt wrong. Terribly wrong.

A blast of cold air greeted her outside, and she turned her face willingly into the wind. As she broke into a jog, Kerry realized this was the second night in a row that she'd fled from a beautiful woman. Was it worse that she'd gotten herself in the same situation twice in two days, or that she had run away each time?

"Pull yourself together," she muttered as she turned the corner onto St. Cross and headed toward the Manor. She had one short week to settle in and prepare before the maelstrom of classes began. One short week to get her head on straight and stop sabotaging herself.

"Focus. No more mistakes."

CHAPTER SIX

Sasha sipped at her tea and pretended to stare contemplatively into the impeccably manicured garden that stretched out below her table. It was beautiful, if you liked orderly paths lined with trimmed hedges, ornamented with flowering shrubs placed at precise, repetitive intervals. She found the entire scene rather dull and much preferred to covertly people-watch behind her large sunglasses— especially because most of the people were not-so-covertly watching her and Ashleigh. The Terrace of the Goring Hotel was one of the most famous tea spots in the city and attracted tourists and members of high society alike. She could practically hear their exclamations and speculations. *The princess is dining with the prince's fiancée! Are they actually friends, or is this a publicity stunt? What are they talking about? How does Ms. Dunning feel about Princess Sasha's vexed public image?*

While the tabloids had gotten wind of her presence at Summa on its opening night, they hadn't discovered that she'd ditched a scheduled event to be there, so she'd dodged that particular scandal. Neither had there been any word from her father, who was returning today from a business trip to Edinburgh. She wondered if he'd managed to see Arthur while in Scotland. Probably not. He was, after all, a stickler for the rules, and Arthur wasn't allowed any sort of leave until the Christmas holiday.

"Did you talk to Arthur yesterday?" she asked Ashleigh. "I haven't spoken to him since the weekend."

"He called this morning to tell me they're heading off on some sort of exercise and it might be a few days before we could speak again."

"How did he sound?"

Ashleigh smiled over the brim of her teacup—a gentle, happy smile that was entirely without pretense. The fondness she felt for Arthur was palpable, and Sasha wondered fleetingly whether she would ever inspire that kind of emotion in anyone. Being wanted had its perks, certainly, but sometimes she hoped for more. For someone who would smile that way when thinking of her.

Her mind's eye flashed to the memory of how Kerry had instinctively shielded her when their kiss had been interrupted. No one short of her own protection detail had ever reacted that way— certainly never a woman whom she'd just engaged in a clandestine tryst. Sasha couldn't deny that Kerry's instinctive selflessness and courage made her even more attractive. Perhaps that was why she'd found herself unable to stop thinking about her, days later.

"He sounded excited." Ashleigh's words cut through her introspection. "You know how he is."

Arthur's boyish enthusiasm hadn't entirely faded, and Sasha hoped it never did. How he managed to retain it in the face of their father's tyrannical handling was beyond her. Then again, their father treated his only son quite differently.

"I hear the King has asked you to fill in for Arthur at his engagements," Ashleigh said. "How has that been?"

Sasha bit back a sigh. Ashleigh was aware of the fault lines that ran beneath their family's civilized veneer, and Sasha felt fortunate to have another ally in her future sister-in-law. But she didn't want to monopolize the conversation with her complaints.

"It's a tug-of-war, as always. Nothing new there. But how are you? Holding up all right?"

"Yes, just fine. Plenty to keep me busy."

"Like this film project." Sasha was more than happy to turn the conversation to something that did not involve family. "What did you think of my initial ideas for venues for the premiere?"

They talked business for a while, and Sasha felt her melancholy slip away as the plans for Ashleigh's event began to coalesce. The film launch was meant to cater to a broadly influential audience— from peers of the realm who had been born into the House of Lords, to up-and-coming avant-garde artists working for social justice. The best sort of party would be one with the formal trappings of an elegant society soiree, which could then be subtly undercut throughout the event. Most of her previous work had been on birthday parties and bridal showers, and Ashleigh's request presented a unique opportunity to showcase the range of her abilities.

As Sasha was wrapping up a voice memo outlining her to-do list, a murmur rippled through the crowd. Moments later, a hush descended, broken only by faint whispers. She glanced up to the sight of her father striding toward them, dressed immaculately in a black suit and holding a briefcase in one hand. Flanked by two members of his security team, he cut an imposing figure. Murmurs of "the King" reached her just before he did. Ashleigh rose immediately, while Sasha took her time getting to her feet. She also kept her sunglasses on.

"Good afternoon, Alexandra. Ashleigh."

"Good afternoon, Your Majesty." Ever proper, Ashleigh delivered the words with a small curtsy.

"Hello, Father."

He only glanced at her before returning his attention to the woman who would soon be his daughter-in-law. "I don't wish to inconvenience you, Ashleigh," he said, "but I'm afraid I need to speak with Alexandra on some business matters."

"Of course, sir." Ashleigh gathered her shawl from the back of her chair and embraced Sasha lightly. "We made some great progress today. See you soon."

With an extra squeeze that Sasha knew was a silent token of encouragement, Ashleigh turned toward the doors leading into the lounge where her own bodyguard waited. Irritated at her father's callous interruption, Sasha dropped back into her chair before he was seated. A minor breach of protocol, but the tiny rebellion felt good.

"I suppose it never occurred to you that we might be discussing business of our own?"

His bushy eyebrows rose. "You're affronted?" He opened his briefcase and pulled out the tabloid that had broken the story of her visit to Summa. It displayed a grainy photograph—clearly taken by someone's phone—of her dancing in the club. Kerry's face was visible in profile, but fortunately, they had been several feet apart at the time.

Sasha felt a sudden pang of guilt for what might have happened had the camera caught them a few minutes later.

"When I rang the Secretary of the Rhodes Trust to ask her how the reception had gone, she mentioned how sorry she was to hear of your illness, and how impressed she was by the generosity of your impromptu visit the next day."

Sasha crossed her right leg over her left and hid behind her glasses, determined not to let him bully her into guilt or defensiveness.

"This rag," he continued, rattling the paper, "tells a different story." When she remained silent, he leaned forward. "Do you have nothing to say for yourself?"

"I don't believe my behavior requires justification."

When his cheeks grew mottled, Sasha struggled to hold back a tight smile. If they had been in his office, he would have been able to give his temper free rein. Here, in public, she had the distinct advantage. He leaned in over the table, and Sasha found herself hoping he would inadvertently dip his dark sleeve into the clotted cream.

"You are going to make amends to the Rhodes trustees," he said, his voice soft and threatening. "You will organize an *appropriate* event for the incoming class of scholars—an *academic* event—and you will pay every penny yourself."

For a moment, Sasha wasn't sure she'd heard him correctly. Once she realized he was quite serious, she couldn't stop her smile from breaking free. At her father's look of consternation, she laughed. Did he truly believe he was punishing her by asking her to plan a party? Not only could she use this opportunity for her company's advantage, she could also test the fortitude of the walls Kerry Donovan had put up between them.

"What exactly do you find so humorous about this situation, Alexandra?"

She stood and reached for her purse. "Only this, Father: that for the first time in my life, you've ordered me to do something I'm actually good at, and that I enjoy." She turned to walk away, then looked back over her shoulder. "Your invitation will be in the mail."

❖

The sun was just beginning to set as Kerry entered the front door of the Iffley Road Sports Complex for her weekly workout and dinner "date" with Harris. Just for him, she'd made one exception to her morning exercise rule, and so far she was enjoying their sessions. Tonight, though, she passed the ID checkpoint with a pit of dread in her stomach. She knew exactly what Harris would want to discuss tonight, and she didn't have any good answers.

As she walked through the atrium, she passed Claudia Tully, captain of the Balliol women's football team. Claudia had been kind to her ever since they'd met at the first team meeting—before anyone knew Kerry would be a ringer. Smart, fun, and happily involved with her boyfriend, Claudia was exactly the sort of friend Kerry wanted to cultivate.

"Kerry, hi!" Her curly brown hair was pulled back into a ponytail, and her cheeks were flushed with exertion.

"Hey, Claudia. Good workout?"

"Not bad. Are you excited for Saturday?"

Kerry grinned. "You have no idea."

On Saturday, Balliol would play Magdalen in the first match of the season. The team had only been practicing since the first day of classes, just over a week ago, but Kerry was so eager for a real match that she didn't care how ill-prepared they were. Besides, as she had to keep reminding herself, this was essentially an intramural league. She hadn't played in an organization this low-stakes since kindergarten. It took some getting used to.

"I can't wait," Claudia was saying. "You'll be our secret weapon. They'll never know what hit them."

"I'm just glad to be playing. I was going crazy without it."

Claudia nodded sympathetically. "I'll let you go. See you at practice tomorrow?"

"Absolutely." And then she remembered. "Oh, hang on. I'm going to have to miss a game. Not next week, but the weekend after. I'm sorry."

Claudia waved away her apology. "Please, don't even worry. It's fine."

After bidding her good-bye, Kerry jogged up the stairs toward the weight room. Still preoccupied with how to formulate a response to Harris's inevitable question, she didn't notice that he was lying in wait for her at the top.

"Hey, you."

Nonchalance, she decided, was the best tactic. "What's up? How was your day?"

"My lecture was boring. But it was the hot prof, so I didn't mind so much."

"Glad to hear it, one-track mind." She slugged him lightly in the shoulder. "How about you help me with my erg technique today? I've never figured out how to use that thing properly, and I'd like to add it in to my cardio regimen."

"Follow me, young Skywalker."

He led the way to a row of erg machines and demonstrated where the straps should rest on her feet. After situating himself onto the next machine over, he grabbed the handle and leaned forward in a low crouch.

"Watch my technique, and remember: first legs, then back, then arms."

"Legs, back, arms," Kerry repeated under her breath as he demonstrated a few strokes on the machine.

"Now you try. I'll watch your form."

Kerry sat all the way forward until her knees were touching her chest. She grasped the handle and pushed backward with her quads, focusing on the sequence Harris had taught her. Legs, back, arms. As she slipped into a rhythm, she increased the pressure of her strokes.

"That's near perfect," Harris said. "Just remember, when you want to row harder, most of that power should come from your legs."

Breathing deeply, she focused on maintaining the proper sequence of motions. Already, she had broken a sweat. Now that she knew the proper technique, the erg would make a valuable addition to her fitness plan.

At the whirr of the machine next to her, she looked over to see Harris settling into his own stroke. His movements were smooth, economical, and powerful—the product of years of repetition—and Kerry tried to mimic his form and fluidity.

"So," he asked after a moment, "get anything interesting in the mail today?"

Despite having expected the question at some point, she faltered. Determined to regain her rhythm before she answered him, she spent several moments focusing on her technique.

"I got the invitation, yes," she finally said.

"She organized it with you in mind, didn't she?"

"What?" Kerry willed her body to continue moving smoothly, despite the storm winds lashing at her mind. "No, she didn't."

"She sure as hell did. C'mon, Ker. This thing is at Balmoral Castle—built when, exactly?"

"Fourteenth century, originally," Kerry said automatically, before realizing she'd betrayed herself.

Harris just laughed. "And the guest of honor is the President of the Royal Institute of British Architects. Face it: Sassy Sasha has made it doubly impossible for you to reject her invitation."

"I don't have to go."

"Oh? Really? You're going to miss out on a chance to explore a Scottish castle and to meet the biggest bigwig in your field?"

Kerry's jaw clenched and she yanked harder at the handle, taking out her frustration on the machine. He was right, and she didn't want him to be. As she had read the elegantly-lettered invitation this morning, her mouth had literally fallen open. She couldn't argue with logic. Sasha had deliberately laid a trap for her, one into which she would willingly walk.

Her heavy sigh was all the confirmation Harris needed. "I didn't think so."

"She's smarter than everyone gives her credit for." When Kerry glanced over again, she found him nodding. His rhythm had never faltered. "Now, can we consider this conversation closed and get back to our workout, please?"

He grinned. "You asked for it. Power-ten, on my mark. And remember—push with your legs first. Otherwise you'll end up throwing your back out and you'll be no good whatsoever to your princess."

Kerry grit her teeth but refused to rise to the bait. Instead, she concentrated on rowing harder.

CHAPTER SEVEN

S asha rested her palms on the stone parapet and inhaled deeply, enjoying the light breeze drifting down off the mountains. High above her head, the wind whisked cirrus clouds across the deep blue sky, and she tracked their progress in the chiaroscuro patterns flickering across the pine-covered peaks that encircled the Balmoral estate. Below, at the bottom of a long, grassy slope, the late afternoon sunlight glinted redly off the surface of the River Dee.

Nostalgia rose in her like a flood, and for one exquisitely painful moment, she could have sworn her mother was standing behind her. She wanted to turn and see that gentle, benevolent smile—to run into her embrace and breathe in her distinctive, warm milk scent.

Sasha dug her fingertips into the stone, anchoring herself— refusing to turn, forcing her body, if not her mind, to remain in the present. Perhaps it had been a mistake to choose Balmoral for this event. She hadn't realized just how much being here would remind her of the many summers their family had spent in the Highlands before her mother's illness. She didn't have idyllic memories from her childhood, but those came close.

Suddenly ill at ease, she adjusted the fit of her cardigan and smoothed one hand down the front of her silk dress. This was no time for indulging in sentimentality. Any minute now, the charter bus conveying her guests from the airport would arrive. To distract herself while she waited, she went over the schedule again in her head.

Upon their arrival, the group would be shown to the dining room, where they would eat a light supper. After the meal, they would retire to the games room for cocktails, cards, and billiards. In the morning, brunch would be followed by a tour of the castle and a wide range of outdoor activities. In the evening, a full dinner would be served, and on Sunday morning, the scholars would return to Oxford.

Such was the official agenda. Unofficially, however, Sasha was on a mission to seduce Kerry Donovan. How that one kiss had managed to get under her skin, she had no idea. The only thing she knew for certain was that her desire to feel the fierce chemistry between them again had shown no signs of abating. She hadn't once sought out other company in the intervening weeks. Every need had been sublimated into the work of preparing for this event.

Out of the corner of her eye, she saw a flash of silver beneath the trees. Moments later, a low rumble reached her ears. The bus. She hurried inside, double-checking her reflection in one of the mirrored windows on the way, pleased at how the colorful fabric of her dress draped across her thighs. As she descended the stone staircase, Sasha heard the spitting sound of gravel beneath tires and knew the bus had reached the roundabout. She nodded to Ian and joined the stewardess of the castle just inside the door. Celia Royston had been responsible for overseeing the building and grounds of Balmoral for as long as she could remember, and Sasha was grateful that Celia hadn't raised any stumbling blocks to her plan for this weekend.

"Thank you for all your help," she murmured as a member of her staff pushed open the double doors.

"My pleasure, Your Royal Highness."

Sunlight flooded the atrium, bringing with it the enthusiastic chatter of her guests as they disembarked from the bus. She didn't hear Kerry's voice, and dread washed over her at the thought that perhaps she hadn't made the trip after all. But she had RSVP'd, and she didn't seem like the sort of person who would break promises. Sasha had to believe she would be here.

Exhaling quickly, she stepped out onto the landing. The group was unloading their baggage from beneath the bus, but a hush fell over them as soon as she was visible. Relief soothed her nerves when she caught a glimpse of Kerry's red hair, and she had to force her gaze not to linger.

"Trustees and scholars, welcome to Balmoral Castle. I'm happy you could join me this weekend." She gestured to her left. "This is

Celia Royston, the castle stewardess. Her staff will direct you to your rooms and describe the available amenities. In half an hour's time, we'll convene in the dining room for supper."

She paused to survey the crowd, and almost immediately her gaze was drawn back to Kerry. Dressed in fitted gray slacks, a white Oxford shirt, and a black jacket that clung to her broad shoulders, she looked at once sophisticated and sexy. Her color was high already, but her cheeks darkened perceptibly when their eyes met. The sudden rush of confidence made Sasha smile in triumph. She still had the power to affect Kerry Donovan, and she was going to use it.

"Do you have any questions?" After waiting a few beats, she nodded briskly. "Very well, then. I shall see you shortly."

She turned away, leaving Celia to explain the layout of the castle and the wing to which they'd been assigned. Sasha had been sorely tempted to house Kerry in the room directly across from her own, but singling her out in that way would doubtless have made her uncomfortable. The most she'd allowed herself to do was to ensure Kerry didn't have a roommate.

Just in case.

❖

Kerry reclined in the cushioned window seat across from her bed, barely resisting the urge to pinch herself. She was a guest of the British royal family, and tonight, she would sleep in a castle. She hadn't told anyone back home about this trip—not even her brothers—because a part of her hadn't been able believe it wasn't some kind of hoax. She'd spent the entire journey here in a state of disbelief, waiting for the other shoe to drop. But it hadn't.

Below, a flower garden, its paths lined with immaculately trimmed hedgerows, gave way to patio paved with gray-blue stone. Some kind of granite, most likely, but she would need to get closer to be certain. Beyond the patio stretched a broad lawn, ending in another, taller line of hedgerows. Mountains—some bald, some forested—dominated the horizon. For one romantic moment, she felt cradled in the protective embrace of the valley as the hills looked on, ever vigilant.

But even that momentary sense of security couldn't calm the butterflies churning in her gut. For the past three weeks, she had worked hard to maintain her focus. Except in her weakest moments—and when the occasional glimpse of a tabloid photo caught her unawares—she had resisted all thoughts of Princess Alexandra. She'd thought herself prepared to see Sasha again, but nothing could have been further from the truth.

She closed her eyes and the image was there, burned into her retinas: Sasha's dark, lustrous hair curling around her shoulders; the hint of challenge in her inviting smile; the way her dress—a riotous explosion of swirling shades of magenta—clung to her breasts and hips. Kerry had been instantly overwhelmed by the memory of that lithe body pressed intimately against hers. She felt like Odysseus in the presence of a Siren, caught unawares without rope or beeswax.

"She could shipwreck me."

If Sasha had in fact designed the weekend with her in mind, then what did that mean? The hubris of the thought still floored her, but she couldn't ignore the evidence. This event seemed like an awful lot of effort to put in for another chance at a one-night stand, especially from someone who had no trouble finding willing partners. Did Sasha want more than an assignation? How could she, when they barely knew each other? Was she simply bored? Was this sort of cat-and-mouse game how members of the royal family got their kicks?

At the sound of a knock, she reluctantly vacated her perch. When she opened the door, Harris barged in without even asking permission, talking a mile a minute. "How are your digs? Can you even believe this place? Oh, a window seat! How quaint!"

Before she could protest, he had taken her spot. Lacing his hands behind his head, he gave her an expectant look.

"What?"

He checked his watch. "We have ten minutes until we need to be in the dining room. What's your plan?"

"My plan?"

"Sassy Sasha has you where she wants you. You're squarely in her crosshairs and you, who schedule virtually every minute of every day, don't have a plan?"

Kerry sat on the bed. "What good would one do me? To hear you talk, I don't have much chance of escaping."

"Is that what you want? To escape?"

Kerry let her gaze drift back to the mountains outside. Out here, free of the paparazzi, she didn't have to worry about becoming a headline. If Sasha pursued her again, she could surrender to her own desire without guilt. But instead of relief, the thought inspired a fresh wave of unease. Did she really want to be a conquest? Before arriving in England, she had been fine on her own, at peace in her decision to put the needs of her heart—and her body—on hold in favor of her career. Her solitary coping mechanisms had worked, until Sasha overrode her careful control. Did she really want to pursue what could only be the most transient of flings? Then again, perhaps that was a good reason to allow herself to indulge. She had to get back on the metaphorical horse sometime, didn't she?

But even as the thought crossed her mind, she mentally shied away from its callousness. "I don't know what I want."

Harris stood and held out his hand. Dressed in khaki slacks and a navy plaid sport coat, he looked positively dapper. "I'm relieved to hear you say that. Guess you'll just have to trust your instincts."

Kerry let him lead her out of the room. As they walked down the corridor, they were joined by several other members of their cohort. Together, they made their way down the wide stone staircase that opened into the main atrium, where one of the liveried staff directed them to the dining room. The long, rectangular chamber had fireplaces set into each short wall. Large bay windows with southern exposure looked out onto an immaculate lawn now shrouded in the shadows of approaching dusk. Kerry tried to concentrate on appreciating the Scots Baronial architecture instead of searching the room for Sasha.

"Looks like we have assigned seating," Harris said. "Let's find our placards."

He located his at a table in the middle of the room. Kerry had to hunt a while longer, but she finally found her place at the table nearest the windows. Harris stopped at the seat opposite hers and whistled.

"Well, well, well. It's your lucky day, Ker." Dry humor saturated his every word.

Kerry's pulse jumped at the thought of spending the duration of the meal facing Sasha. She was just debating whether sitting across from her was better or worse than sitting next to her, when a member of the staff paused to proffer them a tray full of champagne flutes.

"Supper will begin shortly," he said. "Do you need any assistance in finding your seats?"

"No, thank you." Kerry sipped at the bubbling liquor, hoping it would steady her nerves. Sliding into her chair, she waved to Harris as he moved away.

Her table filled quickly with several of her peers along with Mary Spencer and two of the trustees who had accompanied them. As she listened to their excited chatter, she had to concentrate on not turning around to look for Sasha. When asked by one trustee how her studies were proceeding, she forced herself to focus exclusively on him and respond in appropriate detail.

And then Spencer who, had line-of-sight over her shoulder, rose to her feet. "Good evening, Your Royal Highness."

Kerry stood, steeling herself. When Sasha came into view, her heart clattered against her ribs. Up close, the princess was even more beautiful than she had been at a distance earlier in the day. Her glossy lips parted on a smile as she took the hand of each trustee in turn, and Kerry couldn't stop herself from flashing back to their incendiary kiss. Sasha sank gracefully into her chair, and Kerry followed suit, relieved to be off her feet.

"Good evening, all. It's wonderful to have you here. Are the rooms satisfactory, I hope?"

"More than satisfactory, Your Highness," Spencer hurried to reassure her.

"Please do let Celia know if there's anything you require. Now, would you be so kind as to introduce yourselves? And if you are one of the scholars, perhaps share what you are studying?"

Kerry barely heard a word of her friends' descriptions of their academic endeavors. She couldn't stop watching Sasha play the role of consummate hostess. She was clearly in her element as she listened attentively to each person, even taking the time to ask a question or two. When those emerald eyes finally locked on to hers, Kerry caught the humor that sparkled in their depths.

"My name is Kerry Donovan, Your Royal Highness, and I'm studying sustainable architecture."

"Oh?" Sasha feigned surprise very well. "How fortuitous that our guest of honor this weekend—aside from all of you, of course—is Raymond Fletcher, the President of the Royal Institute of British Architects."

"I'm very much looking forward to speaking with him."

Sasha smiled warmly. "He'll arrive later this evening and will be giving the tour tomorrow. I believe his nephew, Byron, will be joining him. Are you familiar with his work?"

Kerry didn't bother trying to hide her surprise. An architect in his own right, Byron Fletcher's meteoric rise to success had compelled him to branch out into other media. He was now a renowned designer with his own set of London-based boutiques. And Sasha had enticed him here?

"I am. It will be an honor to meet them both."

When Sasha switched her attention to Anna, Kerry immediately felt bereft. Sasha was far better than she at maintaining her composure, and for a moment, Kerry wondered whether she'd been deluded into believing Sasha still carried some kind of torch for her. But then Sasha's gaze returned to hers for the briefest of instants—a split second of unanticipated connection—and with a rush of adrenaline, she realized the torch burned brightly still.

The meal passed in a haze of agonizing anticipation that didn't improve in the slightest when the group retired to the downstairs game room. The trustees, along with the most extroverted members of Kerry's group, monopolized Sasha's attention. When she perched on a stool before the beautiful, dark-stained oak bar, they hovered around her like moths drawn to a flame. As much as she wanted to join in their discussion, Kerry didn't think she would be able to get a word in edgewise. And so she found herself drinking Scotch and playing chess with Kieran in the corner, alternately cursing her introversion and admiring the smoothness of the Macallan 30. Harris would have tried to help her, she knew, but he was busy flirting with Brent. Perhaps that was for the best. Any of his schemes would doubtless get her into trouble.

Just shy of ten o'clock, Sasha announced that it was time for her to retire. She didn't even look Kerry's way as she left the room. Kerry glumly checkmated Kieran's queen a few minutes later, not feeling victorious in the slightest. She begged off a rematch and found Harris playing pool with Brent.

"I'm going to sleep. See you at the brunch?"

Harris pulled her into a hug. "Did something happen?" he whispered. "Are you okay?"

"I'm just fine," she said firmly. "Have fun. See you tomorrow."

Kerry's footsteps echoed through the halls as she walked slowly back to her room, and for those few minutes, she indulged herself in the fantasy that this was a Gothic castle rather than a product of the nineteenth-century Gothic Revival. Of course, she knew too much about the medieval period to romanticize it for long. Between the plagues, the wars, and the lack of any modern convenience, it certainly hadn't been an easy time in which to live.

She was so preoccupied with her daydream that she didn't notice the dark blue envelope on the floor of her room until she stepped on it. Someone must have slipped it beneath the door. Heart pounding, her fatigue fell away like a cloak as she bent to pick it up and saw her name written in an elegant script. Not wanting to tear it any more than necessary, she carefully pushed her finger beneath the flap.

Inside, she found a small bone-white card emblazoned with the colorful seal of the royal family. But when she looked closer, she noticed that the crest differed from King Andrew's in a few, very minor respects. The children of a British monarch each had their own crests—she knew that much. Was this Sasha's? She flipped the card over.

Come to the northern wing. Present this card to the guards there.

That was all it said. No "please," not even so much as a question mark. It was a demand, but Kerry wasn't affronted by Sasha's presumptiveness. Quite the opposite. Despite her misgivings, there was never any question of her obedience.

"But you will not sleep with her," she muttered as she slipped the card into her jacket pocket. "Not tonight."

Hurrying back down the hall, she bypassed the staircase and continued on until she reached the intersection leading to the north wing. Immediately, she found her passage blocked by a broad-shouldered man in a dark suit. Not Ian—someone she didn't recognize.

"Good evening," she said, praying her voice would remain steady. "I received this a short while ago."

He perused the card and nodded once. "This way, please."

He led her to the second door on the right and knocked. A few moments later, Sasha opened it. She was still wearing the dress, but she'd abandoned her beige heels in favor of going barefoot. That tiny change made her seem more carefree, somehow. More accessible.

"Hello, Kerry." She turned to the guard. "Thank you, Darryl. That will be all."

The door shut with a hollow click. They were alone together. In Sasha's bedroom. Kerry suddenly found it difficult to swallow. The expression on her face must have betrayed her, because Sasha smiled knowingly and reached for her hand. But instead of pressing her against the wall in a repeat of their tryst at the club, she tugged her forward.

"I'm glad you came. I wanted to show you the view from my balcony."

As she was pulled across the room, Kerry caught a glimpse of a large four-poster bed, complete with a canopy. That was all the detail she managed to catch before Sasha opened a set of French doors and urged her out into the night. The balcony held two deck chairs, but Sasha eschewed them to lean against the parapet.

One step behind her, Kerry paused, riveted by the view. The moon, nearly full, hung precisely between two of the distant mountains. Its light cascaded over the hills, drenching them in silver leaf. When Sasha turned to see what had become of her, the moonlight played across her delicate features, lending them an otherworldly look.

"Isn't it perfect?"

Kerry stepped forward to rest her elbows on the cool stone. "Stunning. I wish I were a painter."

"I prefer photography myself. I snapped quite a few shots before you arrived."

"May I see them?"

Sasha slid her arm the fraction of an inch required to eliminate the space between them. Even that light touch, separated by several layers of fabric, sent a fresh surge of anticipation coursing through Kerry's blood.

"You'll have to be patient. I develop my nature shots by hand."

"I can wait."

"Can you?"

Kerry looked over to see the hint of a smile curving Sasha's lips. Blindsided by the urge to lean in and claim her tantalizing mouth, Kerry balled her hands into fists and averted her gaze. She had to get control of herself. At the light touch on her shoulder, her muscles tensed.

"Is something wrong?"

Kerry exhaled slowly and turned back to face her. The teasing smile was gone, replaced by a puzzled frown, and Kerry wanted to smooth out the furrowed skin between her brows.

"No. Not at all. It's just that I'm confused."

"By?"

Kerry knew she was supposed to play Sasha's flirtatious game, but she simply couldn't find the will. She wasn't naturally good at it, and trying only sapped her mental reserves.

"Why am I standing here with you right now?"

Sasha cocked her head. "Because you accepted my invitations. Both of them."

"Did you…" Kerry felt her face heat at the audacity of the question on her lips. "Did you design some of this weekend with me in mind? That feels so preposterous to ask, but—"

Sasha pressed one finger to her lips to stop her babbling. The gesture brought back an onslaught of memories from their night at Summa, and Kerry trembled despite herself.

"My father asked me to organize an event for your group." When Sasha let her hand drop, Kerry immediately missed her touch. "I wanted to be certain I'd see you again, and so I made arrangements with that goal in mind."

"Why?"

"Why?"

"Why would you want to see me again?"

Sasha searched her eyes for a moment before answering. "You intrigue me. I want to know you better. Why does that surprise you?"

Kerry gripped the stone and leaned back, turning her face up to the sky. "Because we don't have a thing in common. We come from completely different worlds. You're a princess of the United Kingdom. I'm the daughter of a roofer—"

"You're a genius. I'm a bloody imbecile." The unexpected words were saturated in bitterness. "Fine. I understand. I'll walk you out."

She had one hand on the balcony doors before Kerry got over her shock.

"Sasha! Wait. Don't put words in my mouth. Never once have I thought you're a—an imbecile."

"Of course you do. Everyone does."

"That's not true. I don't." She took a deep breath, praying for the right words. "I think you're one of the most captivating people I've ever met. I think there are many, many more layers to you than most people see."

Sasha turned slowly. "Why should I believe you?"

"Why should I believe you?" Kerry threw the words back, refusing to be bullied. But when uncertainty flashed across Sasha's face, the uncharacteristic show of vulnerability made Kerry's heart ache. She held up her hands in a gesture of surrender.

"Let's start over. The truth is that I've been trying not to think about you for the past few weeks, but I've failed miserably. You look beautiful tonight, and this event is simply incredible. I don't know what you want from me, or whether it's something I can give. But truthfully, I'm starting not to care."

Sasha took one step forward and then another. Kerry held her breath and let her hands slowly drop to her sides as she approached. When only a foot separated them, Sasha reached out to adjust the collar of Kerry's jacket. The unexpected intimacy of the gesture made Kerry breathless.

"You're honest. I like that about you." Her quick smile was rueful. "Honesty can be difficult to come by."

"Occupational hazard?" Kerry didn't trust herself to attempt a full sentence.

"Something like that." Sasha brushed her knuckles along Kerry's jawline in a fleeting caress. "Do you really think we have nothing in common, just because we were born into different lives?"

The question pierced to the heart of Kerry's insecurity. "When you put it that way, what I said sounds pretty silly."

"Exactly."

Sasha finally closed the space between them, and Kerry inhaled sharply at the sensation of their bodies pressed together. Tentatively, she rested her hands on Sasha's waist, enjoying the slip-slide of the cool silk beneath her fingertips.

"You've been brave and honest. Now it's my turn." Sasha rested both hands on Kerry's shoulders, peering intently into her face. "All I know is that I've replayed our kiss a thousand times in my memory. For whatever reason, we have incredible chemistry. I want to see if it means anything."

Kerry's head spun at the news that Sasha felt just as intensely about their encounter. Beneath the dizziness, she struggled to formulate a coherent response. "What exactly are you suggesting?"

Sasha seemed amused by the strangled sound of her voice. "I'm simply suggesting that we spend some time together. Does that sound like something you'd enjoy?"

"Yes." The simple syllable was so easy to say. "Very much."

Sasha slid her hands to the back of Kerry's neck and gently began to massage the taut muscles there. Kerry's eyes slid shut automatically, though she managed to stop herself from moaning. Those muscles were a source of near chronic pain, and Sasha's fingers felt so good.

"For this to work," Sasha murmured, "you have to be able to relax. Do you even know how?"

Kerry forced her eyes to open. "I do have some trouble with that."

"We have an excellent masseuse on the premises. I'll schedule you something with him tomorrow."

"No, no, that's really not—"

Sasha tugged at the short hairs on the back of Kerry's head. "Don't argue."

Kerry felt her entire body go liquid at Sasha's assertive tone, and she subtly leaned more of her weight back against the stone balustrade. "Okay," she finally managed. "Thank you. How can I repay you?"

The mischievous smile that rose to Sasha's lips sent a chill shivering up Kerry's spine, but any anxiety she should have felt was obliterated by the surge of arousal that quickened her blood.

"Do you ride?"

Unbidden, Kerry flashed to an image of Sasha on her hands and knees, moaning softly as Kerry cupped her hips and teased her skin with gentle strokes, poised to—

Ruthlessly, she quashed the fantasy. "Wh-what?"

Sasha's fingers stilled and she tilted her head back. "Do you ride horses?" When her smile deepened, Kerry knew her Irish coloring had given her away. "What exactly were you just thinking?"

Kerry cleared her throat. "Ah. Yes, I can ride. I'm no steeplechase champion, but I'm proficient."

Thankfully, Sasha let her get away with the redirect. "Something you're not perfect at? I'm shocked."

"Why do you ask?"

"I want you to ride with me tomorrow morning. Though it will have to be early if we're to be back before brunch." She pursed her lips, considering. "This is the second time already I'll be rising early to spend time with you."

"Is that a good thing or a bad thing?"

"I haven't decided yet." Releasing her grip, she stepped away. Kerry immediately felt bereft. "The stables are a quarter mile's walk from the castle, just past the western gardens. Do you think you'll be able to find them?"

"I have an excellent sense of direction." Kerry tapped the side of her head, even as every cell in her body clamored for Sasha's return.

"Meet me there at seven o'clock sharp." She walked toward the door and Kerry dutifully followed.

At the last possible moment, Sasha turned, rose onto her toes, and pressed the briefest of kisses to the left corner of Kerry's mouth.

"Good night."

The door latched shut, and just like that, she was gone, leaving the faint scent of lilacs behind.

CHAPTER EIGHT

The sun had just begun to clear the jagged horizon as Kerry stepped out of the castle. With Sasha's directions in mind, she turned her back to the brightening sky and began to walk briskly along the gravel path. Tendrils of mist curled around the mountains like the tail of a dark gray cat, and she rubbed her palms together to generate some heat against the damp chill. She was dressed in the warmest clothes she'd packed: jeans and a bulky, hand-knit wool sweater procured last year in Ireland by her aunt. Footwear was her only problem; she'd brought loafers and sneakers, but no boots. Hopefully, she could borrow a pair.

As the path made a sharp curve around a copse of trees, the stable came into view. It was built of the same granite as the castle and topped with a thatched roof. Arched double doors, painted a deep crimson, had been thrown wide open. The scent of hay reached Kerry just as she heard one of the horses neigh, and she quickened her pace. She had learned to ride as a girl, on the farm horses belonging to their neighbors. It had been years since she'd sat in a saddle, though, and she hoped not to make a fool of herself today. But when Sasha emerged from the barn leading a glossy black mare, Kerry forgot all about her trepidation.

Sasha looked like she was about to walk onto the set of an equestrian photo shoot. Polished black boots reached up to mid-calf, giving way to fawn-colored jodhpurs that clung to her legs like a second skin. Her black jacket was lined with tartan flannel, she carried a helmet in the crook of her free arm, and her long dark hair hung down past her shoulder in a neat braid. She was crooning something to her horse, and while her voice was too low for Kerry to make out, she could catch the flickering of the mare's ears.

Despite feeling horribly underdressed, Kerry squared her shoulders and called out a "good morning." The mare's ears pricked inquisitively, and Sasha turned with a smile.

"Hi." Deftly, she tied the horse to a hitching post, brushed her hands on her legs, and awaited Kerry's approach. Uncertain of how to greet her, Kerry stopped a few feet away, but Sasha closed the distance between them and kissed her swiftly on the cheek.

"How did you sleep?"

"Very well, thanks." Kerry gestured to the mare. "Who's this?"

Sasha stroked the mare's nose. "This is Morrigan."

The name sounded familiar. "Morrigan. A Celtic goddess—is that right?"

Sasha looked impressed. "Quite right. She comes of Irish stock, so I thought it appropriate."

"You and me both, Morrigan." When Kerry offered the flat of her palm, the mare nosed at it briefly until she'd determined there was no food to be had and then blew out a petulant sigh through her nostrils. "How long have you had her?"

"About three years now. You'll be riding her stable mate, Finnegan. Would you like to meet him?"

"I would. And can I trouble you for a pair of boots? All I have are these sneakers."

Sasha glanced down. "In this country, those are called trainers." She reached for Kerry's hand. "Let's check the tack room."

"Trainers." Kerry tried to focus on the conversation, rather than the warmth of their interlaced fingers. "I should know that one. I've heard my teammates use it plenty of times."

"You're playing football at Oxford?"

"Yes. For Balliol."

"What position?"

"Midfielder."

Sasha squeezed her hand. "If I were to watch one of your matches, would you score for me?"

Kerry could picture the scenario as though it had already happened: charging down the left flank, angling into the box, leaping for a cross from the right corner. Heading the ball over the keeper's outstretched hands and hearing Sasha's triumphant shout from the sideline.

"Yes."

"Sure of yourself, are you?" Sasha pressed her shoulder against Kerry's triceps. "I like that. Here we are."

The wood-paneled tack room was well stocked, and they found an acceptable pair of boots within only a few minutes. Sasha then led her down the row of stalls before stopping in front of a dapple-gray horse that whickered softly at their approach.

"Kerry, Finnegan. Finnegan, Kerry."

Again, Kerry held out her hand. Finnegan's lips moved softly over her palm, seeking. "Sorry, bud. I don't have any treats." She shifted her hand to his neck and stroked his silky coat for a while. His coloring was beautiful, as though he was the morning mist incarnate.

When she stopped, he butted his nose into her chest. Sasha laughed in delight, and the sound made Kerry's heart flip-flop. She looked over her shoulder to find Sasha leaning insouciantly in the stall corner, arms crossed beneath her breasts. Kerry kept her hand firmly planted on Finnegan's flank to resist the urge to cross the space between them, pin Sasha to the wall, and kiss her until they were both breathless.

"He likes you."

"I wouldn't go that far." Kerry patted the horse's muscular shoulder. "This one seems pretty equal opportunity."

"You're not wrong, actually. He's a beggar for attention. Shall we go?"

Kerry nodded and grasped the reins just beneath Finnegan's mouth. As she led him out of the stall, Sasha handed her a helmet.

"Just in case. You Americans are so litigious."

"Not my family. They'd curse and shake their fists and promptly start planning the wake."

"Are you entirely Irish?" Sasha asked.

"One hundred percent. My family lives in the number one destination for Irish emigrants to the States."

Sasha's perfect eyebrows rose. "Have you ever been? To Ireland, I mean."

"Never. But it's on my to-do list while I'm here in the UK."

As they reemerged into the sunlight, Kerry noticed a chestnut gelding tied up opposite Morrigan, Ian standing next to him. Dressed in jodhpurs several shades darker than Sasha's and a forest green jacket, he glanced at them briefly before bending to inspect his horse's hooves.

"You haven't been properly introduced." Sasha was apparently determined to act as though the moment wasn't awkward. "Kerry, this is Ian, the head of my protection detail. Ian, this is Kerry Donovan, one of the Rhodes scholars."

Kerry stepped forward and extended her free hand. Ian's grip was firm and brief. Businesslike. "Pleasure to meet you."

"Likewise."

The two syllables were monotone, but she didn't sense any animosity from Ian—only a crystalline focus. Sasha placed a hand on her arm and leaned in to whisper in her ear.

"Don't worry. Ian will ride behind us quite a ways."

"I'm—" Mouth suddenly dry, Kerry had to pause. "I'm not worried."

Sasha stepped away, smiling. "No? Maybe you should be. Finn would follow Morrigan off a cliff."

"Now you tell me." Kerry reached for the girth strap on the saddle and tightened it a notch. "My fate is in your hands."

"Indeed." Sasha rose into the saddle in a fluid, practiced movement. Her gracefulness was beautiful, and Kerry was certain she'd look like a lumbering ox by comparison.

"Okay, big guy," she muttered as she struggled to fit her foot into the stirrup. It was high, and she had let some of her flexibility fall by the wayside since the end of her college athletic career. "Don't let me down." She pushed off the ground hard with her right foot and a moment later miraculously found herself seated atop Finnegan's back.

"Not bad," Sasha called, a teasing lilt to her voice. "Now let's see if you can keep up."

At some cue from her mistress, Morrigan trotted off down the path leading past the barn and into the forest. Finnegan immediately followed suit, almost bouncing Kerry right off. Shoving her right foot into the other stirrup, she made a grab for the reins and tried to remember how to post up and down in time with the horse's gait.

The first few minutes were a struggle, but by the time they entered the woods, Kerry had managed to find a comfortable rhythm. Once she stopped concentrating so hard, she was able to appreciate the scenery. Through the swirling mist, the landscape felt like a watercolor painting. Most of the deciduous trees had begun to change color, and Kerry enjoyed the explosions of red and yellow and gold among the dark green of the conifers.

Immediately ahead, Sasha moved easily in tune with Morrigan's brisk trot, her braid bouncing cheerfully between her shoulder blades. Kerry was captivated by the rhythmic flex of her legs. Desire warmed her from the inside out, warding off the briskness of the air. Every once in a while Sasha glanced over her shoulder and smiled. The entire situation was completely surreal, and Kerry rested one hand on Finnegan's shoulder, the powerful surge of his muscles reassuring her that this was not, in fact, a dream.

As they skirted a field filled with long grass and wild flowers, the path became wide enough to ride two abreast. Sasha slowed her mare to a walk and beckoned Kerry forward. Cheeks pink from the chill and exertion, she radiated happiness.

"How is Finn treating you?"

Kerry patted his neck. "He's fantastic, and these views are stunning."

Sasha rose in her stirrups and surveyed the mountains encircling them. "It's very beautiful here, isn't it?" She turned back to Kerry, one eyebrow raised. "How would you feel about picking up the pace?"

Every competitive bone in her body clamored for her to accept the challenge. "Let's do it."

Sasha pushed Morrigan into a canter, and this time, when Finn leapt to follow her, Kerry was ready. She clamped her knees against his withers and tried to relax into the rolling motion of his gait. Ahead, Sasha crouched low over Morrigan's neck, the tails of her jacket fluttering behind her.

At the edge of the field, they turned down a shallow slope and back into the forest. When the trail narrowed, Sasha slowed their pace.

They wound through the trees for several minutes before emerging into another, smaller clearing. Kerry caught sight of several stones poking up above the grass. Before she could ask about them, Sasha dismounted.

"Come on," she said. "I want you to see the ruins."

After swinging down much more awkwardly, Kerry followed her through the tall grass, leading Finn behind. As they approached the center of the clearing, Kerry realized the ruins were in fact a foundation, complete with the remains of a chimney. Some sort of house, perhaps.

"We can tie them here." Sasha beckoned her over to a tall outcropping and looped both sets of reins around the stone. She pulled off her helmet, then withdrew a thermos and a small foil package from Morrigan's saddle bags. "Coffee and freshly baked scones. Let's find a good place to sit and eat."

Kerry began to walk the periphery of the ruins, projecting the stones upward in her mind, visualizing how the house must have looked. It hadn't been large, and she saw signs of only three rooms.

"Do you know what this was?"

"My father claims it was a hunting lodge." Sasha climbed over one of the walls and approached the remnant of the chimney. "This looks like a good breakfast spot."

She sat with her back to the bricks, and Kerry slid in beside her as she unwrapped the scones. Sasha handed her one, unscrewed the thermos cap, and filled it with coffee. After passing it over, she raised the thermos.

"Cheers."

"Thank you for this." When Kerry bit into the scone, its buttery taste combined with the tartness of the currants to inspire a soft moan of pleasure that she couldn't hold back.

Scone poised before her own lips, Sasha cocked her head. "If I'd known you were going to make sounds like that, I would have asked the kitchen for more."

Kerry could feel her face flaming, but she refused to act ashamed. "They're that delicious."

Sasha took a bite and closed her eyes, savoring it. "I agree. And I like how expressive you are."

Her throat suddenly dry, Kerry took a sip of coffee. She had no idea how to respond. How did Sasha make her feel so off-kilter and yet so good at the same time?

"So." Sasha drew her feet beneath her to sit Indian-style against the broken wall. "You know about my family already. Tell me about yours."

Kerry licked the last crumbs of the scone from her fingers as she thought about how to reply. For now, it would be best to keep things simple. "I have three siblings, all older. One sister, Mary, and two brothers, Aidan and Declan. My father owns his own roofing company. My mother stayed at home to raise us."

"Tell me more. What are they like?"

The last thing Kerry wanted was to dredge up her family's sordid reaction to her coming out. She had to keep the atmosphere light. "Well, when she was a teenager, my sister had a photograph of your brother taped inside her locker at school."

"No!"

"Yes. Truly. She had quite the crush."

Sasha clutched her middle as she laughed, loud and long. "That is just too funny," she finally gasped.

"It really is." Kerry swiveled so that her toes were pressed against the wall and then reclined onto her back. While they rode, the mist had almost completely burned off. The sky was a bright, robin's egg blue, broken only by the occasional cirrus cloud.

"Your turn. Tell me something funny about your family. Something that never made it to the media."

Sasha drummed her fingers against the thermos as she mulled over the question. "Once, during a state dinner with several Middle Eastern dignitaries, my younger sister Elizabeth was sitting on my father's lap while he chatted with the Israeli Prime Minister. The PM had a bushy white beard, and she reached right up and gave it a tug."

Kerry laughed. "Please tell me she didn't irreparably damage relations between Israel and the UK!"

"Quite the opposite, actually. I think the prime minister was charmed."

"How old was she?" Kerry sat up to take another sip of coffee. Sasha wore a nostalgic expression she hadn't seen before.

"She was three. My mother was aghast. I'll never forget how quickly she whisked Lizzie away. But the prime minister only laughed."

When silence descended between them, Kerry wondered whether Sasha was caught up in memories of her mother. As much as she wanted Sasha to feel comfortable sharing those memories, she didn't think they'd reached anything near that level of emotional intimacy.

"Let's not betray any more family secrets." Kerry laced her hands behind her head. "How about...what's your favorite book?"

More silence. At first, Kerry thought Sasha was just considering her answer until she caught sight of the troubled look on her face.

"I'm not a very big reader," she finally said.

"All right." Kerry kept her tone light. She didn't know what had bothered Sasha about the question, but the last thing she wanted to do was to upset her. "Favorite film?"

The hint of a smile returned to Sasha's face. "*Sabrina*."

"Original or remake?"

"The original, of course, though the remake is decent." Sasha nudged Kerry's foot. "Your turn."

"*Lord of the Rings*."

Sasha laughed. "What are you, a teenage boy? Do you play... what's it called...Dungeons and Dragons, too?"

"I don't just enjoy those films for the story," Kerry protested, "but also for all the intricate, detailed work they did behind the scenes. Did you know that every piece of chain mail had to be assembled by hand? And the swords were forged by a real blacksmith at his foundry in New Zealand?"

"I see. You're not a teenage boy; you're a nerd." When Sasha very deliberately looked her up and down, Kerry suddenly flashed hot despite the cool breeze on her face. "In the body of a Greek god."

She had to clear her throat before she could be sure of her voice. "I'm going to take that as a net compliment. So thank you."

"How about a more serious question?" Sasha leaned forward. "What's your greatest fear?"

The question reminded Kerry of one of her undergraduate history professors, who had insisted that to comprehend the prevailing mentality of a culture, one had to understand its fears and anxieties. So much for maintaining any kind of emotional distance. Sasha was asking her to bare her soul. She looked from Sasha to the ruins surrounding them and back.

"I study the history of architecture, so I know—I mean, I really know—just how little an entire civilization can leave behind. Not to mention one individual. Even so, I can't help wanting to leave a—a mark of some kind on the world. A positive mark. I suppose my fear is that I won't succeed in that."

Sasha rocked up onto her knees, then stretched out alongside Kerry. "It's a little frightening, isn't it? Our lives are like shooting stars on the canvas of history."

Kerry's heart thundered in her chest—not only at Sasha's proximity, but at her eloquent acknowledgement of the anxiety that lurked at the very core of her being. As Sasha propped her head on one hand and looked down at her, Kerry made the choice to ignore the alarm bells clanging in her brain. Their bodies were separated by mere inches. She licked her lips, hoping her voice wouldn't fail.

"Surely you don't worry about being remembered by history."

"Even the names of kings are eventually forgotten." Sasha rested her free hand in the hollow between Kerry's breasts. Her fingertips twitched against the handspun wool. "We can't know how, or if, we'll be remembered. That's why we have to pause sometimes to simply enjoy what we have."

Dipping her head, she lightly pressed her lips to Kerry's and then withdrew. "Your heart is beating so fast."

Dizzy and aching with desire, Kerry dared to cup Sasha's cheek with one hand. "More. Please."

"I like how it sounds when you say 'please.'" Sasha drew closer, but paused inches above Kerry's mouth. "Say it again."

Kerry curled her free hand around a fistful of grass to stop herself from pulling Sasha's head down. How had such a brief touch infused desperation into her every cell?

"Please."

Sasha's eyes glittered in triumph. She bent her head again, and this time, Kerry surged up to meet her. She felt Sasha's quick gasp of surprise against her face before she fused their mouths together, stroking Sasha's tongue with her own. A soft, needy moan was her reward, making her head spin.

And then Sasha pulled away. Kerry smacked both palms against the ground in frustration, every cell clamoring for her to reverse their positions, tangle her fingers in Sasha's hair, and kiss her until neither of them could breathe.

"Oh? Still not satisfied?" Sasha's smile was insufferably smug.

Pride was far less important than feeling that perfect mouth on hers again. "Please."

"One more. Just one." Sasha licked her lips, and Kerry gave herself up to immolation. Surrender had never felt so much like triumph.

"Please."

Sasha reclined in a chaise lounge, legs crossed at her ankles, watching the impromptu football match through large sunglasses. While some members of Kerry's cohort had decided to avail themselves of the tennis courts, several others had created a makeshift pitch using cricket wickets for goal markers.

A sudden gust of cool air made her reach for the white cable knit cardigan hanging on the back of her chair. She'd dressed festively in Celtic colors—a green and white form-fitting sweater and black, skinny clamdiggers. Several of Kerry's peers had complimented her on the matching green penny loafers that completed her outfit.

A shout went up from the lawn as Kerry broke free from a cluster of players and pounded after a loose ball. After controlling it with a series of light touches, she barreled down on the opposition's final defender. At the last moment, she deftly flicked the ball over his extended foot toward Harris, who was there to guide it through the posts.

Sasha clapped, drawing curious glances from the scholars chatting at a table nearby. She didn't care. They would see only that she was caught up in the game, not that she was applauding the woman who had repeatedly begged for her kisses mere hours before. Heat flashed down her spine at the memory of Kerry's mouth opening beneath hers, of the low groan that greeted the slip-slide of their tongues. That last kiss had lasted an eternity, and when she had finally pulled away, the need eclipsing Kerry's bright blue irises had almost made her forget her promise to move slowly. But for her iron will, they might still be lying in the long grass, exploring each other's bodies.

As the players returned to the middle of the field, Kerry looked her way and smiled. Earlier, during the tour of the castle conducted by Raymond Fletcher, her demeanor had been all professional gravitas. She had listened attentively and asked interesting questions of which Fletcher had clearly approved. While she brought that same focused intensity to football, now an almost puppyish exuberance inflected her every movement. The more Sasha saw of her, the more she found to like. Such a thought should have been frightening, but mostly it just felt...good.

A shadow fell over her chair, and when she glanced up she found herself looking into the classically handsome face of Byron, Fletcher's famous nephew.

"Sasha, darling! Just the person I was hoping to meet out here. So lovely to see you."

"And you, Byron." She swung her legs over the edge of the chair and rose to embrace him lightly. Tan and fit, dressed in immaculate tennis whites, he looked a decade younger than his forty-one years.

He winked at her conspiratorially. "I have a business proposition for you. Is there somewhere we can sit and talk shop, as they say?"

"Certainly." Intrigued by the proposition of a joint venture, she took his arm. Byron's design expertise was coveted by some of the most exclusive venues and events in Europe. If he wanted to partner with her in some way, the opportunity would be a golden one. "My father's study has a beautiful view of the gardens and an excellent selection of bourbon. Will that suffice?"

"It sounds like heaven. Lead the way."

After conversing with Byron for an hour, Sasha had to change for dinner. As she slid her crimson, one-shoulder dress over her head, she reflected on the details they had discussed. The Mandarin Oriental Hotel had contracted with him to organize their Christmas gala for the following holiday season. He had some ideas about how her company could get involved, and at this point she was all ears. Yoking her business to one of the hottest designers and one of the most exclusive hotels in the city could only help her company gain credibility. She wanted it to be successful in its own right, and not simply as a byproduct of her parentage.

Plenty of people, her father included, regarded her business venture as pure vanity. Yes, her company wasn't eradicating malaria or building irrigation ditches in the Sahara. But she provided an important service that made people happy. Happiness was intrinsically valuable, wasn't it? Besides, she organized at least one pro bono event a year, and a sizeable portion of her profits were earmarked for charity. This proposed joint venture with Byron and the film premiere for Ashleigh had the potential to significantly boost her demand. She was finding ways to contribute to society while doing what she was good at. Where was the harm in that?

Upon entering the dining room, Sasha caught sight of Kerry, chatting with a few of her friends near the fireplace. Dressed in a checkered jacket and gray trousers, her colorful hair stylishly mussed, she made Sasha's mouth water. She had just set out to join the group when a touch on her shoulder brought her up short. She turned to the sight of Byron, clad entirely in black, from his jeans to his collared shirt—unbuttoned halfway down his chest—to his sport coat. Cowboy boots completed his obstinately underdressed look.

"Do you have another few minutes? I just finished a chat with my contact at the hotel, and he has some more details to share about the venue."

"Another few minutes" became significantly more, and one of the scholars graciously permitted Byron to switch seats with her so that he could continue to engage Sasha in conversation throughout dinner. Across the table, Kerry seemed deep in discussion with Byron's father, and Sasha fleetingly hoped their chat would lead to professional opportunities for her.

By the time the group withdrew into the games room, Sasha belatedly realized she had allowed Byron to monopolize most of her attention during the meal. Determined to play the role of gracious hostess, she moved methodically from group to group, chatting for several minutes with each in turn. Kerry was nowhere to be found, and at first Sasha thought she might have elected to continue her own conversation upstairs. But when she noticed the elder Fletcher keeping company with two trustees, she began to suspect that Kerry had misinterpreted her interest in Byron.

After an hour, she didn't have to feign a headache in order to find an excuse to leave. Her temples were throbbing, but after sequestering herself in her bedroom, she bypassed her medicine cabinet and headed straight for the desk, where she withdrew a piece of stationary from the top drawer. *I want to see you tonight,* she wrote, haste making her script less elegant than the night before. *This guard will escort you back to my room.* She signed her name, and then on second thought added a postscript. *Please.*

Once she had given Darryl his instructions, she kicked off her shoes, tossed back two aspirin, and began to pace. Kerry probably thought she'd been ignoring her all evening. "Oh, admit it," she muttered, suddenly cross with herself. "You were, but not in the way she thinks."

Several uncertain minutes later, a single knock came at the door. Sasha crossed the room quickly, unable to care that she would be betraying her own eagerness. She threw back the bolt and smiled in relief at the sight of Kerry, wearing orange sweats and a gray tank top, both of which were emblazoned with the Princeton crest. She could have changed back into her evening wear, but she'd elected not to. Sasha wanted to take that as a good sign. Besides, Kerry somehow looked even more attractive in baggy sweats and a tank than she had in her dressy attire.

She ushered Kerry quickly into the room and shut the door, keeping her fingers curled around the handle to anchor herself in place. As much as she wanted to pick up exactly where they'd left off among the ruins, she could sense that their mood had been broken. Kerry was regarding her warily, and Sasha cursed her own idiocy for allowing distance to spring up between them.

"Hi," she said softly.

"Hi." Kerry looked around the room, as though expecting to find someone else. "So I'm not really sure why I'm here."

"Because I said 'please'?"

Kerry flushed. She was remembering the morning. Good.

"You seem to be irresistible."

Sasha took one step forward. "I'm glad you came. I wish I'd had more of a chance to talk with you downstairs. Byron approached me earlier with a business proposition, and we spent most of the night hashing out the preliminaries." She took another step. "If it goes through, it could be a fairly significant venture."

"That sounds promising." The tautness of Kerry's shoulders eased as she smiled. "Congratulations."

"Normally, I might indulge in some champagne." Sasha extended her hand, praying she wouldn't scare Kerry away. "But I'd rather have one more kiss from you than all the Dom Pérignon in the world."

Kerry's laugh sounded forced. "Ever since you came down the stairs in that dress, I've needed to kiss you again."

Their fingers entwined, and Sasha pulled her further into the room. "Come here."

When they reached the foot of the bed, she pushed Kerry backward until her legs hit the mattress. Kerry sat down hard, clutching the coverlet. "I can't lie down," she whispered.

"Oh?" Sasha climbed onto her lap, trapping Kerry in place with her knees. "Why not?"

"Because if I do, I'll lose what little control I have left."

The strangled words made Sasha go liquid deep inside. Suddenly, she wanted nothing more than to make that happen—to drive Kerry to the point of surrendering to their mutual need. Unleashed from her inhibitions, she would be simply stunning—a dangerous, sensual creature.

Combing her fingers through Kerry's hair, she settled herself on those muscular thighs and embraced the warmth of the adrenaline rush. She would content herself with teasing. For now.

"What are you afraid of? That if we sleep together I'll disappear?"

"Yes."

She tugged lightly. "Are you that bad at it?"

Kerry's laugh was breathless. "What do you think?"

Sasha let her hands drop to Kerry's smooth, broad shoulders, then trail down along the prominent bulges of her triceps and biceps. So strong. She reached for Kerry's hands and tugged.

"I think I want your arms around me."

In the next moment, she felt Kerry's right hand at the small of her back, even as her left hand caressed the nape of Sasha's neck. Kerry pulled her closer until those blue, blue eyes filled her vision.

"Now what?" Kerry whispered, breath puffing against Sasha's mouth.

"Now you kiss me. But only for a little while."

Kerry's hand tightened on her neck, igniting a surge of arousal that forced Sasha's hips to edge forward, involuntarily seeking relief against the ridges of Kerry's quads. Gritting her teeth at the storm of sensation, she never once broke their gaze. At her movement, darkness absorbed Kerry's eyes.

"Only for a little while," she agreed, the words barely a whisper.

Leaning forward, she finally took Sasha's lips in a slow, deep kiss. As her tongue stroked rhythmically within Sasha's mouth, her hand massaged Sasha's shoulders to the same slow, tantalizing beat. Utterly lost, Sasha gave herself up to the maelstrom of sensation, praying Kerry would never stop.

CHAPTER NINE

Sasha stood in the shade of an oak tree, thirty feet from where the small crowd was clustered near the midfield line of the pitch. Despite the fact that she was dressed in her incognito attire today—skinny jeans, a University of Connecticut hoodie, her blond wig, and navy trainers—Ian had insisted they remain separate from the group of observers.

The Balliol women's football team was playing New College today, and from what Sasha had seen of the match, it was a fairly equal contest. She'd arrived just as the second half began, frustrated at her own lateness. Her daily meeting with Bloom had run long; she was set to deliver a speech at the groundbreaking ceremony for a new wing of the British Museum tomorrow, and Bloom had forced her to drill and re-drill the text until he was satisfied she wouldn't choke.

She'd been ready to choke *him* when she realized she wouldn't arrive to the match on time, but now that she was breathing the crisp air and watching Kerry work her magic in the midfield, her frustration had begun to melt away. It didn't take long for her to realize that Balliol could have been winning by several goals had Kerry not been an entirely unselfish player. Within the first ten minutes of the half, she had made three separate forays into the opposition's defense. Each time she was challenged, she passed the ball to an open teammate, and each time, the opportunity was squandered. Sasha had a feeling Kerry could have beaten the defenders quite easily and taken the ball to the net herself.

The team didn't have proper uniforms, but they were wearing matching shirts bearing the Balliol crest. Sasha admired the way Kerry's broad shoulders filled hers out. Suddenly, she was flashing back to the last time they'd touched, remembering how Kerry's strong biceps had flexed as she'd dipped Sasha back in her arms to cover her neck and throat with kisses.

"I won't leave a mark," she had whispered. "But I want to."

Sasha shivered, even as the memory made her skin flash hot. In many ways, Kerry was a paradox—an intriguing blend of confidence and humility, sensuality and restraint. During their days apart, they had exchanged a few semi-flirtatious text messages and even one brief phone call that had only whetted Sasha's appetite, not sated it. It had been a little silly to come out here when she was due back in London this evening for a drinks reception hosted by the museum trustees, but she hadn't been able to resist the chance to watch Kerry play.

A shout rose up from the Balliol supporters as once again, she broke free with the ball. This time, instead of targeting one of her teammates, she deftly faked out the woman who stepped up to challenge her. Belatedly, the goalkeeper tried to cut off her angle, but Kerry was already taking aim. At first, it looked as though her shot would go wide, until the ball curved at the last possible moment to enter the upper left corner of the net. Sasha had to clench her teeth to hold back the shout that would likely attract unwanted attention from the other spectators.

"Beautiful," she whispered fiercely.

"That was impressive." Miraculously, Ian's face hinted at admiration before his stoic mask dropped back into place. Sasha smiled. He seemed to be warming up to Kerry. That would be useful.

After the final whistle blew, she lingered beneath the tree as Kerry's teammates slapped her on the back and slung their arms around her. Jealous of their easy camaraderie, Sasha forced herself to stay where she was instead of approaching the knot of players. As they joined their supporters on the sideline, Sasha's jealousy turned to wistfulness. Harris had wrapped Kerry in a gigantic bear hug, and everyone was chattering excitedly about their plans for a celebratory drink at a nearby pub. In that moment, Sasha would have given anything to be one of them—to cast off the yoke of her royal ancestry and discard all its privileges in exchange for one utterly normal afternoon. Would the price be worth the prize? At times like these, she thought it might.

Kerry began to walk toward the road then, flanked by Harris and one of her teammates. Shaking off her funk, Sasha called out, pitching her voice slightly higher than normal. When Kerry looked over her shoulder and frowned in consternation, Sasha had to bite her lower lip to keep from laughing. Sometimes she thought she could go on a tour of Buckingham Palace in this disguise and none of the staff, who had known her since her infancy, would ever be the wiser.

Suddenly, recognition dawned on Kerry's face. "I'll meet you there," Sasha heard her say, before she turned and broke into a jog. She didn't think it a coincidence that the path of Kerry's approach shielded Sasha from the team's eyes.

"Congratulations," she said as Kerry pulled up before her, seeming even taller than normal in her football boots.

Her grin was ear-splitting. "This is a pleasant surprise."

"I told you I'd come see a match." Sasha wanted to reach for her hand, but this location was still too public.

"And I told you I'd score."

"It was a beautiful shot. I'm glad you finally took one."

Kerry laughed. "No one likes a ball hog."

"Your teammates might disagree, where you're concerned." Still feeling too exposed, Sasha gestured toward the tree-lined path that skirted the field. "Let's take a little stroll."

Kerry fell into step, one shoulder brushing hers, body radiating heat like a furnace. "So tell me," she said, her voice rich with amusement, "how did you decide on UConn?"

"It suits my purposes perfectly. American, but not one of the most recognizable names. Only once have I ever been approached by an alum."

"What did you do?"

"I told her I hadn't yet matriculated."

Kerry laughed. "Quick thinking! That was smart."

The adjective sent a rush of warmth through Sasha. "Go Huskies," she quipped, indicating the blue-stitched dog on the front of her shirt. When a curve in the sidewalk revealed a small bench next to a public water fountain, she pointed in its direction. "Shall we sit?"

"Sounds great."

Kerry gestured that she should take her seat first, and Sasha wondered whether she was naturally chivalrous or had been reading the protocol on public interactions with royals. Probably both. She sat near the middle of the bench, and Kerry dropped down beside her, putting a solid foot of space between them. When Sasha slid over so their legs and hips were in contact. Kerry tried to protest.

"I'm all sweaty."

"So?"

Sasha grabbed her left arm and guided it along the back of the bench so she could cuddle into the curve of Kerry's body. She smelled good—musky and warm, like the earth waking up after winter.

"So." Kerry's arm curved to pull her closer, fingers idly playing with the string of her hoodie. "Hi."

"You already said that."

Kerry's broad smile turned sheepish. "Sorry. I'm happy to see you. It's a little distracting."

Sasha kissed her neck, allowing her lips to linger when she found a sensitive patch just below Kerry's ear. The arm around her tightened as Kerry shivered.

"Is that a little distracting, too?"

"You have no idea."

Sasha loved knowing that Kerry's breathlessness had nothing to do with the match she had just played. She smoothed one hand over the mesh material of Kerry's shorts, enjoying the subtle flicker of the muscles beneath.

"I need to introduce you to my brother. You two would get along smashingly. He's quite a good footballer in his own right."

Kerry nodded. "Wasn't there talk of a Premier League team signing him a while back?"

"Oh, he's not nearly good enough for that." Sasha laughed. "It was a publicity stunt, really. QPR made an overture, in the hopes of boosting their flagging attendance. But he would never have seen a minute."

"I take it that wasn't attractive to him?"

"Not at all. Arthur doesn't do anything halfway." She leaned her head back on Kerry's shoulder. "Which team do you support?"

"Everton." Kerry brushed her cheek against the top of Sasha's head. "I read somewhere that your entire family supports Manchester United. True?"

"I'm a Red Devil born and bred. When they next play Everton, I'll arrange for you to sit in our box, if you'd like."

"That would be incredible."

Kerry's smile was genuine, but her tone rather subdued. Sasha wanted to ask what she was thinking but wasn't quite sure she wanted to know the answer. Did Kerry not fully trust the invitation? That wouldn't exactly be surprising, given her track record. Was she apprehensive about meeting the royal family? About the media? About getting more deeply involved with someone still in the closet?

Sasha bit back a sigh. She hated that analogy, but in her case, the shoe fit. Arthur and Lizzie knew she preferred women, but she hadn't discussed the matter with anyone else except Miranda. Doubtless, her father knew as well, thanks to his ubiquitous spies. He had never brought up the subject, probably because her flings had been only that.

One-night stands may have been her *modus operandi*, but she had already seen Kerry on four separate occasions—and that was counting the entire weekend in Scotland only once. Did that pattern constitute the beginnings of a bona fide "relationship?" And if so, shouldn't she feel apprehensive? In a relationship, the other person had a right to make certain claims on her—claims she didn't know she'd ever be able to honor. Did she have the courage to take on the Leviathan of the British political machine and come out to her nation? Did she have the fortitude to weather the resulting media frenzy? Did she have the necessary selflessness to shelter another person for the duration of the storm?

If she feared anything, it was that the answer to those questions was *no*. Someone like Kerry deserved a relationship that wasn't shrouded in lies. So why couldn't she stop wishing she could stay right here, instead of having to go back to London? Why couldn't she stop wondering when they would next be together?

Her thoughts scattered when Kerry lightly rubbed her upper arm.

"You just got really tense. Are you all right?"

"I'd be better if I didn't have to leave in a few minutes." Sasha cupped Kerry's neck in her palm and drew her down for a soft, slow kiss. As it went on, her lingering anxieties faded to the background. Never, ever had anyone kissed her like this. She felt as though they were mind-melded somehow—as though Kerry were inside her head, sensing every desire. When the tips of their tongues brushed ever so lightly, Sasha's head spun and she clutched at the fabric of Kerry's shorts, anchoring herself.

"Wow," Kerry whispered when she finally pulled away. "Just… wow."

"Yes." Wanting to lighten the mood, Sasha curled one finger around a lock of artificial hair. "You haven't said anything about my wig. Like it?"

"It's very convincing." Kerry rubbed a few strands between two fingers. "I like your real hair more, but I appreciate what this wig lets us do."

"You mean…this?" The kiss wasn't slow this time, and Sasha shivered when Kerry bit down lightly on her lower lip. The twinge of pleasure echoed in the pit of her stomach, and she gasped. Immediately, Kerry withdrew.

"Are you okay?" Concern and even a hint of self-recrimination, were plain in her eyes.

"Stop looking at me like that." Curling her fingers around as much of Kerry's thigh as she could manage, she squeezed the hard muscle. "I wish you hadn't stopped. And that I could stay longer."

"Time to go?"

Sasha knew she shouldn't be pleased at the forlorn note in Kerry's voice, but she was. She angled her body so she could rest her other hand on Kerry's abdomen. The muscles flickered beneath her touch, and her fingertips ached to feel skin.

"Sadly, yes. I have a reception to get to."

"And then the groundbreaking ceremony tomorrow, right?"

Sasha raised one eyebrow. "Oh? Keeping tabs on me?"

Kerry's flush was delightful. It was so much fun to make her squirm.

"I like knowing where you are." She frowned suddenly. "That doesn't sound creepy, does it?"

"Not coming from you." Sasha forced herself to stand. "Congratulations again. Go celebrate with your team."

Kerry rose as well. "Will this ceremony tomorrow be televised?"

A spike of anxiety lanced through Sasha. What if she flubbed her delivery, despite all her drilling Bloom had made her do? The last thing she wanted was for Kerry to see her make a mistake. Especially a public one.

"I'm sure you have better things to do. This isn't a very big deal." Standing on her tiptoes, she brushed her mouth over Kerry's one last time. "Go. Have fun."

"Okay." Kerry took a step backward. Sasha hated the space between them already. "Be safe."

"You, too."

Kerry raised her hand in an awkward little wave before turning and jogging back toward the field. Sasha watched her go, wondering about courage and fortitude and selflessness. And whether she would ever be able to take that leap of faith.

"Here we go." Kerry leaned back in her chair at the corner table in the Rhodes House study lounge that she was sharing with Harris, eyes fixed on her laptop screen.

"You found a live feed?"

"Right on the museum's home page. I love the Internet."

He looked up from the journal article he was reading. "When does it start?"

"In just a few minutes. Want to listen in?"

"Sure."

As Kerry worked a knot out of her headphones, she silently cursed the standing appointment she had with one of her advisors on Thursday afternoons. If not for that, she would have taken the train down to London to be at the event in person. At least the ceremony itself hadn't interfered with one of her commitments. She couldn't wait to see Sasha again, and to witness her uncanny ability to charm a crowd.

With a click, she maximized the live feed so that it filled her entire screen. Currently, the camera showed a sizeable group gathered in a sandstone courtyard, waiting for the groundbreaking to begin. The podium stood empty, while nearby, the Union Jack snapped in a brisk wind. When a white-haired man in a suit stepped up to the microphone, Kerry reached over to tap Harris on the shoulder.

"I think they're about to get started."

He shifted his chair until they were sitting side by side, and Kerry handed him the left earphone. The white-haired gentleman introduced himself as the president of the museum's board of trustees. After thanking the financial benefactors who had made the new wing possible, he introduced Princess Alexandra.

Kerry leaned forward as Sasha emerged into the camera's field of vision. She was dressed quite conservatively in a slim-fitting navy suit, and she carried with her a leather-bound folder that she opened on the podium. The camera zoomed in just as she smiled at the crowd, and Kerry's breath stuttered in her chest.

Harris nudged her. "You're drooling."

She never looked away from the screen. "Can you blame me?"

"Ladies and gentlemen," Sasha began, her amplified voice ringing out clear and pure like a bell. "It is an honor to be with you here today, on such an august occasion for the citizens of the United Kingdom and the world."

Sasha paused briefly as her gaze fell to the paper. "The holdings of the British Museum represent the most comprehensive record of human history on our planet. Thanks to the generosity of thousands of private donors, construction will begin today on a new wing that will allow the public even greater access to invaluable artifacts. While the advancements of this digital age allow—"

A sudden gust of wind rattled the microphone and caught the paper on which her speech was written, lifting it into the air and propelling it toward the Beefeater guards standing near the flagpole. The camera zoomed out to catch some aide scurrying toward the guards, who remained motionless and stoic as he retrieved the speech.

"Apparently Mother Nature wants me to be brief." Sasha's comment prompted a laugh from the crowd.

She accepted the now-battered sheet of paper, and the camera zoomed in again. Suddenly, her smile disappeared and she swallowed hard. Kerry felt herself grip the edge of the table as panic flickered across Sasha's face. She rotated the speech ninety degrees, then back. A hush had fallen over the crowd, but as she continued to remain silent, the microphone began to pick up a current of murmuring.

"What's the matter?" Harris asked.

Kerry shook her head. "Come on," she whispered. "You've got this." She'd been doing so well. What had just happened?

"This…this digital age…" Sasha swallowed hard again. "Presents many, ah, opportunities? Archives, and…and…"

Kerry watched her blink furiously, as though she were trying to focus on something blurry. Or perhaps she was hoping to hold back tears? Sympathy and concern twisted in her gut, making her feel ill.

"It's like all of a sudden, she can't *read*." Harris leaned forward, squinting at the screen. "Did the speech get wet or something?"

Epiphany struck. Sasha's reputation as an intellectual weakling and the wild child of her family. Her insecurity about her own intelligence. *I'm not a very big reader*, she had said. Without a script to read, she charmed a crowd effortlessly. But now that she was bound to a text, she could barely string three coherent words together. Kerry hadn't thought to add up the pieces before now, but when she did, a clear picture emerged. One of her cousins suffered from the same condition.

Sasha was dyslexic.

"This is bad," Harris muttered as Sasha continued to struggle through the remainder of the speech. The syntax of most of her sentences was completely jumbled, and it was impossible to follow a logical thread through the speech. "The media is going to crucify her."

Kerry's heart was racing and her palms were moist. She wanted nothing more than to whisk Sasha away from the judgmental crowd—to take her someplace quiet where she could hold her and comfort her and try to convince her that she didn't have to feel ashamed. She had to grip the table tightly to keep herself from jumping up and running to the train station.

Harris's palm came to rest on her jittering leg. "Hey, take it easy. This will be bad for a day or two, but it'll blow over soon."

She nodded, heart in her throat. As much as she wanted to share her revelation, it wasn't her place. Clearly, Sasha wanted this kept secret. The real question was why, if her father knew about her dyslexia, would he set her up for this kind of public humiliation? Unless he didn't know. But how was that possible?

Mercifully, Sasha's last few sentences were coherent. As the camera panned away, Kerry caught a glimpse of her trembling hands and her heart broke all over again.

"I have to get down there."

"Right now?" Only when Harris answered did she realize she'd spoken out loud. "And skip out on your professor?"

"Damn it." Frustration welled up in her, and she smacked her fist against her thigh. "You're right. I can't."

Harris grabbed her hand. "Jesus, go easy. You can always leave later on. But are you sure she'll want to see you? She's got to be pretty embarrassed."

Kerry shook her head emphatically. "I don't care. I have to try." She snapped her laptop shut and pushed back her chair. "I'm going back to my room to pack so I can leave from my meeting."

"Just be careful, okay? Call me if you need anything."

On impulse, she leaned across and kissed him on the cheek. "You're the best. Thank you."

Several hours later, she leaned her cheek against the cool window of the train and watched the sun set over the London skyline. It grew larger every second, and for the tenth time in as many minutes, Kerry checked her phone. She'd left a voice mail message for Sasha from the Oxford station, and she'd sent a text just half an hour ago. The lack of response was disheartening. She'd wanted to believe that Sasha wouldn't shut her out, but apparently, Harris had been right.

Of course, she was probably dealing with quite a bit of backlash already. The fallout of her botched speech had begun immediately, thanks to social media. Her name had been trending on Twitter since noon, and Kerry had already seen two of her so-called "friends" on Facebook sharing a video clip from the ceremony. Their cruel comments had made her actually see red.

As the train pulled into King's Cross station, she double-checked the map of the Tube on her phone. It was public knowledge that when in London, Sasha resided in Clarence House, the royal residence attached to St. James Palace in Westminster. Perhaps by the time she made her way there, she would have a reply from Sasha on her phone.

But when she emerged from the Underground half an hour later, her phone continued to taunt her with a blank screen. As she paused on the sidewalk opposite the gate to Clarence House, a cold drizzle began to fall. Perfect. For one insane moment, she considered approaching the guard booth and asking to see the princess.

"They'll probably arrest you," she muttered. Shoving her hands in her pockets, she turned back toward the Tube station, looking for a place to take shelter from the rain. When her stomach rumbled, reminding her that she'd forgotten to eat lunch, she settled on the Red Lion pub. She sat at the bar, ordered a pint of London's Pride and an order of the bangers and mash, and decided to send one more text. The last train back to Oxford left just before midnight.

I'm in a pub around the corner from Clarence House called the Red Lion, she wrote. *I'll be here until eleven o'clock. I need to see you. Please.*

Before she could second-guess her wording, she hit "Send." While waiting for her food, she forced herself to get a jumpstart on the reading she needed to do for next week. It was slow going, especially since she couldn't seem to stop herself from checking her phone every five minutes, but she had managed to make it through a chapter and a half before she felt a light tap on her shoulder. Adrenaline flooded her system as she spun on her stool...only to see Ian, dressed in his customary dark suit, gray trench coat speckled with raindrops.

"Good evening, Ms. Donovan," he said formally.

She blinked at him dumbly for several seconds before collecting her wits enough to return the greeting. She had no idea what else to say. Why had he come? What did he want with her?

"Is she all right?" Kerry finally asked, not wanting to mention Sasha's name in the crowded pub.

His mouth tightened. "Frankly, no. She refuses to speak with anyone. I saw your message on her telephone and I'd like to take you to her. If you're still willing."

"Even though she doesn't want to see me?"

"I don't believe she knows what she wants, frankly. She's in a very dark mood, and she's been drinking. At this point, I'm willing to risk her ire."

"That makes two of us." Kerry stood, threw a few pound notes onto the bar, and grabbed her backpack. Ian had sought her out. He thought she could help. Silently, she vowed not to disappoint him, or herself.

"I'm ready. Take me to her."

CHAPTER TEN

I an led her back to the main entrance of Clarence House, where he flashed his credentials at the guard booth. After producing her driver's license, Kerry was granted entry through a small door to one side of the main gate. As they walked briskly down the gravel driveway, Kerry admired the elegant stucco façade of the residence. Clarence House had been conceived during the Regency and built shortly thereafter, but the building had been given a near-complete overhaul after suffering bomb damage during World War II. Little of the original structure remained, and Kerry had read that it was quite modern inside. She was about to find out for herself.

She caught only a glimpse of the foyer—its gleaming wood floor giving way to cream-colored walls punctuated by several large oil paintings—before Ian led her upstairs. Four flights later, Ian paused on the landing before a large oaken door.

"This is Her Royal Highness's suite of rooms." He produced a set of keys and fitted one into the lock, then gestured toward the bench resting against the opposite wall, where the other security officer Kerry had met at Balmoral was seated. "Either Darryl or I will be right there should you happen to need any assistance."

"Thank you." Kerry felt a surge of trepidation. What sort of "assistance" did Ian think she might need? What exactly was Sasha up to?

"I shall ask Her Royal Highness's valet not to attend her tomorrow morning, if you think it best," Ian continued.

Her valet? Kerry's brain spun into overdrive as she tried to formulate a response. Sasha's morning routine was apparently worlds apart from her own. Unsurprisingly. "I'll manage, thanks."

"Very well."

When he pushed open the doors, she was struck first by the darkness and then by the music. After pausing to let her eyes adjust to the gloom, she saw that a long corridor awaited her, culminating in a set of double doors. They were slightly ajar, and flashes of light danced in the gap. The music died, to be replaced by the low murmur of voices. Was Sasha watching a film?

Kerry startled at the quiet snick of the door shutting behind her. Ian had well and truly thrown her into the lion's den, but right now, there was no place she'd rather be. At the sensation of thick carpeting beneath her feet, she slipped off her shoes and left them just inside the door.

The voices grew louder as she walked slowly down the hallway, their dialogue tantalizing her memory. Whatever Sasha was watching, she'd seen it before but couldn't quite place it. Feeling like an interloper despite the fact that Sasha's own guard had granted her access, she took a deep breath as she stopped in front of the doors. And then she pushed.

The doors opened soundlessly to reveal Sasha in profile, seated on a black leather couch, a half-empty snifter in her right hand. Wearing only a black tank top and matching bikini underwear, she was focused on a large television on the wall, but as Kerry lingered in the threshold she turned her head. Surprise flashed across her face before she laughed, quietly and without real mirth.

"Perfect. How did you get here?"

Kerry felt like she had just found herself in a minefield, filled with foreboding that whatever step she took would be the wrong one.

"It's true what they say about British trains," she said lightly. "Regular and reliable."

Sasha turned back to the television. "I don't want you here. Please go."

Despite having expected this sort of reaction, Kerry couldn't suppress the stab of hurt that pierced her stomach. She almost turned around. Sasha was a princess, after all. What right did she have to disobey? But Sasha was also woman she cared for. A woman in pain.

"I'm not going anywhere. And since Ian was the one who brought me here, I don't think he'll throw me out."

"He put you up to this."

"He didn't put me up to anything." Kerry made her voice soft but firm. "I came as soon as I could. He saw the messages I'd left on your phone."

"I'm sure you can appreciate why I haven't touched my phone in hours." Sasha drank from her glass. "I've been sitting here praying one of your precious celebrities dies or gets pregnant."

The rawness beneath her words tore into Kerry's chest, but she had to tread carefully. Sasha would reject out of hand anything that even remotely resembled pity.

"May I come in?"

She didn't look away from the screen. "If you must."

Kerry crossed the threshold and sat gingerly on the matching chair to the right of the sofa. Uncertain, she turned her attention to the screen, only to realize she recognized the movie.

"*The Age of Innocence*?"

Sasha raised her glass in a salute. "One of my favorites. I may be a fuck up, but at least I've avoided a loveless marriage. So far, anyway."

Kerry gripped the arms of her chair, reminding herself not to take the bait. If she expressed sympathy, Sasha would use her as the focal point for her anger. And while Kerry would gladly have painted a bull's-eye on her own belly if it would help, she knew that in this case, turning herself into a target wouldn't do a hint of good. Sasha needed to talk about the real problem.

"Have you ever read the novel?" When she remained silent, Kerry pushed harder. "It's a beautiful book. I read it in my first year of college for a seminar on the literature of New York."

Finally, Sasha leaned forward, her face a mask of pain and fury illuminated only by the light of the screen. "What do you want me to say? I can't bloody read, all right? Wasn't it obvious today?"

Kerry reached for her hand and held on even when Sasha would have snatched hers away. Tenderly, she stroked her thumb over Sasha's knuckles. They were slightly abraded, as though she had hit something.

"Don't misrepresent yourself," she said quietly. "You can read. You're just dyslexic."

Sasha blinked, shock trumping her anger. "How did you—but—everyone else in the world is saying I was drunk or high or that I'm just a dumb slut—"

"I'm smarter than almost everyone else in the world." Kerry dared a small grin, mostly to hide her boiling rage at the catalogue of insults. Sasha needed her to be calm right now. "Also, my youngest cousin has it. A pretty mild case, but some of the signs were familiar."

Sasha worried at her lower lip with her teeth. Her gaze darted back and forth between the television and the floor. She looked like a trapped animal. Kerry just kept on stroking the back of her hand, hoping the touch would soothe her. Hoping she would open up.

"Mine is…moderate." Sasha threw back the rest of her drink and rather unsteadily set the glass on the coffee table. "When I was young and began to fall behind in school, my father thought I was lazy. Even after I was finally diagnosed, he seemed to consider… this…a personal failing on my part."

Kerry couldn't believe what she was hearing. "A personal failing? Did anyone bother to tell him that dyslexia is genetic?"

"He certainly doesn't have it." She smiled wanly. "He believes that if I concentrate hard enough, I'll be able to force my mind to work properly."

"And that's not how it works for you."

"Not at all." Sasha looked down at their joined hands. "I do much better when I'm relaxed."

"So this morning…" Kerry thought back to exactly what had happened. Sasha had seemed to have the event well in hand at first.

"It was so silly." Withdrawing her hand from Kerry's grasp, she slid back against the couch and pulled her knees up to her chest. The unconscious defensiveness of her position made Kerry want to hold her.

"I was fine until that gust of wind knocked over my papers. But when that happened, I worried one of the sheets would get lost, or that they would be out of order. When the anxiety hit, I…" she trailed off, squeezing her eyes shut as though she could block out the memory.

This time, Kerry didn't resist her instincts. She slid onto the couch next to Sasha and wrapped one arm around her thin shoulders. Her body was rigid, and Kerry sensed she was fighting back tears. As much as she wished Sasha felt comfortable letting go in her presence, she could understand not wanting to show weakness. She focused on taking slow, even breaths, hoping the steady rhythm would prove soothing.

After several tense minutes, Sasha finally relaxed into Kerry's embrace and opened her eyes. This close, Kerry realized they were bloodshot with exhaustion.

"Let's get you to bed," she whispered.

"Are you finally propositioning me?" The words were one hundred percent "Sassy Sasha," but the tone was hollow.

Kerry stood and offered her hand. As Sasha rose, she swayed once and reached out to grip Kerry's upper arm for balance. The movement drew their bodies flush, and suddenly Kerry's head was spinning too. Sasha flexed her fingers and licked her lips.

"I need to see you naked. If you look even half as good as you feel…"

Kerry swallowed hard, wanting nothing more than to give in to their mutual desire. But not like this. Not like this. She lowered her head, lips caressing the delicate shell of Sasha's ear.

"I want you so much, but I'm not going to sleep with you tonight. You're so tired, and you've had too much to drink. I want you to remember our first time perfectly."

Sasha shivered at the words, and Kerry pulled her even closer. Struggling to tamp down the fire in her veins, she stroked her palm along Sasha's spine. She wanted to comfort her with promises—that everything would be better tomorrow, that the world would forget quickly, that her father would handle the fallout with compassion rather than judgment. But she had no control over any of that. All she could control was herself.

"Don't be angry with me, okay?"

Sasha took a step back and looked up at her with a small smile. "I'm not. How could I be?" She cupped Kerry's cheek briefly. "I'll be right back."

Kerry watched her walk unsteadily toward the bathroom. When the door closed behind her, she took her first good look at the rest of the room. A four-poster, king-sized bed stood with its headboard against the far wall, flanked by two marble-topped nightstands. In the far corner, a table and two chairs were arranged near a fireplace. She approached the bed, switched on the nearest lamp, and turned down the covers. As she tried to figure out the television remote, Sasha emerged from the bathroom wearing a green silk nightgown the precise color of her eyes. Its hem came to mid-thigh, the material caressing her breasts and hips as she moved toward the bed.

Kerry groaned in spite of herself. "You're not making this easy."

Sasha's gaze carried a hint of its former fire. "Who said I was obliged to?"

"Touché."

She slid under the covers and patted the empty side. "It's too late for you to go back to Oxford tonight. Stay."

"I will." Kerry felt her smile turn rueful. "But I can't sleep there."

Sasha sighed. "The guest room is the first door on the left as you walk back down the hall, and you should help yourself to anything you need. But will you at least come here? Just for a moment?"

When Kerry perched on the edge of the bed, Sasha ran two fingers up and down the length of her forearm. She shivered.

"You like that?"

"I like it anytime you touch me."

Sasha raised her hand to cup the back of Kerry's neck. "When you finally let me, you'll regret having put me off for so long."

But Kerry shook her head. "No, I won't." She pressed one firm but gentle kiss on Sasha's lips, wanting to linger and knowing she couldn't. "When we make love for the first time, I don't plan on having any regrets at all."

Sasha's breath hitched, and she stared up at Kerry with an unfathomable expression. Kerry squeezed her hand once and then withdrew.

"Good night." She headed toward the door, but Sasha's voice made her pause.

"Kerry. Thank you."

She turned back, savoring the sight of Princess Alexandra reclining on one elbow, looking at her with a mixture of desire and affection.

"Sweet dreams."

She left the door cracked behind her and quickly found the guest room. Its bathroom contained a medicine chest with several spare toothbrushes—the one item she'd forgotten—but as she stood contemplating the queen-sized bed, she realized it simply wouldn't do. She grabbed a pillow and a spare blanket from the closet and crept back into Sasha's room.

Sasha was already asleep and snoring lightly, dark hair fanned out against the pillow, one hand clutching the covers to her chest. Simply stunning. Reluctantly, Kerry tossed her own pillow onto the couch and spread out the blanket. Was she crazy for not taking Sasha up on her invitation? Now that Sasha was sleeping, couldn't she indulge her need to be close by sliding under those covers?

Kerry lay back on the couch with a sigh. Too tall to fit comfortably, it took her several minutes to find a relatively un-cramped position, but she simply couldn't move to the bed. She didn't trust herself.

She didn't trust herself at all.

Sasha woke to the sensation of a distant drumroll in the back of her head. When she opened her eyes, the throbbing intensified. It took her several disoriented moments before the events of the previous day filtered through her headache. The botched speech. Enduring her father's subsequent tirade over the phone. Retreating to her rooms to lick her wounds. Kerry's arrival.

Kerry.

She sat up too quickly and squeezed her eyes shut as the pain sharpened. Once it had receded back to a dull ache, she dared to take a look around the room. It was empty, but a glass of water and two aspirin sat on her nightstand, and her snifter was no longer on the coffee table. Kerry had cleaned up after her. What an impression she must be making.

After taking the pills, she brushed her teeth, pulled on a pair of skinny jeans and a black, v-neck sweater, and then went on the hunt. It was just past seven o'clock, and she hoped Kerry was still asleep. But when she quietly pushed open the door to the spare bedroom, she was greeted by the sight of a bed that hadn't been slept in at all. Had Kerry already left? Belatedly, Sasha realized she didn't even know whether Kerry had academic obligations on Fridays. How much rest and studying time had she sacrificed by coming down to London?

Just as she was giving in to self-recrimination, Sasha turned into the kitchen and was greeted by the aroma of coffee and the sight of Kerry, hunched over her laptop, crimson mop of hair still wet from a recent shower.

"Good morning," she called softly, wondering if Kerry could hear the relief in her voice.

She turned quickly, a smile lighting up her freckled face. "Hi. How are you feeling?"

"A little achy. Thank you for the medicine."

Kerry waved aside her gratitude as she stood. "Coffee?"

"Please."

"How about some toast? Think your stomach could handle it?"

Sasha frowned. "How did you know I was feeling a little queasy?"

"Educated guess. And some past experience."

"Toast would be wonderful, if you really don't mind." But when Sasha sat in the vacated chair, Kerry paused in the act of pouring.

"You might not want to look at my computer."

A quick glance revealed that Kerry had been looking at Twitter. Facebook was open in another tab. The video of her mangled speech had gone viral, and the pain in her head intensified as she wondered just how many thousands upon thousands of people had laughed at her expense.

"How bad is it?"

"It's not great." Kerry's voice was steady, but her free hand drummed a beat on the countertop. She was clearly agitated on Sasha's behalf and trying to hide the extent of her dismay.

"I need to see what they're saying."

She returned to pouring the coffee. "Okay."

As Kerry began to fiddle with the toaster, Sasha took a deep breath and focused her attention on the screen. At first, the words swam wildly before her eyes and she had to look away. Her stomach churned. But then two warm hands came to rest on her shoulders, and Kerry's breath tickled her neck.

"Can I help?"

The question was simple, direct, devoid of all condescension. Miraculously, when Sasha raised her eyes back to the screen, most of the text was standing still. "Actually, you can. Stay right there, please."

"Your wish is my command." Kerry lightly massaged Sasha's shoulders as she read. While a few of the words still shivered or jumped, the majority of the lines remained anchored in place. The responses weren't flattering in the slightest—most commenters had decided that her IQ was barely higher than that of a chimpanzee—but none of the vitriol stung quite so badly today as it had last night.

When the toast popped up, Kerry's hands tightened on her shoulders. "Let me grab that."

Having seen quite enough, Sasha gently closed the laptop. "Where did you sleep last night?"

"On your couch."

"My couch? You're about a foot too long for it!"

Kerry shrugged in the act of buttering the bread. "It worked out just fine."

Her tone brooked no argument, so Sasha let the subject drop. A moment later, Kerry set the plate in front of her and slid into the adjacent seat.

"Thank you." Sasha rested her free hand on Kerry's knee as she bit into her toast. "You didn't have to do this. Any of it."

"I wanted to."

"I hope you didn't miss anything important?"

Kerry shook her head. "My last class of the week finishes on Thursday afternoons. But please let me know when I should leave. Aren't you traveling somewhere today?"

"To Wales, with my father. We'll be there through the middle of the week, mostly visiting schools and charities."

"Do you enjoy that kind of thing? Or no?"

"The sycophantic bureaucrats can be rather annoying. But the children make me laugh." Sasha felt herself smile. "Once, a cheeky little girl had the nerve to tell me that I couldn't possibly be a 'real princess' because I wasn't wearing a crown and a pink dress."

"She didn't!"

"Oh, but she did. Her teacher was mortified." She traced the contours of Kerry's powerful leg muscles, enjoying this casual intimacy. Here they were, chatting over the remains of breakfast like a normal couple. It felt uncommonly good. "We don't leave until late this afternoon. Will you stay? At least for a little while?"

"I'd like that." But instead of looking pleased, she seemed pensive. "Your father—did you speak with him yesterday?"

"Oh, yes. I didn't do much speaking. He, on the other hand, did quite a bit of shouting."

Kerry covered her hand, lacing their fingers together. They fit so well. "I'm sorry."

Sasha didn't answer. There was nothing to say. Her father was a force of nature. He couldn't be controlled. The most she could hope for was to weather his storm. She knew his opinion of her would never change. But what about Kerry? Was she only being kind and solicitous because she was a good person? Or because of their incredible chemistry? She was a Rhodes scholar—brilliant and driven. How could she not feel derision for a grown woman who could barely read? Sliding her hand out from under Kerry's, she fiddled with the hem of her sweater.

"Does it bother you?"

"What, exactly?"

"My dyslexia."

When Kerry leaned forward, Sasha read only earnestness in her face.

"The only thing that bothers me is how people mistreat you because of it."

"But you're so bloody smart. Doesn't it disturb you that I don't share your passion for books? You obviously love to read." She looked away. "I hear it's great fun when the words aren't writhing around on the page."

This time, Kerry reached for both her hands, compelling her attention.

"First of all, being dyslexic doesn't mean you're unintelligent. You read people so well, and I have yet to meet a better storyteller. You're utterly captivating. You can charm a crowd like the Pied Piper. What are all those qualities, if not intelligence?"

Unable to speak or swallow for the sudden lump in her throat, Sasha squeezed Kerry's hands. No one had ever spoken of her own gifts so eloquently before—not even her siblings, when they were trying to make her feel better.

"And as to your other point," Kerry continued, "why can't you share my passion for books? There's no reason why we can't read things together. Do you enjoy listening when someone reads aloud?"

"That's so patronizing."

She frowned. "Oh, no. It's really not. Most stories are meant to be heard, not read silently. Poetry too, of course."

Sasha was having a difficult time believing her. At university, she had received special accommodations that included having some of her course texts and all of her exams read out loud. At the time, it had seemed like a massive inconvenience. She'd never considered that it might be enjoyable.

"You would want to read out loud to me?"

Kerry squeezed again. "Very much."

Despite her avid reassurance, Sasha still felt skeptical. Her thoughts must have been transparent, because Kerry let go of her hands and flipped her laptop open.

"What if we tried it right now? I'll read you one of my favorite poems. You can see what you think."

She had to admit, the thought of Kerry reading poetry to her had a certain appeal. Was there any harm in trying? Just once?

"All right."

"Have you ever heard of T.S. Eliot?"

Sasha tapped the side of her head. "I dimly remember hearing his name in the mandatory literature class I nearly failed at university."

"Well, he was an American, but also a complete Anglophile. He actually became a naturalized British citizen. The poem I'm going to read to you is called 'The Love Song of J. Alfred Prufrock.'"

"So it's a romantic poem?"

Kerry grinned as if she knew a secret. "Not exactly. You'll see." After clearing her throat, she began. "Let us go then, you and I, when the evening is spread out against the sky…"

She was an excellent reader, enunciating each line clearly while also maintaining the poem's internal rhythm. Slow but not ponderous, the words fell from her lips like some sort of magical charm, enfolding Sasha in suspended animation. Despite the pleasure she took in Kerry's physical appearance, Sasha soon closed her eyes to allow the cadence of the words to wash over her.

"…Till human voices wake us, and we drown."

Sasha was so caught up that she didn't immediately realize the poem had come to an end. Only when she felt Kerry caressing her face did she emerge from her reverie.

"You have frown lines here." Kerry smoothed her thumb along the narrow strip of skin between Sasha's eyes. "What did you think?"

She couldn't help leaning into the gentle touch. "It wasn't at all what I was expecting from something called a love song. It was—not sad, exactly. Melancholy?"

"I think that's the perfect word."

"What do you love about it? Why is it one of your favorite poems?"

Kerry leaned back in her chair and cocked her head, considering. "I suppose I love it because it's a warning against mediocrity. A reminder not to get so caught up in daily life you don't ever try for more."

"More. What does that mean to you?"

"Well, I think it comes down to the question he asks in the middle. 'Do I dare disturb the universe?' I love that. Do you have the courage to take action, even when it might create chaos?" She flashed a bittersweet smile. "I used to think about those lines a lot, when I was getting ready to come out to my family. I had a Post-it note on my computer: 'Dare to disturb the universe.'"

Sasha could easily imagine a younger Kerry—more naïve but just as ambitious—struggling with that decision. Especially if she came from a fully Irish Catholic background.

"How did they react?"

A knock at the door interrupted whatever Kerry had been about to say. With a rueful glance, Sasha rose to answer it. When she saw Ian through the peephole, she let him in.

"Good morning, Your Royal Highness." His face was pinched with fatigue.

"Good morning. Is something the matter?"

"Your father has moved up your departure time. He wishes to leave within the hour."

Sasha wanted to stomp her foot like a child. "Did he give a reason?"

Ian scowled. "The paparazzi are out in force. By changing your schedule, he hopes to dodge the worst of them."

Sasha cursed beneath her breath. Always a bother at the best of times, they swarmed like bees whenever the barest hint of notoriety surfaced. Her blunder yesterday must have sent them into a frenzy. At the sound of footsteps behind her, she turned to the sight of Kerry looking unsure of herself.

"Is there anything I can do?"

Sasha went to her quickly, rising onto her toes for a too-brief kiss. She didn't want to say good-bye like this—especially when she would be across the country for the next several days. And then epiphany struck. Her schedule was clear next weekend. The week would be bearable if she gave herself something to look forward to. What's more, she could show Kerry her appreciation by making one of her lifelong dreams come true.

"Yes. There is." She cupped Kerry's face in her palms. "Come with me to Ireland. Just us. Next weekend. We'll leave on Thursday evening and I'll have you back in Oxford by Sunday night." She brushed one thumb across Kerry's mouth. "Say yes."

Kerry blinked down at her, looking dazed. "Yes."

"Good." Galvanized, she faced Ian. "You'll find her an escort to King's Cross?"

"Of course, ma'am."

Sasha squared her shoulders, thinking of the mob scene awaiting her outside the gates. Did she dare disturb the universe? Today, the answer was yes.

"I want to face the fucking paparazzi myself. Let's give them a few shots of me looking unconcerned about anything."

"But, Your—"

Sasha raised a hand to counter his protest. "I know you don't like it. But today, I refuse to slink around in the shadows. Not for them—not for anyone."

She stalked back toward her bedroom, forcing herself not to sneak one last look over her shoulder at Kerry. She had to focus. It was time to choose the perfect outfit for a hostile crowd.

CHAPTER ELEVEN

At three o'clock, Kerry descended the stone staircase outside her professor's office feeling like she was stepping into someone else's life. On the street below, a black car idled at the curb. Waiting for her. The driver must have been watching, because as she approached he got out, relieved her of her bag, and opened the door. She murmured her thanks as she slid inside.

During the brief drive to Oxford's regional airport, she checked her phone. No word from Sasha, other than the brief text she'd received this morning: *See you soon.* Not only had they not been able to communicate very much throughout the week, but Sasha was also being deliberately obtuse about the specifics of their trip. She had told Kerry only that they would be traveling by private plane and that she should "pack casually." Consumed by curiosity and excited to finally see her ancestral homeland, Kerry had had difficulty concentrating all week.

The car pulled into the airfield, and after an ID and bag check from security officials, the driver continued on toward where a small silver plane was being fueled.

"Here you are, ma'am."

"Thank you."

He handed off her bag to a member of the ground crew who directed her up the gleaming staircase. It was a struggle not to take the steps two at a time. When she poked her head inside the plane, she was greeted by the sight of Sasha leaning back in a black leather seat, phone held up to her ear. Her black skinny jeans and deep red cashmere sweater clung to every tantalizing curve, but she seemed thinner than she had last week, and Kerry struggled not to betray her concern as she approached.

Sasha smiled brightly and gestured toward the chair next to her. As Kerry settled into its roomy embrace, she realized she'd be forever spoiled for all future commercial flights.

"I've got to go, Liz. Yes, I'll let you know. Love you, too."

One minute, Sasha was disconnecting the call with her sister. The next, her hand was braced against Kerry's chest and she had joined their lips together. When Kerry groaned, Sasha took advantage of the moment by sliding her tongue deep inside Kerry's mouth.

Kerry very nearly forgot herself. Twisting in the chair, she clutched at Sasha's hip and answered the kiss in kind. *More.* It was the only word she could think. She wanted to feel the weight of Sasha's breast in her palm and taste the heat of her skin and hear her cry out in pleasure as—

Shuddering, she pulled away, gasping for air. Sasha's hand slid down to her stomach, the warmth of her palm soaking through Kerry's sweater. Her eyes were wide and dark and hungry, and Kerry wanted to fall into them. Forever.

"What was that?" she finally managed to ask.

"That was my way of telling you how much I've missed you." Lightly, she began to trace the ridges of Kerry's abs through the fabric. Kerry felt her eyelids flutter at the sensation. "And also a preview of tonight."

Her eyes flew open. Sasha was regarding her with an expression half-determined, half-beseeching. More than anything, Kerry wanted to surrender. What if that was exactly why she shouldn't?

Her anxiety must have been obvious, because Sasha's gaze softened. "What's the matter?"

At that moment, Ian and Darryl boarded the plane. Thankfully, they sat in the very back row, out of easy earshot. When the pilot's voice came over the loudspeaker announcing their imminent departure, Kerry buckled her seatbelt and returned her attention to Sasha, who seemed genuinely concerned. She owed her an honest answer.

"I guess I'm just feeling…uncertain."

Sasha's smile was rueful. "I am, of course, aware of my reputation. If I was too forward, I apologize. The last thing I want is to make you feel pressured."

"It's not that I feel pressured." Kerry jumped on the phrase, wanting to deny it firmly. "It's just that...I want you so much. Maybe too much. This intensity is new to me and I—I'm a little afraid of what will happen if I give in."

The plane began to taxi down the runway. Sasha linked their fingers together and rested her head on Kerry's shoulder. "The very first time I saw you, in the club, it was so simple. Attraction. Chemistry. Whatever you prefer to call it." She slid her hand back up to rest over Kerry's heart. "But it's become much more than that. For me, at least."

"For me, too." Kerry's throat felt as dry as the Sahara. What exactly was Sasha saying?

"I don't have a word for...this...yet." Sasha gestured between them. "Except maybe connection. I feel connected to you. But it's not enough. I want more."

"More." The echo of her earlier thought was comforting. "So do I."

"Then stop fighting it." As she spoke, the nose of the plane rose into the sky. "Trust me."

"I do."

But even as she spoke the words, Kerry knew they weren't completely true. She trusted Sasha in the moment, and even in the immediate future. But whenever she tried to see past the next few weeks, a wall slammed down in her brain. Sasha was a British princess. Even in the twenty-first century, she was expected to marry a man and produce an heir lest anything happen to her brother. What future could they have? She suddenly found herself thinking back to that early conversation with Harris in which he'd cited the rumor of Sasha's bisexuality. Would Sasha even want to be with a woman, long-term? Great Britain allowed civil unions now, but no royal had ever taken advantage of that fact. Would whatever connection Sasha felt to her ultimately be able to trump the imperatives of her culture's millennium-old traditions?

Feeling her anxiety rise, Kerry took a deep breath and tried to keep things in perspective. Outside, the fields and farmhouses of the Oxford countryside grew steadily smaller as the aircraft climbed higher. She was embarking on a romantic long weekend to a place she'd always wanted to visit, with a woman who made her heart race. Why ask complicated questions that neither of them could answer? Why not simply enjoy the moment?

Sasha had also been watching the landscape, but as the plane ascended above a thin layer of cloud cover, her grip on Kerry's hand tightened.

"Tell me. Who taught you to fear your own desire?"

The question surprised her. "That's what you think?"

"Isn't that more or less what you just said? About being afraid to give in?"

Kerry blew out a sigh. "Maybe you're right. Organized religion, I suppose. Our parish priest was always full of stories about the horrors of hell a woman would have to endure if she did anything other than save herself for the man she married."

Sasha threw up her hands. "No wonder the monarchy used to have a rule about becoming involved with Roman Catholics. You lot are hopeless."

Kerry laughed, but as the question lingered in her mind, she grew quiet. Had Sasha's keen insight picked up on an aspect of herself she had never recognized?

"Now that I think about it, my family reinforced the priest quite effectively."

"Oh? How so?"

Kerry felt herself blush. "I remember one incident in particular. I was a teenager, and my mother caught me…taking matters into my own hands, so to speak." She risked a glance at Sasha's face but found only curiosity and concern. "She gave me quite the scolding—made it sound like I had committed some sort of terrible crime—and forced me to promise never to do 'that' again."

Sasha seemed torn between outrage and sympathy. "Well, that's bollocks! What did you do?"

"I remember feeling so confused. I couldn't understand how something that felt good and wasn't hurting anyone could be wrong."

"So smart, even then." Sasha pressed a gentle kiss to the skin just below her ear. "Please tell me you didn't let her bully you."

Kerry grinned. "Not even for a second. That admonition went in one ear and out the other."

"Oh, but it didn't." Sasha's expression became serious. "That's why I asked the question in the first place. Somewhere, deep down, I think you're still afraid. But you don't need to be." She moved closer and let her fingertips slide up and down Kerry's thigh. "Will you do something for me?"

"I'll certainly try my best." Kerry knew the words sounded breathless, but she didn't care.

"Tonight, when we're together." Sasha moistened her lips with the very tip of her tongue. "I want you to let go with me. Trust me with that part of you."

A bolt of heat sliced down Kerry's spine at the words, electrifying her senses. Her skin tingled as if it had absorbed a charge, and she could feel the hair rising on the back of her neck. She wanted to speak, but her tongue felt heavy in her mouth. Instead, she nodded dumbly.

"Good." Sasha sat back in her own seat, a smile playing around the corners of her mouth. "Now. Aren't you curious to know where we're flying? Given your pestering all week, I thought that would be the first question out of your mouth."

Indignation finally helped Kerry find her voice. "There was no 'pestering.' And you kissed me silly before I could so much as open my mouth!"

"Mm. So I did. I take it you would, in fact, like to know our destination?"

"Please." Kerry injected as much sarcasm as possible into the single syllable.

"Do you happen to know where your ancestors—the Donovans—are from in Ireland?"

"From the province of Munster," Kerry said. "At least, that's what my paternal grandfather always told us."

"Correct. And do you know the name of the most beautiful county in the province of Munster?"

"Is this a trick question? Beauty is subjective."

Sasha's eyes sparkled. Clearly, she was enjoying her power trip. "Not in this case. It's a fact. County Kerry, home of the famous Dingle Peninsula and Skellig Islands. Not to mention any number of charming towns and villages."

Kerry laughed. "I take it we'll be touring my eponymous county for the weekend?"

"Yes. Does that make you happy?"

Beyond words, Kerry leaned over and kissed her. Already, Sasha had exceeded her every expectation. Kerry could only hope she would be able to do the same.

Concealed beneath her wig and behind a pair of boxy spectacles entirely for show, Sasha felt quite pleased with herself as she watched Kerry sip from her cappuccino and survey the restaurant. Thus far, the trip was going exactly to plan. From the airport, they had driven to the small city of Tralee. Their hotel was a converted eighteenth century manor house, and their room—the best suite in the establishment— boasted a view of the River Lee, a king-sized bed, and a spacious bathroom equipped with a Jacuzzi.

After consulting with the hotel manager about restaurant recommendations, they had made the short walk into town to dine at a favorite local spot. They'd enjoyed their meal at a table near the fireplace, where they'd spent their time people watching and discussing some of the differences Kerry was already noticing between Ireland and her Irish American community in New York. Sasha had enjoyed the chance to hear more about her home, but mostly, she just enjoyed hearing Kerry talk. Eloquent and expressive, she tended to use her hands more when she became enthusiastic, and Sasha's gaze had been repeatedly drawn to her slender fingers tipped with unpainted, close-cropped nails. As the meal went on, her desire had risen slowly and inexorably, like the tide.

Now they were just finishing their coffee, and Sasha was trying not to betray how much she wanted to leave. Finally, Kerry set her empty cup down on the saucer.

"That was delicious. Thank you."

"It was. And my pleasure. Shall we go?"

Kerry took Sasha's coat from the hook nearby and held it while Sasha slid first one and then the other arm inside. Kerry's fingers brushed the nape of her neck as she adjusted the collar, and Sasha had to bite her lip to keep from making a sound. If she was already this sensitive to Kerry's touch, how on earth would she feel in just a few minutes?

Just a few minutes. The thought made her dizzy with anticipation, and she slipped her arm through Kerry's as they walked out into the night. Wispy clouds partially veiled the moon, lending the quiet street a ghostly aura. Kerry looked around eagerly, visibly soaking in her surroundings. She was experiencing this first taste of Ireland with a childlike enjoyment that was positively endearing.

By unspoken agreement they had kept their dinner conversation light. Now, though, Sasha wanted to reclaim the atmosphere they'd found in the airplane. She slid her arm around Kerry's waist, relishing the freedom to be close. Thankfully, with her disguise, they appeared to have evaded the paparazzi. Ian followed a discrete distance away, but she was adept at pretending he wasn't there. While she and Kerry would have to de-couple as a precaution before walking into the hotel, here in the near-deserted streets, she could be exactly who she was.

"I've been wondering something since our conversation this afternoon," she said, injecting a deliberate note of flirtation into her voice.

"Oh? What's that?"

"How old were you when you figured out how to...how did you say it, earlier? Take matters into your own hands?" Feeling Kerry's body jerk at the question, she smiled into the darkness.

"I was eight." Kerry slid her fingers into Sasha's back pocket. "You?"

Acutely aware of the warm hand cupping her, she had trouble forming the words at first.

"Twelve or thirteen, I suppose. It was definitely in boarding school." She bumped Kerry's hip with her own. "Eight is impressive. You were precocious at everything, I take it?"

"Maybe so." As they turned onto the gravel walk leading to the front door of the hotel, Kerry slid her hand out of Sasha's pocket and put a few feet of space between them. Sasha missed her immediately.

In the lift, Kerry leaned back against the railing. Sasha forced herself to remain in the opposite corner, but she couldn't stop herself from mentally planning out exactly where she would begin once she had Kerry in private.

"What does that look mean?" Kerry asked.

"That I'm going to devour you."

Kerry's eyes glazed over at the words, and Sasha barely managed to wait for the doors to reveal a deserted hallway before grabbing her hand and pulling her into their suite. After securing the deadbolt, she hooked her thumbs through Kerry's belt loops and pushed until her back was against the door, then drove her hands beneath the sweater. Kerry's head thumped against the hard surface and she groaned as Sasha raked her fingernails down the hot skin of her muscular torso, bumping over the well-defined ridges. Sasha loved coaxing those needy sounds from Kerry's throat. She wanted to hear more.

In one smooth movement, she pushed up Kerry's sweater and sports bra, exposing her breasts to the air. Full and firm, they fit perfectly into her palms. Desperate to taste her skin, Sasha leaned in to draw one coral nipple into her mouth while pinching the other. Kerry growled out her name and drove one leg between Sasha's thighs, then wrapped her arms tightly around Sasha's waist to pull her forward.

The pressure was exquisite, and for an instant, Sasha teetered on the brink of surrendering control. But no. No. She had waited too bloody long for this, and she was not about to be usurped. One hard twist to Kerry's nipple made her knees buckle, and Sasha quickly took a step backward.

"Don't you dare try that again," she said, reveling in the magnificent vision of Kerry, breasts and stomach exposed, chest heaving. Completely at her mercy. "I've waited forever to touch you."

"I'm afraid I'll come apart as soon as you do," Kerry gasped. "It's been a while."

The confession only ratcheted up Sasha's desire. Her need was primal, fundamental, infused into the core of every cell. "No more fear," she murmured fiercely. "I'll take care of you. I promise."

Only when Kerry nodded did Sasha move closer. "Shirt off. Now."

As she complied, Sasha deftly unbuttoned Kerry's fly to reveal black boxer briefs. She seized both hems and pulled hard then sank to one knee. Her stomach clenched at the sight of Kerry, slick and swollen, her body begging for touch. After one light kiss at the apex of her thighs, she pulled away. Kerry's tortured moan sent a rush of power sweeping through her.

"Shh. I'll be back. Take those off completely and come to the bed."

While Kerry complied, Sasha turned down the bedcovers and dimmed the light. But when she heard Kerry approaching, she turned and stopped her with a gesture.

"Stay right there. Watch."

Slowly, she inched her sweater up along her abdomen before raising it above her head. Sasha tossed the shirt aside, thrilling to the sight of Kerry, nude, standing before her with a look of pure lust on her face. Muscles taut and fists clenched, she was the paragon of strong, feminine sensuality. Quickly, Sasha shimmied out of her jeans until she was clad only in the elegant but sexy black lace set she'd picked out this morning.

She took one step forward and then another. Another. And then she turned, presenting Kerry with her back.

"Help me with the clasp, please." A quaver in her voice betrayed her own need, but she was beyond caring.

Kerry's fingers fumbled at the back of her bra before she disengaged the hooks. With an aching slowness, she eased the straps down Sasha's shoulders, thumbs brushing the sides of her breasts as she freed them. Suddenly dizzy, Sasha found herself swaying, but Kerry steadied her with one hand on her hip. Her fingertips slipped beneath the waistband of the underwear.

"These as well?" she whispered.

"Yes." Sasha heard her own breaths become ragged as Kerry complied, her light touch skimming down Sasha's legs. Once she was naked, Sasha felt Kerry's fingers trail back up to trace the tattoo on her right ribcage. Her skin pebbled in response.

"This is beautiful," Kerry murmured. "What is it, exactly?"

"My mother's coat of arms."

She gasped when she felt Kerry's warm breath against her ribs. Kerry's hands cupped her hips, and a moment later Sasha felt her lips tracing the lines of the crest. Heat surged beneath her skin even as tears pricked her eyes at the worshipful touch.

"Enough," she breathed, fearing she would soon be overcome.

Kerry stopped and gently spun Sasha to face her. Down on one knee, she looked the part of a knight awaiting command. "Tell me what you want," she said softly, "and it's yours."

She was giving up control at precisely the moment she could have taken it. The realization thawed Sasha's paralysis, and she pointed at the bed. "I want you on your back."

Kerry was smiling ever so slightly as she eased between the sheets, turned onto her back and laced her hands behind her head. But then Sasha climbed up to kneel between her legs, and the smile was eclipsed by need. Sasha dropped her hands to Kerry's strong thighs and leaned forward, pressing her palms into Kerry's skin and then pushing up, up along her rib cage, up until she was firmly kneading Kerry's breasts. When her eyes closed at the pleasure, Sasha pinched her nipples, hard. Startled, Kerry's gaze returned to hers.

"I told you to watch."

"Feels so good," Kerry panted. "I don't think I can."

"You can. And you will, if you don't want me to stop."

Kerry's hips bucked again. "Please don't stop!"

"Then watch." Drunk on Kerry's surrender, Sasha slid her hands back down, thumbs dipping into the indentations between Kerry's straining abs before continuing on to her inner thighs. Settling back on her heels, she urged Kerry's legs apart.

"You are exquisite," she murmured, running her fingers ever so lightly over Kerry's most delicate skin and thrilling at the jerk of her hips. She gently spread her open, wrenching the sound of her name from Kerry's throat. Never had she coaxed such responses from the body of a lover. It was intoxicating.

Dipping her head, Sasha licked her slowly, savoring that first glorious taste. As the rich flavor coated her tongue, she couldn't help but lean in, increasing the pressure. Kerry shuddered, muscles tensing, and Sasha forced herself to pull back.

"No, please—" Kerry's fingers fluttered against Sasha's face before clutching a fistful of the sheet.

Sasha looked up to meet imploring eyes the shade of fresh bruises. She raised one finger to her lips and wet the very tip with her own tongue. Arousal sang through her as those eyes darkened even further. For a long moment, she remained poised at the entrance to Kerry's body, breath cascading over the sensitive whorls and folds. And then, ever so slowly, she pushed inside.

Immediately, Kerry clamped down around her. Delighted by her responsiveness, Sasha fluttered her tongue and pushed deeper, one fraction of an inch at a time. And then, quite suddenly, Kerry's body grew rigid. Sasha glanced up, watching the approaching ecstasy play across her face.

"I'm—"

Sasha hollowed her lips and crooked the very tip of her finger, and then Kerry was shattering beneath her, hips surging, groaning Sasha's name. Sasha didn't pull away until the tautness disappeared from Kerry's muscles. Raising her head, she feasted her eyes on the body she had just worshipped, so powerful even in repose. Pride and desire and something else—something visceral and magnetic—swirled in the depth of her chest.

"You are a work of art."

Kerry's smile was brilliant. "Come here," she whispered.

When Sasha stretched out on top of her, Kerry buried the fingers of one hand in her hair and pulled her down for a long, slow kiss. The knowledge that Kerry was tasting herself was inexplicably arousing, and Sasha couldn't keep her hips from shifting restlessly against Kerry's thigh. That small indicator of arousal must have been all Kerry was waiting for. Quite suddenly, Sasha found herself on her back with Kerry looming over her, hands pressed to the sheet on either side of her head.

The smile disappeared. Sasha watched the storm of emotion rage across Kerry's handsome features. She reached up to grasp Kerry's chin, locking their gazes.

"Touch me. I'm not going to break."

With a groan, Kerry lowered her head for a bruising kiss that left Sasha gasping for air. No sooner had it ended than Kerry's mouth was at her breasts, teeth grazing each nipple. Sasha clutched her head to pull her closer.

"Yes. Oh, yes."

Kerry slid one hand between them and paused again, fingertips twitching against the skin of Sasha's lower abdomen. Dizzy with need, Sasha gloried in the fierceness of Kerry's expression. She was keeping her promise—letting go of the fear. It was beyond erotic.

"Take me."

The first brush of Kerry's fingers set off sparks beneath Sasha's skin. At first tentative and exploring, her fingertips slipped and slid through her wetness, searching. And finding. Sasha's head snapped back in pleasure as Kerry made her touch firmer.

"You feel perfect." The ragged words were a harsh whisper in her ear. Before Sasha could process them, Kerry's lips had closed around her earlobe. Twin bolts of arousal arrowed through her, colliding in her chest. Her hips lifted. Kerry pressed and circled.

"Ker—" The unexpected climax tore the breath from her lungs. She forced her eyes open just enough to witness the awe on Kerry's face as the ecstasy took her.

Before she could even begin to catch her breath, Kerry was sliding down her body. Grasping both thighs, she pushed Sasha's legs apart. At the first warm, silky stroke of her tongue, Sasha whimpered. At the second, she reached down to wind her fingers through Kerry's wavy hair. When she tugged lightly, Kerry's groan sent an answering echo of pleasure skittering beneath her skin. As Kerry lapped and sucked, Sasha pulled her closer, grinding against that incredible mouth.

"There!" she gasped as Kerry dragged her lips over a particularly sensitive spot. "There, oh yes, there—"

Her mind dissolved into a blizzard of sensation. Dimly, she heard herself sobbing for breath. As the pleasure slowly ebbed, Kerry's tongue grew softer against her. Still shuddering, she gradually relaxed into the tender strokes.

And then Kerry slid one finger deep inside her body. Sasha cried out as her back arched helplessly, every nerve jangling. Struggling to open her eyes, she shook her head.

"Too much. I can't."

Kerry kissed her inner thigh. "Shh. You can. Relax and let me touch you."

Her mouth returned, gentle as a butterfly's touch, playing counterpoint to the slow glide of her finger. The pleasure rose slowly this time, layer building upon layer like the tuning of a symphony. Sasha gave herself over to the gradual crescendo, head moving restlessly back and forth against the pillow. When the strands of ecstasy finally coalesced and released deep inside, light and warmth spread through her body like ripples on the surface of a lake.

"Beautiful." She heard the word from far, far away. "So beautiful."

For a time, she floated somewhere between consciousness and a dream. Dimly, she was aware of Kerry sliding into place beside her and pulling the covers over them both. With an effort, she turned and buried her face in Kerry's neck, inhaling deeply. Strong arms enfolded her, pulling her even closer, melding their bodies together.

Her last thought before sleep claimed her was that she finally knew the meaning of contentment.

CHAPTER TWELVE

Kerry's internal alarm woke her faithfully at six o'clock, as it had every morning since she'd adjusted to Greenwich Mean Time, but this day could not have been more different from its predecessors. Her eyes opened to the sight of Sasha's smooth, pale shoulder, mere inches from her lips. Her arm encircled Sasha's waist, palm possessively cradling her breast. Inhaling deeply, she caught the faint scent of lilac, and she was overwhelmed by visceral memories of the night before.

Sasha above her, inside her, beneath her. Her fierce commands and sensual pleas. The intoxicating sweetness of her skin.

Kerry's fingers flexed involuntarily and Sasha murmured in her sleep. Desire spiraled through her as she felt Sasha's nipple harden against her palm. Not wanting her restlessness to wake the sleeping princess, she slowly eased herself out of the bed and stole into the bathroom. Bracing her arms on the sink, she examined her own reflection.

Her hair was a bit more tousled than usual, but otherwise she looked no different. How strange, to feel utterly transformed inside and yet see no external evidence. Closing her eyes, she retraced the night with her mind—every sound, every touch, every taste. What did it mean that she had never felt more *herself* than in those moments of intimate joining with Sasha? Her skin ached, and suddenly she couldn't bear the closed door standing between them.

After brushing her teeth and doing her best to flatten her rowdy hair, Kerry padded back into the room. Far too restive to fall back asleep, she could at least indulge her need to be close to Sasha by doing some reading while watching over her slumber. But as she bent to grab a book from her bag, the sound of rustling fabric reached her ears.

"Kerry?"

She turned to the sight of Sasha, propped up on one elbow, blinking sleepily. The sheet just barely covered her breasts, and one shapely calf lay outside the nest of blankets. Kerry's heart stuttered and she abandoned her book without a second thought.

"Good morning." She perched lightly on the edge of the bed and dared to comb two fingers through the long, dark locks spilling artfully onto the white coverlet. "It's early still. You should go back to sleep."

Sasha reached for her hand. "Lie down with me."

"I'm not sure I can—"

"Just for a few minutes. Please?"

Helpless to resist, Kerry let Sasha draw her down onto the mattress. Immediately, Sasha snuggled into Kerry's side and threw one leg over her abdomen.

"Mm," she purred. "You smell good."

Within moments, she had fallen back to sleep. Kerry lay quietly, still gently stroking Sasha's hair and enjoying the pressure of Sasha's leg against her thighs. She felt anchored. Wanted. At peace. Always on the go, she suddenly didn't want to move a single muscle. Lassitude settled over her limbs and she closed her eyes, giving in to the unfamiliar desire to rest.

Her next conscious sensation was the slow movement of fingertips over her scalp. As their pressure increased, Kerry couldn't hold back a sigh of pleasure.

"Don't open your eyes," Sasha whispered from above. "Just feel me."

As the massage went on and on, Sasha's fingers moved down the nape of her neck until she dug her thumbs into the knots on either side of Kerry's spinal column. Miraculously, Kerry felt the ever-present tension in her shoulders begin to ease under that firm, soothing touch. Sure hands smoothed out her bunched muscles until she felt as though she were floating gently atop a becalmed sea.

When Sasha's touch finally retreated, Kerry's eyes fluttered open. She was lying on her stomach, cheek pressed to the soft white pillow. The room was bathed in bright sunlight, and as she rolled over onto her back, Sasha stretched out beside her.

"Hello again." Sasha leaned in close, pressing her breasts against Kerry's side.

"I fell back asleep. I never do that."

She skimmed her fingertips down the center of Kerry's chest. "I feel proud."

Kerry reached up to stroke Sasha's cheek. "You should. And thank you for that massage. It was lovely."

Sasha bent to kiss her—a light, lingering kiss that only left Kerry craving more. Wrapping one arm around Sasha's shoulders, she pulled her on top, snugging Sasha's pelvis into the hollow of her hips.

"Better."

Sasha nipped at Kerry's chin. "You feel incredible."

"I do." Kerry saw no sense in denying it. She didn't want to move back—only forward. "You're a remarkable lover."

Her eyes darkened. "I think that's my line. When you let go, you are simply magnificent."

Kerry felt her face heat. She didn't know what to say. Emotion churned sluggishly in her depths, dimly-realized and somehow frightening. She didn't want it to feel like falling. Not yet.

"So tell me," she said, running her fingertips lightly down Sasha's back. "What's on today's agenda?"

Sasha rested her chin on Kerry's breastbone. "In a few moments, I'll let you up so you can experience your first Irish breakfast. Then, we'll drive to Killarney, where we'll be spending the remainder of the weekend."

"I can't wait. This trip has already exceeded my wildest dreams, and it's barely even begun."

"Good."

Sasha leaned forward to kiss first her left nipple, then her right. Suddenly throbbing, Kerry felt her stomach contract as her vision went hazy.

"So responsive," Sasha murmured. "If I weren't so eager to show you your native land, I might never let you out of this bed."

"I wouldn't complain," Kerry gasped, but Sasha was already rolling off to one side. She swatted playfully at Kerry's thigh as her feet hit the hardwood floor.

"Come on now, lazybones."

Indignant, Kerry sprang out of the bed, but before she could retaliate, Sasha had disappeared into the bathroom, silvery laughter echoing behind her.

❖

The wind ruffled Kerry's hair as she rounded a sharp curve in the trail, bringing with it the scent of honeysuckle and loam. A few feet ahead, Sasha was gesturing to a large boulder just off the path. Dressed in hip-hugging jeans and her UConn sweatshirt, its hood helping to hold the wig in place despite the crisp breeze, she looked fashionably athletic and entirely carefree.

"Shall we sit for a spell?"

At first, her words didn't register. Sasha was beautiful all the time, but Kerry preferred this flushed, fully human version to the highly coiffed façade she presented to the media. As she joined her, Kerry traced a loose wisp of her faux hair. Sasha stuck out her tongue.

"I've never worn it so many days in a row. It's starting to itch."

"Well, do you think you might be able to do without it for the rest of the trip? Have you seen any sign of photographers?"

"None whatsoever." Sasha sipped from her water bottle and glanced around the small clearing. "Maybe I will take it off, and just keep the hood up."

Kerry watched, entranced, as she whisked the wig off her head and shook out her long, dark tresses. Fingertips itching, she drank deeply from her own water as Sasha stowed the hairpiece in her backpack.

"That feels fantastic," she said. "As does this climb. Much more satisfying than those bloody stair machines in the gym."

Kerry laughed. "I couldn't agree more."

After arriving at their hotel in Killarney, Sasha had laid out the plan for the afternoon: a tour of the nineteenth century Muckross House—a product of famous Scottish architect William Burns—

followed by a trip to Torc Waterfall and a hike up to the top of Torc Mountain. It was the perfect way to spend a beautiful autumn day, and Kerry was touched by the forethought Sasha had put into their itinerary.

Sasha capped her bottle and stood. "Let's keep moving. I can't wait to see the waterfall from the top."

Thoroughly charmed by her enthusiasm, Kerry followed closely behind her as she set a brisk pace up the remaining ascent. Soon, the surrounding forest gave way to a grassy, rock-strewn slope. Ahead, a stone cairn marked the summit. As they approached it, the ambient roar of the waterfall resolved into clear splashing sounds.

Sasha halted next to the cairn and spun in a slow circle. "Spectacular."

"You are," Kerry said, softly enough that any nearby tourists wouldn't overhear. "It's true."

Sasha rolled her eyes, but the hint of a smile at her lips betrayed her pleasure. "Not me, you dolt. This view."

Wrenching her gaze away from Sasha, Kerry finally surveyed the panorama before her. She had an unimpeded, three hundred and sixty degree view of the Irish countryside, and it was indeed spectacular. To the west, a lake lay nestled in the valley created by the juncture of three low mountains. To the north, the stone turrets of Muckross House gleamed in the late afternoon sunlight.

"Kerry! Come and see." Sasha had descended a short way down the slope along a ridge that ended abruptly in a sheer cliff. It was the perfect vantage point from which to watch the water hurtle over the outcropping and drop into the deep pool far below.

Sasha reached for her hand as she approached. The falls throbbed beneath them, its power traveling up through the soles of Kerry's feet, quickening her blood. The rich scent of the earth filled her lungs as the cool fingers of the wind stroked through her hair and the rising mist caressed her face. The land itself was embracing her, cherishing her, and Kerry suddenly felt a sense of belonging that was at once utterly foreign and yet somehow familiar.

Sasha's grip tightened, and she looked over in concern. "You're trembling. Are you all right?"

Kerry swallowed hard. How could she explain without sounding like a sentimental fool, especially when she hardly knew what was happening herself?

"This place," she stammered. "It…affects me."

Sasha's expression softened. She looked around quickly before leaning in close, her lips grazing Kerry's ear. "Welcome home."

Kerry pulled back just enough to see her eyes. They were the same shade of green as the surrounding fields, and for one insane moment, she very nearly blurted the revelation aloud. Behind them, a shrill chorus of young voices echoed from the rocks. Sasha released her hand and stepped away. The spell of the land died as suddenly as it had risen. In the next moment, children were swarming over the summit, laughing and shouting—a school group, by the looks of their identical uniforms.

"Shall we go back?" Sasha asked, watching them with bemusement.

"All right." Kerry worked to keep her voice light. She couldn't help but be disappointed by Sasha's withdrawal, but what else could she expect? This entire trip was clandestine, and not only because of her gender. Even the straight royals often tried to hide their romantic involvements from the world for as long as possible. All other obstacles aside, did she really want the kind of media attention that would accompany being Sasha's "official" girlfriend?

By the time they returned to the trailhead, Kerry had managed to reason herself into a happier mental space. They had a full day and a half left together and much more exploring to do. She wanted to appreciate this trip for what it was, not what it wasn't. Sasha had put a great deal of time, effort, and money into making one of Kerry's lifelong dreams come true. The last thing she wanted was to seem ungrateful.

Sasha rested her palm on Kerry's knee as they pulled out of the parking lot. Behind them, the underbellies of the clouds were just beginning to smolder as the sun began its descent behind the mountains.

"Did you enjoy that?"

"Very much." With one finger, Kerry traced aimless patterns along the back of Sasha's hand. "Thank you for an incredible day."

"It isn't over yet. We have dinner reservations in town, and then I thought we might do some dancing."

"Oh?" Kerry's head spun at the thought of trying to dance with Sasha in some hot, crowded, throbbing nightclub. How on earth she would manage to remain platonic, she had no idea.

"Apparently there's a ceili—a traditional Irish dance—at a pub near our restaurant." Sasha glanced over quickly. "Would that be fun for you?"

Kerry couldn't hold back a laugh at just how far off her mental image had been. At the flash of hurt that crossed Sasha's face, she hurried to explain.

"I've been going to ceilis since before I could walk. They're quite popular in my hometown. And I would love nothing more than to attend one with you." She squeezed Sasha's fingers lightly. "If it's anything like what I'm used to, I may even be able to lead."

"I may even let you," she replied archly. "Though don't think for a moment that your lead will extend beyond the dance floor."

"Oh?" Kerry's throat constricted at the sensual note in Sasha's voice.

In the dying light, Sasha's eyes gleamed like a cat's. "If yesterday was any indication, you need to learn some patience. Tonight, I plan to make you wait."

Kerry's view of the road blurred as Sasha's words sparked a rush of flame beneath her skin. The inferno stole her breath in a quiet gasp, and now it was Sasha's turn to laugh. She lifted her hand to brush her knuckles across Kerry's cheek.

"Breathe. I told you I'd take care of you. I meant it."

CHAPTER THIRTEEN

Sasha woke slowly, her consciousness spiraling up toward the sunlit world she could dimly sense beyond the blankets nestled around her like a warm cocoon. When she breathed in, she detected the faint aroma of Kerry's rich, earthy scent. A frisson of desire skittered down her spine as memories of the previous night flooded back into the forefront of her brain. After another full day of touring—this time along the Dingle Peninsula—they had opted to retire early. For a while, they had simply cuddled and channel-surfed until the edges of their kisses grew sharp with need. Kerry had taken the lead effortlessly, surging above her with gentle purpose.

The tone of their lovemaking had been palpably different from the nights before. The urgency of discovery had given way to tenderness, and Kerry's slow, stroking touches had set Sasha ablaze. But even as they had taken their fill of each other, Sasha had sensed a new kind of desperation at the core of their joining. It was their last night in Ireland. Was Kerry also wondering whether the magic they had found would be able to follow them back across the channel?

The thought dissolved her inner peace and she opened her eyes, propping herself up on both elbows to look for Kerry. The room was empty, but a note was waiting on the nightstand. *Good morning,* it read. *You're beautiful. I've gone for a short run. Back around nine o'clock. –K*

Sasha had to smile as she imagined Kerry's lean frame stretched out in motion along some nearby winding road. She could easily picture her glistening body slicing through the mist like a blade, and suddenly she envied the very air. Glancing at the clock, she saw that it was nearly nine. When Kerry returned, perhaps she could entice her into sharing the shower. To conserve water, of course.

A knock sounded at the door, accompanied by Ian's greeting. Frowning, she quickly threw on a robe. They were leaving at half past ten. What did he need at this hour?

When he stepped inside, she first noticed the grim set to his mouth. Then she saw that he was holding a folded-up newspaper. The bottom dropped out of her stomach. Oh, no. No. They'd been cautious! Not as cautious as they could have been, but she'd seen no sign of the paparazzi since she'd left the UK. Surely, she would have realized if they had picked up her trail. Over the years, she'd become nearly as adept as her security at ferreting them out of the shadows.

"How bad?" Her voice was nearly unrecognizable to her own ears. Now her father would have yet another weapon in his arsenal against her. And not only would the media turn her life into even more of a circus than it already was, but they would also turn their all-seeing eye toward Kerry. She would be sucked right into the heart of the maelstrom, and—

"We dodged a bullet, I believe." Beneath the terseness of his clipped words was an unexpected note of amusement.

He flipped open the paper to reveal a grainy photograph of the two of them leaving the ceili on Friday night. The headline above danced and shimmered, refusing to resolve, and Sasha focused on the picture. Her own face was fairly recognizable, but the camera phone used to snap it had only caught an oblique shot of Kerry's profile. Blinking fiercely, she closed her eyes and took a long, deep breath. When she opened her eyes, the words were clear. *Sasha's New Bloke?*

Sasha stared in disbelief between the large, bold words and the image below them as realization struck. Kerry's short hair, her strong jawline, and her clothing—low-slung jeans and a button-down shirt, that night—had all conspired to deceive both the amateur paparazzo and the editors of the gossip rag that had won the bidding war for this photo. The thundering panic slightly eased its grip on her heart.

"That's an interesting twist."

"Indeed." Ian refolded the paper. "Nevertheless, depending on what you wish to do, it may be necessary to take some additional precautions."

"What I wish to do?" She sank into a nearby chair, feeling her fingers tremble slightly under the influence of adrenaline. Her brain seemed filled with haze. She should never have relaxed her guard and abandoned her disguise, no matter how uncomfortable it was.

"You have several options, of course." Ian's voice was carefully neutral. "Stop seeing her. Continue to see her, but take stronger measures to keep it secret. Or go public."

Sasha's head snapped up. Go public? Was he mad? They had just barely escaped public detection, thanks to a fortuitous misunderstanding! But when she met his gaze, she saw only steadiness there. He wasn't counseling her one way or another—simply laying out the options.

At that moment, the lock turned in the door. Kerry stepped into the room, disheveled and sweaty and smiling. When she saw them, she froze. The smile dropped away.

"What happened?"

"Show her, Ian."

Ian held out the paper. Kerry stepped forward to take it from him, and Sasha watched her eyes flicker back and forth across the page. A moment later, she dropped into a crouch at Sasha's feet.

"Are you all right? I am so, so sorry. This is all my fault. I should never have suggested you take off your wig." Jaw clenched, she shook her head fiercely. "What a fucking fool I was."

Sasha was struck dumb by Kerry's reaction. Had she given even a moment's thought to the implications for herself? When she reached out to touch Kerry's face, her fingertips came away moist with sweat. Dimly, she registered the sound of the door closing behind Ian as he gave them privacy.

"Stop. I'm fine. Just a little surprised. But I'll be damned if I allow you to take the blame for this. Don't you dare." Hooking her fingers behind Kerry's jaw, she tugged lightly. "Do you hear me?"

Kerry squared her shoulders and swallowed hard. "What do you want to do? Do you want to put...this...on ice for a while? Or, ah, longer? Would that be best?"

Sasha couldn't believe what she was hearing. Kerry was offering to—to what? Break up? Was that the right word, when they'd never really agreed on any terms to begin with? When they'd never admitted to anything other than insane chemistry and a fledgling connection?

"Is that what you want?"

Kerry shook her head emphatically. "What? Of course not! How could you possibly believe that after what we've shared for these past few days?" She reached for Sasha's hands. "I may be more book smart than world smart, but by now I've seen the kind of pressure you're under. I don't want to add to that. So tell me what you want from me, and if it's in my power to give you, I will."

Sasha dug her thumbs into Kerry's palms, anchoring herself against the surge of emotion. How could she help Kerry comprehend something she didn't fully understand herself?

"I don't want to stop seeing you."

Kerry exhaled softly. "Okay. Good. Me, neither." She even managed a tight smile. "In that case, what should we do?"

Sasha stood and went to the window, pulling back the curtain to look out on their view of the verdant rolling hills. This country was still so wild—fundamentally untamed. As the imaginary walls of her position and obligations pressed in around her, she envied the land its freedom.

"We'll just have to be careful," she said without turning around. "Much, much more careful."

Kerry met Harris outside the gates of Holywell Manor just as the last rays of the sun fled the sky, abandoning the clouds to the darkness. Despite having a mountain of work to do before the morning, she hadn't been able to concentrate at all since being dropped off by one of Sasha's staff members in the early afternoon. They had flown into a small airport on the outskirts of London, and after one last, too-brief kiss inside the belly of the plane, Sasha had been whisked back to her royal obligations. Kerry hadn't heard a peep out of her since then— not even a text to say she'd returned home safely.

Kerry didn't know whether she had the right to feel horribly alone and adrift, but she did just the same. Hopefully, talking things out with Harris would help her to process everything that had happened—the good and the bad. A stiff wind blew up as she approached him, and he shivered dramatically.

"I'm absolutely dying to know all about your trip," he said, slinging one arm around her shoulders, "but do we really have to go for a walk? Can't we get a drink someplace nice and warm?"

"No. We can't." One look at his face told her he had picked up on the somber note in her voice.

"Oh, no. What happened?" His arm tightened around her. "What did she do?"

"She was born." For the first time since her morning conversation with Sasha, Kerry released her hold on the bitterness she felt about the whole situation. From beneath her free arm, she produced the copy of the gossip rag she'd purchased at a magazine stand.

Harris took a few steps until he was standing beneath a street lamp, then whistled under his breath. When he looked back to Kerry, all trace of his prior teasing was gone.

"Close one."

"Too close," she agreed. "Let's keep walking."

He handed the paper back to her. "I think I understand why we're not sitting someplace warm having a drink."

"Exactly." Her stomach twisted at the memory of the anxiety and dismay she'd seen in Sasha's face upon returning to their room this morning. She wanted to do everything in her power never to contribute to that expression again, and she still felt awful about the role she had played in Sasha's discovery by the tabloids. But a niggling voice in the back of her head refused to stop wondering how they could possibly have a meaningful relationship someday if Sasha remained so fearful of them being seen in public together. Or was a meaningful relationship not something she was interested in at all?

Harris linked his arm with hers. "Start at the beginning."

Kerry took a deep breath and launched into a summary of the trip. As she recounted the highlights—Sasha's thoughtfulness at arranging architecture-themed excursions, the beauty of the Irish landscape, the growing strength of their connection—Harris remained quiet. Finally, she arrived at the events that had transpired that morning, including Sasha's decision to make their future meetings even more clandestine.

"Insofar as I'm able to, I understand where she's coming from. And she's right. This relationship, or whatever I should be calling it, is so new. I get the feeling this isn't her usual *modus operandi*."

"Believe me, it's not," Harris said. "Until quite recently—in other words, until *you*—not a week would go by without some sort of speculation about her latest fling with some high-profile actor or athlete or trust fund baby."

"I don't know what to do," Kerry admitted. "I don't want to put her in jeopardy of any kind. And in a way, I can empathize with her situation. I lived in the closet for almost two years in college." She thought back to Virginia, then, and to how frightened she had been that anyone would discover their relationship. At first, she had hidden it even from her teammates. But even after her peers had accepted them, she hadn't been able to confess to her family until it was far too late.

"I thought I had to live that way. And maybe at first I really did, while I was coming to terms with myself. But after a while it just became habit. Looking over my shoulder all the time, always worrying what others thought. In hindsight, I realize that wasn't really living. Being in the closet cost me my first relationship. I hated every second of it. I don't want to go back there."

She lapsed into a silence only broken by the crunch of their shoes on the gravel path leading toward the park. After a few moments, Harris squeezed her arm in reassurance.

"The good news is that you're self-aware. You're walking into this with open eyes, and even with some experience on the other side of the tracks, so to speak. If it makes sense to jump back into the closet with her while you figure out whatever potentiality exists between you, then at least you know what you're doing."

He stopped and took her by both shoulders. "Just promise me that when the time comes, you'll stand up for yourself. You deserve a princess, Kerry, but a princess who will hold your hand in public. Not one who insists on keeping you hidden in her royal boudoir."

For the first time since she had watched Sasha disappear into her Bentley at the airfield, Kerry felt a smile tug at her lips. She stepped forward and pulled Harris into a long hug. With a friend like him supporting her, she could keep the tendrils of anxiety at bay.

"I promise."

❖

"And then he walked out—just walked right out the door, leaving her standing there in the midst of their own party. He's not been back since, either." Miranda rolled her eyes, added a dash more olive juice, and proceeded to shake the cocktail in a rather more melodramatic fashion than was strictly necessary.

"That certainly doesn't sound pretty." Sasha hoped her response was adequate. She had only half paid attention to Miranda's long and sordid tale about two of their recently married acquaintances. The other half of her mind was wondering about Kerry. Was she already asleep? Or more likely, studying? Was Kerry missing her? Had she thought any more about the photograph?

"It's a disgrace, really."

A moment later, Sasha accepted her brimming martini from Miranda and took a quick sip. As the cold vodka slid down her throat and into her empty stomach, she hoped it would settle her nerves. She perched on the loveseat while Miri gracefully settled into an armchair.

"It's been so frustrating not having you in town," Miranda said, crossing one leg over the other. "I'm glad you're home."

"It does feel like forever since we've been able to catch up."

Miranda leaned forward conspiratorially. "So. You simply must tell me. Who were you with in Ireland? I couldn't recognize him from that atrocious photograph."

Sasha closed her eyes. This was it—the reason she was here instead of in her own bed. She needed Miranda's help. So why did she feel as though she was about to commit some sort of betrayal?

"I was with Kerry."

Miranda's face was blank. "Who is Kerry?"

"Kerry Donovan. The Rhodes scholar I met a few weeks ago. She was at that club in Oxford. Remember?"

"Oh, yes." Miranda set her drink on the table and frowned. "You've kept in touch with her?"

"I've seen her a few times. Once in Scotland for that event my father made me do. And then last week I went up to Oxford to watch her play football."

Miranda's frown had grown deeper. "And you just whisked her off on a trip to Ireland?"

"Yes." Sasha felt herself smile. "She's Irish-American, but she had never been to Ireland before, and so—"

"Sasha." Miri cut her off, her tone grave.

"What?"

"This…thing. With the American. Is it serious?"

Sasha gripped the edge of the sofa as her temperature rose. "She has a name, Miri."

"At the moment, I don't particularly care what her name is. I want to know whether this is just a flirtation that's lasted longer than usual, or whether you actually have feelings for this woman."

"I don't know!" Sasha set down her glass before she accidentally snapped the stem. "All right? I don't know."

Miranda's eyes narrowed. "I don't think I believe you."

"I *might*." Unable to sit still, Sasha began to pace. "I feel… something. I want to see what this connection—or whatever it is— turns into. But how can I do that, when there's a camera phone on every corner and a telephoto lens in every bloody window?"

"Let me get this straight," Miranda said. "So to speak. You want to continue seeing this Kerry, but in absolute secrecy? First of all, there's no such thing. And secondly, you do realize what you're risking if you pursue this, do you not?"

"What I'm risking?" Sasha braced on arm on the mantle and turned back toward Miranda. "You mean risking that my country might actually come to know me for who I really am? What a travesty!"

"Oh, hush." Miranda waved her comment away. "Your subjects don't want you to transform into a precious, rainbow-winged butterfly. They want you to remain exactly as you are." She jabbed one finger into her leather armrest for emphasis. "Sassy Sasha."

Sasha thought she might be ill. Miranda was supposed to be her best friend. To support her. To have her best interests at heart. What kind of advice was this?

"So the best thing you can do to hoodwink the public," Miranda continued, "is to get the rumor mill churning again. For weeks, there hasn't been so much as a whisper about you with someone. Someone acceptable. That has to change. You need to be seen."

Sasha opened her mouth to disagree, then shut it. Maybe Miri had a point. She should at least hear out her logic. "What exactly are you suggesting?"

"I'm suggesting that you behave the way you always have." Miranda rose and went to her, reaching out to lightly stroke her back. The musk of her perfume was cloying. It made her miss Kerry's pure, earthy scent all the more. "Go to clubs and parties. Dance. Flirt. Be photographed. If you give the paparazzi enough of what they want to see, they won't go looking for more. And when they're not looking, you can do whatever you want, with whomever you want."

Sasha nodded slowly. The vodka was beginning to kick in, dulling her mind and her senses, and the mental fog promised relief from her anxiety. She could do what Miranda was suggesting—play her part on the public stage and later retreat to Kerry's arms. She could live two lives.

For a little while, at least.

CHAPTER FOURTEEN

"Ms. Donovan?"

Kerry jerked awake at the sound of the driver's voice. The car was beginning to slow, and when she leaned forward, she saw the illuminated façade of Clarence House just up ahead.

"We've nearly arrived," the driver continued. "You'd best conceal yourself."

"Of course. Thank you." Blinking away her fatigue, Kerry struggled to focus. It was highly unlike her to doze off under any circumstances, and yet she had somehow fallen asleep in the car that was bringing her to London to be reunited with Sasha. Mindful of the driver's instructions, she reached for the blanket on the seat next to her. Sasha's text this morning had advised her to hide under it as the car entered the front gate. Feeling rather silly, she unbuckled her seatbelt, lay on the bench, and pulled the scratchy wool over her head and body.

Her eyes felt as gritty as the fabric. The week had been long and grueling as she worked to catch up on her assignments after a weekend abroad, and sleep hadn't come easily without Sasha beside her. What's more, she was discouraged by her performance on the soccer field this morning. Having studied until late into her Friday night, she had woken up early for a match against Merton College. It had resulted in Balliol's first loss, and she could blame no one but herself. Her touches on the ball had been off and her passes inaccurate. Eventually, she'd asked Claudia to sub her out.

The car stopped at the guard booth, and as one of the security personnel conversed with the driver, the unmistakable flare of a flashbulb made her twitch. Forcing herself to be still, she held her breath until the car carried on. Pressing the heel of her hand to her suddenly galloping heart, Kerry tried to be reasonable. There was no way the paparazzi could have caught a shot of her. At most, they had captured the car and the guard's backside. She wanted to laugh at the thought, but the sound stuck in her throat. The stakes were just too high.

The car drove around to the back of the house and pulled into a parking space. "Here we are, Ms. Donovan," said the driver.

Relieved, Kerry threw off the blanket. After thanking him, she opened the door and took a deep breath of the fresh night air before noticing Darryl, who stood a few feet away with his hands clasped behind his back.

"Hello, Darryl," she said, feeling a bit like a wayward adolescent as she clambered out of the car.

"Good evening, Ms. Donovan. This way."

He led her inside and up a small narrow staircase. The chipped, uneven steps were a far cry from the ornately carpeted flights she'd ascended last time she was here. Apparently, clandestine lovers used the servants' stairway.

"Princess Alexandra has not yet returned to the residence," Darryl said over his shoulder. "But you are welcome to wait in her rooms."

Kerry glanced at her watch. Sasha had asked to meet at Clarence House at ten o'clock. The car had run into some unexpected traffic, and it was quarter past now. Shrugging to herself, she followed Darryl through a nondescript door that opened onto the landing outside Sasha's apartments. Whatever engagement she'd had tonight must have run longer than expected. Still, as Kerry entered the empty suite, she couldn't help but feel like an interloper.

"I'll be just outside," Darryl said, swinging the doors shut behind her.

"Thank you."

Kerry walked slowly down the hall and into Sasha's bedroom. For a moment, she contemplated undressing and waiting for Sasha naked in her own bed. But as appealing as the thought was on one level, she hadn't just come here to make love. They had barely spoken all week. She wanted to know what Sasha had done, what she'd been thinking of, how she was feeling. More than anything, she wanted to recapture the closeness they'd found in Ireland—a closeness that included the physical but extended far beyond it.

After stowing her bag neatly in a corner, she settled back onto the sofa. There was always more reading to be done, but tonight she needed a break. Once she had reacquainted herself with the remote, she flipped through the channels until she found a sports highlights show. Thankfully, instead of having to watch repeat footage of men trying to break each other's necks, she could catch up on all the spectacular Premier League goals while waiting for Sasha to return.

The sound of a slamming door roused Kerry from her second impromptu nap of the day. Disoriented, she raised her head and immediately grimaced at the crick in her neck. She'd fallen asleep sitting up on Sasha's couch. Glancing blearily at the clock on the television, she realized it was almost midnight. Where on earth was—

"Hi." The single, sultry syllable came from the doorway where Sasha stood wearing a velvet green dress with a plunging neckline just short of scandalous. "You look fantastic."

"Hi." Kerry swallowed hard as Sasha executed a tight pirouette. The fabric draped artfully over her shoulders to pool at the small of her back, revealing the smooth, milk-white expanse of skin. "And... wow."

Within moments, Sasha was straddling her on the couch, fingers combing through her hair. Kerry inhaled deeply, but the familiar aroma of lilacs was all but drowned out by the scent of rum. Even as every cell in her body lit up in response to Sasha's closeness, warning bells throbbed in her brain.

"Are you drunk?"

"No." Sasha leaned in and nipped at Kerry's earlobe, then laughed softly. "Well, maybe a little tipsy."

Kerry let her palms come to rest on Sasha's waist. "I missed you."

"Mm. Same." Sasha slid back along Kerry's thighs and pressed light, sucking kisses to her neck. "Your skin tastes so good. I want you."

The wet heat of Sasha's mouth trailing along her collarbone was quickly fraying Kerry's self-control. Desire coiled in her belly like a beast, ready to devour her. Making her tremble. She wanted to surrender, but not like this.

"Slow—slow down." Kerry ran her hands up Sasha's back and tangled her fingers in the long, dark strands of hair. "I want you, too. But can we talk a little first?"

Sasha sat back, a pout on her lips. "Can't you see how wound up you've made me?"

Kerry stroked her face gently. "You just got here. I'm not sure I had all that much to do with it." She leaned in to join their lips in a soft kiss. "Tell me about your night. Were you at a family affair, or something more official?"

"Miranda and I went to Mahiki to celebrate the engagement of one of her university friends." She held her hand up between them, showing off a shimmering gold plastic wristband. "The DJ tonight was incredi—what?"

Realizing the stab of hurt she'd felt must be apparent on her face, Kerry schooled her features and shook her head. But even as she tried to wrestle her emotions back under control, she couldn't keep her brain from peppering her with questions. Had Sasha deliberately let her believe she was at some official function, or had Kerry simply assumed it?

"Nothing. You were saying, about the DJ?"

Despite her intoxication, Sasha was too savvy to be fooled. "I've wounded your feelings."

Kerry sighed. "No. I'm being too sensitive. I just didn't realize you were going out socially tonight." She skimmed her fingers up and down Sasha's spine. "Now you'll think I'm petty. Or worse, controlling."

"I don't think you're either." Sasha slid off to one side and nestled into the curve of Kerry's arm. "I should have been more clear. I just didn't want you to feel left out or get the wrong idea. And now, of course, that's all backfired. Next time, you should come with."

"You have every right to go out with your friends. I don't need to be there."

"To be honest, I would much rather have been here with you the whole night." Sasha ran two fingers along the seam of Kerry's jeans. "But Miranda suggested the best way to distract the paparazzi is for me to be seen more in public. A misdirection of sorts."

"Miranda told you that?" A surge of anxiety pulsed through Kerry's chest as she remembered Harris's description of Sasha's "normal" behavior. "What does that mean for…this?"

"*This* is what I'm trying to protect." Sasha stared up at Kerry, her eyes liquor-bright but serious. "If I have to do a little partying to keep the media at bay, then I will. I don't want them getting in our way."

Kerry nodded. Sasha's use of "our" made her feel good. On the other hand, she couldn't suppress the surge of jealousy that had clawed its way into her throat. The beast had slipped its chains. "So if I see a photograph of you flirting with some impossibly wealthy eligible bachelor," she said, angling her body toward Sasha's, "how exactly would you like me to react?"

Sasha must have sensed the change in mood, because she lay back to pillow her head on the armrest. When she slid one leg on either side of Kerry's torso, Kerry's pulse soared.

"You should remember I'm only pretending." Sasha laced both hands behind Kerry's neck to pull her head down. "That it doesn't mean a thing. That I may tease them, but I'll never let them do this."

The kiss was not gentle. At the sensation of Sasha's tongue thrusting deeply into her mouth, Kerry's hips bucked. As their pelvises ground together, Sasha wrapped one leg around Kerry's, heel digging into her calf muscle. When Sasha slid one hand between their bodies, Kerry raised her head with a soft groan. Within moments, Sasha's fingers slipped inside her jeans and dove beneath the waistband of her boxer briefs.

Sasha's touch stilled as she blinked up in awe. "So wet." Moving her fingertips back and forth, she gently sought out the focal point of Kerry's need. "So hard. So beautiful."

Electricity hummed down Kerry's spine and her eyes slammed shut. With a gasp, she forced them to open, needing to see Sasha's face. Overwhelmed, she could grasp only one thought. She had to feel her. Now.

Pushing up on her left elbow, she skimmed her palm down the warm fabric covering Sasha's abdomen and thighs. As she reached beneath the hem, her fingers encountered a damp swatch of silk. Twitching it aside, she touched Sasha as she herself was being touched. Triumph sang through her veins as Sasha's teeth closed down on her lower lip in pleasure. Edging lower, she slid first one, then two fingers just inside.

"You feel so good," she stuttered, even as Sasha drew intoxicating circles against her own skin. Instinctively, she shifted her own hips in counterpoint to the swirling strokes that threatened to send her over the edge. "Love how you hold me…in you."

Hooking her fingers higher, she fluttered them gently and was rewarded by the sound of her name drawn out on a moan. Almost immediately, Sasha began to pulse around her. As their gazes met and held, Kerry felt herself begin to fall.

"I—I'm—"

Sasha grabbed the front of her shirt and yanked her even closer. "Oh, yes. Kerry. Yes."

As Sasha's body clenched around her, ecstasy struck Kerry like a lightning bolt. Gasping Sasha's name, she gave herself up to the fury of her own release.

When consciousness returned, Kerry found herself fully on top of Sasha, head buried in the curve between her neck and shoulder. Not wanting to crush her, she levered herself up and gently eased her fingers from the warm embrace of Sasha's body. Only then did Sasha rouse. Blinking, she reached out to grip Kerry's arm.

"Don't—don't go."

At the vulnerability of her expression, Kerry turned onto her side and carefully wrapped her arms around Sasha, pulling her close. She kissed her forehead and stroked her hair, feeling as though her chest might explode at any moment.

"Shh. I'm right here."

Sasha burrowed even closer, relaxing into her embrace. "Be patient with me," she murmured, her words slightly muffled by Kerry's shirt. "I just need a little time."

"I know." Kerry closed her eyes, enjoying the closeness she'd craved all week. "I'm not going anywhere. Promise."

❖

As the car pulled up to the curb, Kerry stared out the window at the wooden double doors, above which *boujis* was inscribed in large, white script. This was it—the club Sasha was patronizing tonight. The line to get in wrapped around the block. Everyone in it was young and beautiful and obviously far more sophisticated than Kerry had ever been in her life. She swallowed hard and fiddled with her shirt collar. Harris had officially approved her attire—washed out jeans, a black linen shirt, and a gray sports coat. Thankfully, he hadn't made her buy new shoes. Her scuffed Doc Martens were apparently "classic perfection."

Of course, he had also claimed that Sasha wouldn't be able to keep her hands to herself once Kerry arrived. That was patently untrue. Sasha would be keeping her distance tonight—at least, until they could meet up at Clarence House in the wee hours of the morning. For the entire drive down from Oxford, Kerry had been trying to prepare herself for the sight of Sasha flirting with rich, handsome men. As much as the idea made her feel nauseous, she could understand the stakes. In order to hide their relationship, Sasha would have to present a convincing trail of bread crumbs leading elsewhere—namely, into the most exclusive nightclubs in the city. She would need to leave either in the company of men, or with an established friend like Miranda.

Even as Kerry tried to psych herself up for the spectacle of the next few hours, she couldn't help but wish they could dispense with all these cloak-and-dagger machinations. But that wasn't possible for any royal. Arthur and Ashleigh had admitted in interviews that they'd been obliged to sneak around during their early courtship, and Sasha's rumored conquests were the perpetual grist to the rumor mill. Only Elizabeth had escaped the glaring spotlight so far, but Kerry imagined that would change now that she was at university.

"Here we are, ma'am," the driver said as he opened her door, jolting her out of her introspection. "I'll await your call."

"Thank you." Kerry slid across the leather seats and stepped out onto the sidewalk. As she approached the entrance, she could feel the curious stares of those in line. At the whirs and clicks of nearby camera shutters, she stiffened in alarm before reminding herself that this was the point of her entering and leaving the club separately from Sasha—so that they wouldn't be visibly linked by the ever-vigilant paparazzi.

After producing identification for the two impassive bouncers, Kerry waited while one scrolled through his phone. A moment later, he pushed open the door without saying a word. Immediately, the pulse of a DJ's electronic beat filled her ears like a heartbeat. Shoulder blades prickling with self-consciousness, Kerry slid past the thick, dark curtain shielding the interior from prying eyes.

The club's décor made her dizzy. Each wall was a gigantic screen on which blue and purple psychedelic patterns swirled in time to the music. Black couches and tall tables lined the periphery, while shimmering violet lights played across the glittering surface of the bar. The VIP entrance Sasha had told her lay just beyond the bar, and she quickly made her way across the room, deftly threading between knots of young, well-dressed patrons sipping drinks and talking loudly over the music. At the far end of the chamber, a raised stage was crowded with those brave enough to dance.

The VIP area was separated from the remainder of the club by another thick curtain, and once again she relinquished her ID into the hands of another bouncer. This time, he pulled the curtain aside and ushered her in. This room was much smaller and more intimate. Each table was topped with a pewter bucket holding a magnum of Moët. As she took in her lavish surroundings, Kerry recognized a male movie star whose name escaped her, but who appeared in all the romantic comedies these days. She didn't care. The only person she cared about was—

When the princess's distinctive laugh rose over the music's low throb like a descant, Kerry felt as though an invisible hand had reached inside her chest to squeeze her heart dry. Turning in the direction of the sound, she stared into the far corner at Sasha who was flanked by two men. One of them held the large bottle and was tipping it slowly toward her waiting, open mouth. The liquid foamed out of the neck in a golden, bubbling torrent, and Sasha caught it expertly, swallowing once, twice, three times. Kerry's mouth went dry with desire even as her stomach twisted like a fish on a hook.

And then something compelled the princess to look up. Sasha froze for a heartbeat, lips moist and eyes bright. Even separated by the width of the room, Kerry felt a charge pass between them, addictive and electric, and she felt herself falling faster.

A moment later, Sasha's mask slid back into place. "Kerry! Come meet my friends!" She slung both her arms out along the bench, hands dangling near the men's shoulders. "Alastair and Eugene went to university with me. Kerry is an American here on the Rhodes."

"Pleasure," said Alastair, sounding bored.

"Hello," said Eugene, favoring her only the barest of glances. He smoothed one palm down Sasha's thigh to lightly rub her knee. "Ready for more then, Sash?"

Kerry shoved her hands in her pockets to keep herself from jumping over the table and ripping the oversized bottle out of their aristocratic hands. So much for all her mental preparation. At the slightest challenge, her precious control had nearly gone out the window. She had to remember the facts. Sasha was a consenting adult. If she wanted to tease the animals this way, it was well within her rights to do so. Besides, she was playing a game. Acting a part. If she was doing so convincingly, well, hadn't she been practicing all her life?

As she fought to suppress her rage, a slender arm slipped around her waist accompanied by the spicy scent of perfume. Startled, she glanced over to the sight of Miranda wearing a short, shimmering gold dress, nearly reaching her own height with the help of matching heels.

"Kerry, how lovely to see you again! Come and sit by me."

Before she could reply, Miranda took her elbow and sashayed them over to the table next to Sasha's. After sliding onto the blue leather bench, she patted the spot beside her with one hand while reaching for the champagne with the other. While she slowly filled Kerry's glass, she introduced the others at the table. Sasha's cousin, Lucy, sat directly across from her, perched on the knee of a ruggedly handsome man named Fergus who was apparently a famous cricket player. Next to them was Jillian, a childhood friend of Sasha's from Roedean. Kerry had read up on the illustrious boarding school while she was procrastinating from her schoolwork a few weeks ago. Some called it the female equivalent of Eton.

Acutely aware of her manners, Kerry only sipped at her champagne despite wanting to down the entire contents of the flute. Around her, the conversation flowed in elegantly clipped syllables punctuated by bursts of laughter. At first, Kerry remained quiet, completely at a loss for what to say in such company. Their conversation topics ranged from holidays in Kenya to the newest watering hole in Mayfair, and she felt completely out of her depth. She tried to chime in on occasion, but mostly she just kept sipping, and risking the occasional glance in Sasha's direction. When the movie star and two of his male friends joined her table, the spike of jealousy pierced through Kerry's chest like a javelin. Eugene and Alastair weren't enough? Now she needed to seduce Hollywood royalty, too?

"You look as though someone murdered your puppy," Miranda said, her breath cascading across the shell of Kerry's ear.

But then Jillian, who also seemed aware of her discomfort, engaged her in discussion about her course of study. For several minutes, they chatted about academics, before Lucy stood tipsily and exhorted them all to follow her to the dance floor. When Sasha got to her feet, movie star in tow, Kerry decided to stay put. She wasn't a very good dancer, anyway.

Oddly enough, Miranda had stayed behind as well. "So," she said, angling her body toward Kerry's while refilling her glass. "How are you managing?"

"Managing?"

Miranda's gesticulation took in the entirety of the club. "All of this."

Kerry wasn't about to admit to Miranda—whose glossy hair, perfect face, and glamorous outfit made her seem like a high-society robot instead of a human being—that she felt like a fish out of water.

"I'm fine, thanks. This is a great spot."

"*Boujis* is one of my favorites. Sasha's, too." She cocked her head. "Speaking of whom, how is your relationship faring? Smooth sailing, I hope?"

Kerry didn't have to feign the smile she felt on her face at Miranda's use of "relationship." Instinctively, she turned to watch Sasha sway to the music, wholly independent despite the crowd of admirers surrounding her. "She's wonderful."

"My favorite person in the entire world. I'm glad to see her happy. It's been some time since she's chosen to date someone." Miranda gave her a conspiratorial look. "You're the first woman, in fact."

Kerry almost choked, and her eyes watered as champagne bubbles went right up her nose. "I am?"

"Oh, not the first woman she's had, of course. She's been snogging girls since boarding school. But the first she's actually dated."

Kerry was starting to feel dizzy, and not because of the alcohol. Was she really Sasha's first true girlfriend? And in her case, what did that even mean? "How many relationships has she had?" she asked, unable to stop herself from probing for details.

Miranda toyed with the stem of her flute, the bright polish on her long nails glittering under the lights. "Let me see. Three… no, there have been four men. None of whom lasted for more than a few months." She shrugged delicately. "Dating a princess can be a challenge. As you are no doubt discovering in the wake of that photograph."

Kerry took another drink to hide her dismay. Sasha had never managed a relationship longer than a few months? Had she broken them off, or had these four men been unwilling to stand in her shadow?

"Sasha is well worth any challenge," she said, trying to maintain an even tone. Her instincts were screaming at her not to betray too much emotion to Miranda.

"Oh, certainly," she said airily. "She inspires loyalty in every life she touches. And who can blame her for having a roving eye?"

Studiously, Kerry kept her focus on Sasha, who was dancing more slowly now near the movie star. Did she really have a roving eye? Was Kerry doomed to be one more notch on Sasha's bedpost, or did they have a chance to build something deeper, stronger, and more enduring? It wasn't a question Miranda could answer, but perhaps Kerry could use her chattiness to her own advantage.

"Are you suggesting I should be worried about her and that movie star?"

"Luke Boyd? Of course not. He's gay."

Like mist before the sunrise, Kerry's darkening mood lifted, and she laughed. Sasha was playing an elaborate game, but Boyd was in on the joke. Smiling broadly, she drained the rest of her glass and stood. The revelation made her want to dance—though not too close to Sasha, of course.

"In that case," she said, looking toward Miranda as she stepped away from the table, "Let's celebrate."

CHAPTER FIFTEEN

The next morning, Kerry rested her chin on the Princess Royal's bare shoulder, looking on as she pulled up the website of a popular British tabloid. Sure enough, a coyly smiling Sasha, linked arm in arm with Luke Boyd as they exited *boujis*, stared back at them from the laptop screen beneath the headline: "Sasha Boogies At Boujis With Boyd."

"Brilliant," Sasha murmured.

"Like clockwork." Kerry drew her hair aside to kiss the nape of her neck. "You know exactly how to work the system."

"What do I get for being so clever?"

Kerry reached around her to close the laptop and put it on the nightstand. Sasha fell back onto the bed, eyes sparkling with mirth, lips curved in an inviting smile. When they had finally reunited at Clarence House late last night, Sasha had effortlessly taken control. Now, she was surrendering it.

"What did you have in mind?" Kerry asked, hearing the hoarseness in her own voice as she took in the sight of Princess Alexandra sprawled across their mussed sheets, her dark hair rippling over the pillow.

"Surprise me."

In the next moment, Kerry had covered Sasha's body with her own. After pressing several lingering kisses to her neck, she gently took Sasha's earlobe between her teeth and was rewarded by a soft moan. "You are a work of art," she murmured as she reached down with her free hand to cup Sasha's hip and pull their bodies closer together. "Flawless."

Sasha tugged at her hair. "Less talking. More sex."

Kerry captured both her hands and held them above her head, ignoring the token protest as she ground her pelvis slowly against Sasha's. "Patience, Princess. I'm going to take my time savoring you."

"I could scream. My protection detail would barge in and arrest you."

Enjoying the ease of their sensual banter, Kerry laughed and leaned in closer. "Oh, you will scream. My name. In passion." She brushed a soft kiss across Sasha's lips. "I think Ian will get the hint and stay away."

"Again." Sasha's hips flexed restlessly. "Kiss me again."

Kerry lowered her head but paused mere inches from Sasha's inviting mouth. "Say please."

❖

The tabloids were obsessed with "Sasha and Luke" for two weeks before it became clear—thanks to photographs that emerged of her dancing at Mahiki with the heir to the throne of Luxembourg—that Boyd was no longer on the royal radar. At first, Kerry found the media's obsession laughable. They thought they were revealing news, when really Sasha was adroitly leading them on a wild goose chase.

Kerry had quickly learned not to read the comments on the newspapers' online articles about "Sassy Sasha." The tasteful protestations of attraction didn't bother her so much—she could, after all, empathize. But many people either spoke of her in vulgar, wildly inappropriate terms, or they denounced her activities in harsh language. Seeing the ignorant public's opinion made Kerry's blood boil. What would they say if they knew she was putting on an elaborate performance to protect their fledgling relationship? Would they still be so critical?

Sometimes, even Kerry's peers weighed in on Sasha's love life. A drunken Kieran had once dubbed her "sexy as fuck" during a pub crawl—prompting Harris to kick Kerry in the shin under their table—while Anna had alternately lauded Sasha's fashion sense while disapproving of her "wild child" tendencies. Whenever the Princess Royal became a topic of conversation, Kerry resolutely kept her head down and her mouth shut.

But as the cool October days gave way to a blustery November, Kerry began to increasingly doubt her ability to keep up the charade. It had become difficult for her to stomach the weekly sight of Sasha flirting with men whom the public would—she had little doubt—vastly prefer to herself as a partner for their princess. Besides, nightclubs were fun on occasion, but they lost their novelty quickly. After two weeks of watching Sasha from the sidelines of one exclusive and outrageously expensive venue after another, Kerry decided to forgo the all-night partying and meet her in her apartment.

For the fourth weekend in a row, she had made the trip down from London to a deserted Clarence House. This time, Sasha had promised she would quit her club of the week early and be waiting for her, and yet when Kerry stepped inside, she found the rooms dark and empty as always. Instead of retreating to the couch, she went to the kitchen, took a beer from the refrigerator, and sat at the small table. As she spun the bottle in her hands, she listened to the rain and wind lash at the trees outside. Mother Nature seemed frustrated, and she could empathize. On the one hand, Miranda's plan for Sasha appeared to have worked; the paparazzi had stopped hounding her quite so mercilessly now that she was back to handing them easy fodder. But on the other hand, Sasha had become increasingly embroiled in her own game. Sometimes Kerry wondered if she even remembered why she was playing it in the first place.

It was getting more and more difficult to watch from afar while Sasha deliberately played a caricature of herself for the benefit of the public. No matter how she tried not to look, she couldn't avoid the ubiquitous images of Sasha on the arm of some hot male musician or athlete or entrepreneur. Glossy magazine covers and sensationalist tabloid headlines taunted her on every news stand. It had gotten to the point where she couldn't even shop for groceries without her stomach turning.

At times, she felt as though she had been pulled into some sort of bizarre love triangle between Princess Alexandra and her assortment of male decoys. Yes, she and Sasha were able to spend at least one night a week together. But after a bout of frenzied lovemaking followed by a few hours of sleep, they always woke into a world they couldn't share with each other—a world that held no place for them as a couple. Inevitably, Sasha would have to get up to attend a charity polo match in Ascot or an extended family outing at Sandringham Estate or a state dinner at Buckingham Palace. The royals, she was coming to realize, lived their lives almost entirely in a fishbowl.

As she picked at the corner of the label on the bottle, Kerry reminded herself that even had she been a man, her place at such functions would not have been guaranteed. Over the past few weeks, she had been reading about the beginnings of Arthur and Ashleigh's romance, just to get a sense of perspective. They had been together for almost a year before Ashleigh had begun to accompany Arthur to official events. Was that even what she wanted—to be held up to the scrutiny of the masses the way Ashleigh was now? And what did Sasha want? Admitting to a relationship with another woman would rock the royal boat as it had never been jostled before. Did Sasha have any desire to "go public," or was she simply having fun?

The beer label ripped beneath her fingers and she sighed in frustration. She wanted to be sympathetic and compassionate, but more and more, being Sasha's secret was chafing at her sense of self worth. Was this how Lancelot had felt about Guinevere?

And then she had to laugh at herself, because Arthur was Sasha's brother, not her husband. And because she had no wish, however romantic parts of the story might be, to insert herself into such a tragic tale.

The sound of the door opening pulled her from her thoughts. Taking a long pull from the bottle, she readied herself for Sasha's excuses. Moments later, she appeared in the doorway, dressed in a shimmering gold gown that almost swept the floor. Tonight's outing must have been classier than the average nightclub.

Sasha regarded her silently. "I've let you down. You're angry with me."

Kerry spread her hands. "That's not the right word."

Sasha stepped over the threshold and took a seat across the table. "But you're definitely not happy."

"No," Kerry said. "I'm not."

Sasha glanced at the clock on the wall. "I realize I broke my promise to be here, and—"

"That isn't the problem." Kerry picked at the corner of the Hobgoblin label.

"Then what is?"

Beneath the coolness of Sasha's tone, Kerry could detect a note of...perhaps not fear, exactly, but concern. Maybe even anxiety. Was that a good sign? An indication that she genuinely cared?

"I know this is complicated. So complicated." Exhaling slowly, she tried to walk the emotional tightrope between her feelings for Sasha and her frustration with her. "But it's been almost two months since you told me you needed to buy yourself some time so that you could decide what you really wanted. Instead, you've gotten completely caught up in the game you're playing with the media. Recently, I've gotten the feeling that it's more important to you than I am."

Aside from the flush that rose to her cheeks, Sasha betrayed no indication that Kerry's words had affected her. Crossing one leg over the other, she presented a nearly impassive façade. "What are you saying, exactly?"

"I wish I knew where I stood with you. You seem content with this system we've put into place, but I—I'm not."

"You're not?"

She shook her head, feeling miserable. "I'm not trying to bully or pressure you. I'm just trying to tell you how I feel."

"Do you honestly believe I enjoy living a double life? Pretending for the cameras? Watching every word that comes out of my mouth?"

Just as Kerry was opening her mouth to reply, Sasha's phone rang. She glanced at her purse. "That's my father. I'll return his call later." She leaned forward, intent on Kerry's face. "Tell me what you want from me."

Faced with this icily composed version of Sasha, Kerry had to remind herself that while she might not be a princess, she too had rights. "I want us to have an honest conversation about where this— us—is going. In Ireland, you talked about our connection. Do you still feel that? Do you think, someday, that you'll want to make this relationship public?"

Speaking the words made her mouth go dry, and she swallowed hard. "I know something like that would take time. And I can wait, if I have to. But not forever. I won't hide forever. I lost my first love to the closet in college. I won't lose myself."

Sasha's fingers twitched against the lacquered surface. Otherwise, she betrayed no movement. "Let me be certain I understand you. You're asking for clarification about my intentions with respect to… this." She gestured between them.

Feeling suddenly shaky, Kerry took another sip of her beer. "Yes."

"And while you would consider continuing to keep…this…a secret for a short time, you refuse to do so in the long term. Is that correct?"

"Yes." Kerry's stomach was in knots. She might as well have been speaking to a robot, for all the emotion Sasha was showing. What did that mean? Was this the end? If it was, she sensed no relief on the horizon of her psyche—only sadness and pain and longing.

Sasha's phone rang again. At first she ignored it, but as the ringtone resolved she looked over at her purse in concern. "That's Ashleigh," she murmured. "Just a moment. I have to…hello? Ash? No, I—*what*?"

As Kerry watched, the color disappeared from Sasha's face and she swayed in her chair. In an instant, Kerry was kneeling at Sasha's feet and lacing their fingers together. Something had happened. Something awful. In the face of Sasha's palpable fear, Kerry's frustration melted away. She felt the world snapped into crystalline focus as adrenaline surged through her blood. She had to stay calm. She had to be strong. Sasha needed her. That was the only thing that mattered.

"Now. I'm leaving now. I'll be there—Ash, please, just—I love you. Yes. Soon."

When the phone dropped from Sasha's hand, Kerry was there to catch it.

"Sweetheart?" The term of endearment came without thought. "What's happened? Can you tell me?"

Pale and trembling, Sasha turned to her with a grief-stricken expression. Kerry brought her hand to her mouth and kissed each knuckle gently, willing her to find the words.

"It's Arthur. He's—he's had an accident." She gulped for breath. "He's in a coma."

CHAPTER SIXTEEN

The city passed in a blur of rain-washed light. Sasha leaned her head against the window, wishing the cool glass could ease her fevered mind. Outside, people were going about their daily lives—enjoying their Saturday night, despite the weather. Meanwhile, she had slipped into a parallel universe in which the very idea of enjoying anything ever again seemed ludicrous.

Arthur. Her brilliant, charming, loyal brother. Arthur, who had always let her have a head start in their childhood footraces. Arthur, who had once given the jacket off his back to a homeless boy on the street. Arthur, who had comforted both her and Lizzie so well in the wake of their mother's death. Arthur, whose patient explanations over the phone had made it possible for her to pass her history course at university. Arthur, who had asked friends, family, and strangers alike to donate to charity in lieu of sending wedding gifts. Arthur, the golden boy not only of the United Kingdom, but of the entire Commonwealth. And beyond.

"It should have been me," she whispered.

"Pardon, ma'am?" Ian asked gently.

"Never mind. I'm sorry."

She couldn't stop mentally retracing Ashleigh's words in a futile search for more information. This afternoon, Arthur had been out on a training mission in foul weather. There had been some sort of accident, and he had been evacuated by helicopter to the nearest trauma center. Shortly thereafter, he had been transferred to the London Brain Centre at Wellington Hospital. Their father, whom she had called back immediately, had been unable or unwilling to offer any more details.

A crowd was already gathering outside the hospital by the time Sasha's car pulled up. At first, she felt outrage that so many photographers were hoping to capitalize on her family tragedy. But then she saw the signs interspersed with the telephoto lenses. *God bless you, Prince Arthur. Praying for you, Arthur. We love you, Arthur.* The news had barely broken, and already people were showing their support—abandoning their Saturday night plans and braving the discomfort of the elements to hold a vigil for their fallen prince.

She stepped out of the vehicle before Ian could open his umbrella. Rain pelted down furiously as the crowd surged and cameras flashed. She didn't care about any of it. She had to get inside. Members of both the royal guard and the police force closed around her in a phalanx as she moved toward the doors.

Once inside, Ian offered his handkerchief. She took it gratefully and wiped her face, nose crinkling as she caught the scent of antiseptic. The sharp odor sent her flashing back in time to her mother's illness: the months spent in and out of the hospital, its pale walls closing in on her at the end. Her stomach roiled, and she pressed the cloth more firmly to her face.

"Are you all right?" Ian's hand was at her elbow.

Not trusting her voice, she nodded. When she felt her fingers trembling against her face, she willed them to stop. She had to be strong. For the sake of Lizzie and Ashleigh and even her father. Arthur had always been the strong one. Now it was her turn.

Exhaling slowly, she raised her head. The guards had remained outside. Ian stood at her right hand, and a nervous-looking man in a pair of scrubs lingered a few feet away.

"Can you take me to my brother?" she asked him.

"The physicians are still running some tests, Your Royal Highness," he said. "But I can take you to the private waiting room where your family is gathering."

"Yes. Thank you."

As they fell into step behind him, she tried to return the handkerchief to Ian. He pressed it back into her hands.

"Keep it. I have plenty."

"Thank you." She subtly leaned her shoulder against his. "For everything."

"It's always an honor, ma'am."

As they continued down the maze of corridors, Sasha found herself wishing that Ian weren't the only person at her side right now. She missed Kerry with a ferocity as sudden as it was unexpected. Despite the tension of their earlier conversation, Kerry had been a rock as Sasha attempted to pull herself together. She had led Sasha into the bedroom and helped her pick out clothing to wear. While she was changing, Kerry had poured her a glass of water, and while she drank it, Kerry had rubbed her back. And as Sasha was about to leave, Kerry had pulled her into a gentle embrace.

"I'll be thinking of you," she had murmured before leaning in to kiss her with infinite gentleness. "And praying for him."

By now, she was probably on her way to the train station. The thought made her feel even more alone.

The hospital employee stopped in front of a door of frosted glass. "Here you are, ma'am."

Ian pushed the door open to reveal her father, phone to his ear, in mid-pace across the room. He gestured for them to come inside. As she entered, she turned to see Ashleigh rising from an armchair. Her eyes were rimmed with red, and she pressed her quivering lips together, clearly trying to be brave. But it wasn't her turn.

Sasha opened her arms, and that was all the invitation Ashleigh needed. She threw herself into the embrace, sobbing quietly against Sasha's shoulder. Sasha closed her eyes and stroked the back of Ashleigh's head, just as she remembered her mother doing when she'd suffered some scrape or bruise as a child.

"He's going to be all right," she murmured. "He's got the best care. And the whole world behind him. But most importantly, he has you."

Ashleigh didn't answer, but gradually, the shaking of her shoulders began to subside. Finally, she raised her head. Even with puffy eyes and tearstained cheeks, she was exceptionally beautiful. She and Arthur would have such lovely children.

A stab of fear sliced into her chest, but she grit her teeth and stood strong against it. Leaning forward, she kissed Ashleigh on the forehead, then stooped to take a few tissues from the box on a nearby table.

"Thanks," Ashleigh whispered.

Sasha tried to smile. "I'll be back in a moment." She had to speak with her father. Now off the phone, he stood at the window, one hand braced against the frame. "Father."

He turned slowly to look down at her out of too-bright eyes. Otherwise, his craggy face was impassive. In that instant, she thought about the chasm that gaped between them—the thousand misunderstandings and cruel words and hurtful deeds. Right now, none of it mattered. She could only imagine how difficult it was for him to be standing here, contemplating the loss of his son after already losing his wife. Stepping forward, she grasped his shoulders and pressed her cheek against his chest.

"I love you."

He remained motionless for several seconds before patting her awkwardly on the back. She wondered what he was thinking—whether he, too, wished she could have taken Arthur's place. Gathering herself, she stepped back.

"He's going to be all right."

"Yes." He nodded once.

"What more do you know? Anything?" As she asked the question, Ashleigh stepped up beside her and linked their arms together.

"No. But hopefully these tests will be able to give us a much clearer sense of his...prognosis."

"Have they let you see him?"

He shook his head.

"And Lizzie? She's on her way?"

He glanced at his watch. "She should be here within the hour."

"Very well." She surveyed the room, taking it in for the first time. Two chairs and a sofa were arranged around a small glass table. Two vending machines hummed quietly in the far corner. The place positively reeked of fear, and she had to swallow hard before she trusted her voice again.

"I'm going to try the hot chocolate that machine is advertising. Would either of you like something to eat or drink?"

"No, thank you." Her father turned back to his contemplation of the window.

"I'll come with you," Ashleigh said, still clutching her arm.

Sasha got them each a cocoa and they sat on the sofa, sipping the watery drinks, knees touching. They didn't speak. She thought of Arthur, somewhere nearby, lying still and unresponsive as the doctors hovered over him. The image made her shiver, and she mentally reached out for a memory of Kerry. The broad smile that was the hallmark of her enthusiasm, the cadence of her rich alto voice as she read aloud, the fierce tenderness in her eyes as she touched Sasha with possessive reverence.

Miraculously, Sasha felt her anxiety ease a little. Thinking to send Kerry a text, she removed her phone from her purse. But as she looked down at the blinking cursor, she couldn't think of the right thing to say. Before Ashleigh's call, they had been poised at a pivotal moment. Kerry wanted their relationship to be open—at least, eventually. While she certainly wouldn't be pushing for that now given Arthur's accident, her desire wouldn't simply fade away, never to return. If Sasha had no intention of ever granting Kerry's request, she had no right to lead her on now. It all came down to the fundamental question. Was she willing to come out?

"Do I dare disturb the universe?" she murmured, thinking of how Kerry's face had lit up while she was explaining the significance of the poem.

"What was that?" asked Ashleigh.

The door opened and a doctor, dressed in a white lab coat over pale green scrubs, entered. Sasha jumped to her feet, Ashleigh one beat behind her. Her father turned, hope and fear warring plainly on his face.

"Your Majesty." The doctor inclined his head, then turned to Sasha. "Your Royal Highness. Ms. Dunning. My name is Philip Herren, and I am the neurologist in charge of Prince Arthur's case. The prince is currently in critical, but stable, condition." He gestured to the chairs. "If you would be so kind as to sit, I will explain some of the details."

Sasha sank back into her chair. Critical, but stable. The phrase raced through her brain like a dog chasing its tail, going nowhere. Ashleigh found her hand and clutched it tightly.

"By all accounts, Prince Arthur endured a serious blow to the head. He also suffered several contusions and a broken right wrist, which we have already set. In cases such as his, the primary danger is swelling of the brain, which can lead to permanent damage. We've inserted an intraventricular catheter into his brain in order to monitor the pressure. If necessary, we'll remove a small section of his skull to accommodate any brain swelling."

Silence fell. Her father looked as though he wanted to speak, but couldn't. Ashleigh looked as though she might burst into tears.

"What are his chances of waking up without any lasting damage?" A tiny part of Sasha felt absurdly proud that her voice remained steady.

"He is young, healthy, and strong," Dr. Herren said. "He has a very good chance, provided we can keep the swelling under control. Even in the best-case scenario, however, it may be days or weeks before he wakes. These next twenty-four hours will be especially critical. We'll know more tomorrow."

"May we see him tonight?" Ashleigh asked.

"Briefly, yes. I can take you to him now, if you wish."

Sasha rose quickly, but her father held up one hand. "Doctor, before we go, is there anything..." He paused, wrestling with a surge of emotion. "Is there anything you require that you don't currently have? Anything at all..."

Dr. Herren's fingers twitched, and for a moment it looked as though his innate compassion might compel him to touch the King. But then, remembering himself, he slipped his hands into his pockets.

"Your Majesty, right now I have full confidence that this is the best facility in the world for Prince Arthur's present needs. If I ever believe otherwise, you will be the first to know."

"Thank you." The King cleared his throat and squared his shoulders. "Take us to him, please."

As they left the room, Sasha slipped her left hand into her father's right. When she squeezed tightly, he returned the pressure. Chin raised high, she prepared herself for what she was about to see. No matter what, she would remain strong. For Arthur.

❖

It was nearly four o'clock in the morning by the time she left the hospital, and then only because her father insisted they all return home to get some rest. Arthur's condition hadn't changed in the intervening hours. Thankfully, Lizzie had arrived just in time to spend a few minutes with him before Dr. Herren had cited the risk of infection and shepherded them back to the private waiting room.

Sasha wrapped her arm around Lizzie's waist as they walked through the nearly deserted corridors behind Ian. Like her, Lizzie had a suite of rooms in Clarence House, and they would take a car back together. She didn't speak. There was nothing to say. When Lizzie stumbled once, Sasha pulled her even closer. She was exhausted. They all were. And they hadn't even made it through the first twenty-four hours yet.

Ian spoke quietly into his wrist mic and then turned toward them. "There is still a substantial crowd outside the hospital. You'll be given a police escort to the car."

"Thank you." Sasha turned to Lizzie and tucked a loose strand of blond hair behind her ear. "Are you ready?"

When Lizzie nodded, Ian led them around the corner. Waiting in front of the double doors stood a group of policemen. As they closed ranks around the two of them, Sasha caught sight of the crowd. It had tripled since her arrival. At least.

"My God," Lizzie breathed. "Look at them all."

"The princesses!" someone called as they walked out into the night. The cry was taken up and spread throughout the people, followed by a cheer that resolved into their brother's name, chanted over and over and over.

Sasha felt the tears running down her cheeks, but for once she didn't care what she looked like to the waiting cameras.

"Thank you," she said, as they made their way slowly through the masses. And louder, "thank you." She glimpsed men and women and even some children, many still drenched from the earlier downpour. Her people. Gathered here for her brother. She reached out one hand and felt their fingers against hers—slender fingers, callused fingers, tiny fingers. Her people.

And then, as the crowd began to thin, she saw Kerry. She stood near the edge of the throng, wearing a raincoat that matched the color of her eyes. Those eyes were brimming with tears, and one had even escaped to trickle down the gentle slope of her cheek. Sasha wanted to chase its path with one finger and then brush it away.

"Kerry," Sasha whispered.

She hadn't gone back to Oxford. She had come to the hospital. To keep the vigil for Arthur. To be close. As their eyes met, Kerry kissed the tips of her fingers and raised her hand.

"Sasha?" Having felt her trail behind, Lizzie was looking at her in confusion.

She hurried forward, then glanced once over her shoulder. Kerry had been swallowed by the crowd, but she could still feel the pull of her gaze and the memory of their last, tender kiss.

CHAPTER SEVENTEEN

K erry rose from the kneeler, crossed herself, and turned into the side aisle. As she had entered the chapel at Magdalen College, she'd felt a little silly. Now, after lighting a candle and offering up a prayer for Arthur, that feeling had dissipated. She might not know exactly what she believed in anymore, but she believed in something. Some power, some force, some being—something benevolent and creative and compassionate. In her prayer, she had asked for healing for Arthur, guidance for his doctors, and comfort for his family. Especially Sasha.

She had received only one message from Sasha—a text, shortly after they had seen each other at the hospital. *Thank you,* was all it said. Kerry had replied, *Please let me help. Whatever I can do. Anything.* But she had heard nothing back.

Nearly three days had passed since Arthur's accident, and the prince's condition had cast a pall not only over all of the United Kingdom, but also the world. But as most of the global community rallied behind the royal family, some media outlets used the tragedy as a way to stir up drama. When the monarchy announced late Sunday morning that it had been necessary for Arthur's physicians to drain some cerebrospinal fluid in order to relieve the pressure on his brain, several of the more sensationalist reporters had questioned what would happen if Arthur died of his injuries, pronouncing Sasha a "brainless socialite" who was unfit to rule. Just thinking about their ignorant criticisms set her teeth on edge. She wanted to protect Sasha from every last word, and she couldn't.

"Being with me would just make it worse," she murmured as she stepped out into the dark. The rain, which had lasted on and off for days, had finally given way to a clear, wintry night. Shivering, she jammed her hands into her pockets and began to walk quickly up the hill.

And then her phone vibrated.

Heart suddenly racing, she fumbled to pull the phone out of her pocket, reminding herself all the while that it was probably Harris checking in on her.

But it wasn't.

I'm nearly at Oxford. I need to see you. I've booked a room at the Old Bank. They're expecting you. As Kerry looked down at Sasha's message, utterly incredulous, another came in. *Please.*

She didn't think. She ran. The Old Bank Hotel was on High Street in the center of town. She could be there in less than ten minutes. As she ran, thoughts flooded her head. Ultimately, they all boiled down to two: Why was Sasha here? Had something worse happened to Arthur?

A few blocks away, she slowed to a walk. It wouldn't do to enter one of the finest Oxford hotels at a dead sprint. By the time she reached the revolving doors, her breathing had evened out. As she moved toward the desk, she flipped open her wallet and held out her identification.

"Ms. Donovan," the clerk said smoothly. "Of course." He handed her a keycard. "Room six nineteen."

Too impatient to wait for the elevator, Kerry took the stairs two at a time. The suite was empty. She turned on the lamp near the bed and then moved to each window, lowering and closing the blinds of each in turn. And then she sat on the bed, eyes trained on the door, beyond all coherent thought. Only moments later, the door opened and Sasha slipped inside, closing it quickly behind her. Her face was unhealthily pale, and the skin beneath her eyes was dark with fatigue, but she was still the most beautiful woman Kerry had ever seen.

"Sasha?" Two syllables contained the thousand questions Kerry couldn't seem to articulate.

"Thank you." Her gaze dropped to the floor. "For being here. I just—"

"Sasha." Once Kerry had her attention again, she managed a lopsided smile. "Please come here and let me hold you while we talk."

Looking as though she might cry, Sasha walked forcefully across the room and into Kerry's arms. Kerry let the momentum draw her down to the bed and rolled them over until they lay side-by-side. A tremble in her hand betrayed her emotion as she reached out to touch Sasha's face.

"How is he?"

Sasha's sigh caressed her wrist. "No change."

"And you?"

"I'm holding up." She edged closer, sliding one foot between both of Kerry's. "Thank you for being at the hospital, that first night."

"I missed you so much." Gently, she traced her fingers along Sasha's jawline. "I wanted to show my respect for your brother, but mostly, I wanted to be close to you."

When Sasha reached for her hand and drew it over her waist to rest in the small of her back, Kerry moved forward until their bodies were touching.

"It should have been me."

Sasha's voice was muffled against Kerry's shirt, but the words were clear enough to break her heart. She kissed the top of Sasha's head. "It was an accident, sweetheart. It shouldn't have been anyone."

"But if it had to be someone, it should have been me!" She pulled back slightly, eyes feverish and sparkling. "Arthur is so good. So smart and selfless and kind and generous. The world needs him."

"Yes, it does. But the world also needs you. Think of the charities you sponsor. Of all the children's lives you've changed and the people you've inspired." Kerry cupped Sasha's face, desperate for her to understand just how precious she was. "Please don't talk this way. I need you. I love you."

And then she froze. Before the confession had slipped her lips, she hadn't fully realized just how deep her feelings for Sasha ran. But it was the truth. She could feel it in every cell of her body, just as she'd felt that visceral connection to her native Ireland.

"I love you," she whispered as Sasha blinked in surprise. "I do. And right now, I don't want you to say or do anything. I just want you to let me hold you. Please."

After a moment, Sasha nodded. Closing her eyes, she burrowed closer. Kerry breathed in the scent of lilacs and gently rubbed the small of Sasha's back, stroking her hair with her other hand.

"What if everyone's right?" Sasha murmured, the words almost too soft for Kerry to catch.

"About what?"

"That I'm unfit to rule. If I have to."

Kerry's arms tightened around her. "Not everyone is saying that. And the ones who are, are wrong. You would make a wonderful queen."

Sasha pulled back just enough for their eyes to meet. "A dyslexic, lesbian queen."

Kerry tamped down her surprise at the way Sasha had identified herself. "Your dyslexia doesn't define you. Neither does your sexuality. You would be a warm, compassionate, empathetic queen. And if you ever did decide to champion issues like gay rights or learning disabilities, well, just think of how powerful a spokesperson you would be."

Sasha made no reply. Instead, she closed her eyes and returned her head to Kerry's shoulder. Not wanting to push, Kerry resumed her rhythmic strokes, wanting only to make Sasha feel comforted and secure. After a long time, Sasha's body grew heavy and her breathing deepened. Only then did Kerry let herself drift into a light doze. Every time Sasha stirred or murmured in the thrall of some dream, she was there to coax her back into sleep with a soothing touch.

It was just past five in the morning when Sasha suddenly sat up, wide awake and clearly in search of something. She relaxed when she saw the time. Kerry, who had struggled into a sitting position next to her, tucked a loose strand of hair behind Sasha's ear.

"Time to go?"

"Yes, I should get back. I'd like to be at the hospital when the morning shift begins." Sasha lightly stroked Kerry's thigh and pressed a kiss to one corner of her mouth. "How do I begin to thank you?"

"You don't have to." Kerry slid off the bed and extended her hand. "I'm so glad you came here last night."

"Even though I'm not giving you what you want?"

The question puzzled Kerry until she realized Sasha was alluding to their conversation back in London, on the night of Arthur's accident. Her heart clenched at the realization that Sasha had been preoccupied with such a thing on top of all the fallout from her brother's condition. She took hold of Sasha's shoulders.

"I don't want you to think about that," she said. "Promise me you won't. I just want you to take care of yourself, and to let me help whenever you'd like. I can come to you next time. Any time."

Sasha actually smiled. She reached for Kerry's hand and tugged. "Will you walk me to the car?"

"Gladly." Kerry opened the door a crack, then more widely to scan the hall in both directions. The only other person in the corridor was Ian, who rose from an armchair near the bank of elevators as they emerged. The ride downstairs was brief, and the lobby was deserted save for one man behind the desk. The large bay windows revealed a predawn world bathed in ethereal gray tones.

"I know you could easily go home," Sasha murmured as they moved across the room, "but I want you to crawl back into that bed. I'd like to think about you sleeping there, on my way back to London."

"I can do that." When she halted just before the revolving door, Sasha looked over in confusion. "I'll stay inside, just to be safe."

At first it seemed as though Sasha might protest, but then she evidently thought the better of it. "Very well." She glanced over toward the front desk, and Kerry followed her gaze. The employee on duty was staring down intently—probably at his phone—and quite suddenly, Kerry found herself in Sasha's embrace. Twining her arms around Kerry's neck, she merged their mouths in a kiss that was at once soothing and passionate. Giving herself up to it—to them— Kerry groaned softly as the tide of emotion washed over her.

As quickly as it had begun, the kiss was over. Sasha, her lips moist and her eyes slightly glazed, backed away until she was at a safe distance. "Good-bye. I'll see you soon."

"Anytime you like."

Sasha nodded. For a moment, it seemed she was on the cusp of saying something else, but then she turned decisively and walked out the door without a backward glance. Kerry watched her get into the car and followed its progress until the taillights faded into the distance. Only then did she turn around and go back upstairs.

The room felt large and empty without Sasha, but the pillow she had used still faintly smelled of lilacs. Curling her arms around it, she focused on taking slow, deep breaths as she silently recited another prayer for Arthur. When fatigue hemmed her in, pressing her down into the mattress, she didn't fight the impulse to drift off.

What felt like moments later, she was roused by the insistent buzzing of her phone on the nightstand. Fumbling groggily for it, she caught sight of the clock and realized she had slept for almost three hours. Thankfully, she didn't have any obligations until the early afternoon.

"Hello?"

"Where are you?" Harris sounded frantic. "Are you okay?"

"I'm fine." Kerry curled herself into fetal position around the pillow and tried to find the volume button. His voice was far too shrill. "Why wouldn't I be? And I'm in a hotel on High Street. Sasha showed up last night."

"I know."

"You know?"

"Of course I know. That photograph is everywhere!"

"Photograph?" A wave of foreboding washed over her. "Damn it, Harris, start making sense. What are you talking about?"

"You really have no idea." His tone was deadly serious. "I don't know how to tell you this. If you have a television in your room, turn it on. You are all over the news right now, Kerry. Someone managed to snap a photograph of you and Sasha kissing, and it's gone viral."

"What?" Panic sluiced down her spine, knotting her stomach and making it hard to catch a deep breath. When she reached for the remote, her hands shook. "How?"

"I don't know!"

After several attempts, Kerry managed to power on the television. Heart thumping wildly, she thumbed through the menu until she found a news program. The headline made her feel as though she were in free fall.

Sassy Sasha Has Lesbian Fling While Brother Remains Unconscious.

Over the roar in her ears, she heard the anchor explaining how Sasha had been photographed in a kiss with a woman, whom a hotel employee had identified as one Kerry Donovan, at the Old Bank Hotel in Oxford early this morning. When the picture flashed on the screen, Kerry sucked in a sharp breath and gripped the bed sheets. The captured moment was the kiss they had shared in the lobby hours before. Had the paparazzi been lying in wait across the street? How had they found out about Sasha's trip in the first place?

"They're going to crucify her."

"I wish I could tell you you're wrong, but it's already happening." Harris paused. "And they're saying some pretty awful things about you, too."

"I don't care about that." Kerry jumped up and paced over to the window. When she twitched aside the curtain, she could see a crowd beginning to gather on the sidewalk below. "Fuck. The press is waiting outside. I need to find a back door."

"No. Stay put. I'm coming down there. I'll find one for you, and we'll slip out together."

"Harris, I don't want you to put yourself in the midd—"

"Either you let me help you, or I'm calling the police. They're bound to step in soon, anyway. Is that what you want?"

Kerry's heart felt as though it would burst out of her skin in another moment. "Not if I can help it."

"Then you stay put. I'll be there in ten minutes, tops. Do you hear me?"

"Yes."

"What room are you in?"

"Six nineteen."

"Okay. Good. I'm hanging up now. Don't you dare move until you hear from me again."

"I won't," she said. But he had already disconnected the call. She was alone.

Shivering in the throes of adrenaline, Kerry stared numbly at the television as the anchor repeated that Sasha had been caught on film in a passionate embrace with another woman. The broadcast cut away to Main Street, where a reporter was interviewing passers-by about their opinions. One elderly man claimed her tryst brought down irreparable shame on the house of Carlisle and threatened the existence of the monarchy. A mother walking her twin girls to school chastised Sasha for setting a bad example. As the criticism continued to roll in, Kerry cradled her throbbing head in her hands. She could process only one thought.

They were over. The paparazzi had caught them. They were over.

CHAPTER EIGHTEEN

Sasha sat on her couch, knees drawn to her chest, staring at the blank television screen. Waiting for the inevitable knock at her door. The day had dawned bright and cold, but the sunlight outside mocked her. An invisible storm had been unleashed, and she was at its center. When she closed her eyes, she could feel the battering winds.

She could also see Kerry's face. She had replayed their last moment together a thousand times since it had happened. That sweet, passionate kiss had given her the strength to climb into the car that would return her to the hospital—the strength to face another day at her brother's bedside. When the news broke, her protection detail had immediately whisked her back to the shelter of Clarence House. Here, she could remain shielded from the press for as long as she wished. But who would protect Kerry?

The university would try its best; Sasha knew that much. But the simple fact was that Kerry was much more accessible than she was, and that made her much more vulnerable. Worst of all, there was nothing she could do. The juggernaut was in motion. Even if she made no comment or publicly disavowed any sort of relationship, the photographs alone were enough to incite a media frenzy. There was nothing she could do.

And then guilt twisted her stomach, because that wasn't actually the truth. There was one thing she could do. If she acknowledged their relationship and brought Kerry under the protection of the monarchy, at least they could weather the storm together. But how could she possibly do that now? Arthur's condition remained critical and uncertain. Could she ask her family to shoulder the burden of her coming out when they were already mentally and physically exhausted? Could she in good conscience take attention away from Arthur's recovery by making an announcement about something as trivial as her relationship status? The photographs from this morning were already creating an uproar that would distract from what was truly important. And her critics would use them as yet more evidence of her personal failings.

Rubbing her temples, she took several deep breaths in an attempt to calm her racing heart. And then a loud knock sounded at the door. Oddly, she felt relief. At least she wouldn't have to dread this particular encounter anymore.

"What have you done?" No sooner had she closed the door behind her father than he had rounded on her, index finger pointed accusingly. He was dressed immaculately as always, but his eyes were bloodshot and his raised hand trembled.

"What were you thinking? To go off and have a bloody *fling* in the middle of this? With a woman? When your brother is lying in a coma?" He grasped her shoulders, hard. "He could be dying, Alexandra! Dying! Can't you stop thinking about yourself, just this once? Can't you show Arthur—not to mention the remainder of your family—the respect we deserve?"

Sasha wanted to protest. She wanted to tell him that Kerry wasn't a fling. She wanted him to know how kind she was, how generous, how intelligent. She wanted to tell him that for the first time in her life, she thought she might actually be falling in love. But in the wake of his pain and wrath, she couldn't find the strength to explain herself. Mutely, she nodded.

"You have utterly disgraced this family, and we are all paying for it," he fumed. "Elizabeth's protection detail was very nearly overwhelmed when she attempted to go to class this morning."

"What?" Sasha thought she might be sick. Lizzie was being harassed as well?

"The moment she stepped out of doors, she was bombarded by questions about her elder sister's *sex* life."

"I'm sorry," she whispered, unable to think of anything else to say.

"Tell that to her!"

"I will."

"The media is turning this into a circus," he continued. "All we can do is restrict their access to you as much as possible. Your security will be doubled, and you will travel only between here and the hospital. If you wish to go anywhere else, you will have to come to me first. Are we clear, Alexandra?"

"Yes." Silently vowing not to be a coward, she met his angry eyes as she whispered the word. "Yes, Father."

"Good." He loomed over her, powerful and menacing. "Return to the hospital once you've pulled yourself together. Your family needs you."

As the door slammed in his wake, Sasha felt her legs tremble. She reached out to the wall for support, only to find herself sliding down, down, down to the floor. A drop of moisture plinked onto the gleaming hardwood. Then another, and another. Dimly, she realized they were her own tears.

"I'm sorry," she said again, not knowing whether she was speaking to Kerry or to herself. "I'm so sorry."

❖

Kerry slid into her customary seat in the lecture hall and immediately opened her notebook, ignoring the whispers that filled the air around her. It had been three long days since photographs of "the princess affair," as it was being called, had hit the Internet. Gritting her teeth, she opened her laptop and pulled up a Web browser, then typed in the URL of *The Times*. Skipping past the headline containing her own name, she glanced over at the text box proclaiming the latest news about Prince Arthur's condition. Apparently, despite a measurable reduction in the swelling of his brain, he still hadn't regained consciousness. With a sigh, she closed her computer and glanced down at her syllabus in an attempt to force herself to focus on today's topic. "The Non-Euclidean Geometrics of Deconstructivist Architecture."

"Just fantastic," she muttered beneath her breath. Then again, perhaps a difficult lecture topic was exactly what she needed to distract her from the chaos awaiting her as soon as she tried to leave the building.

Foiled in their attempts to gain access to Sasha aside from a few distant photographs of her entering or leaving the hospital, the paparazzi had descended en masse upon Oxford. While both city and university police were doing everything in their power to maintain order, the crowds had grown increasingly disruptive. Some students had even joined in the frenzy. Kerry couldn't go anywhere without being followed, pointed at, and shouted to.

Worst of all, she'd had no word from Sasha. While she couldn't stop herself from continuing to hope for some kind of message, realistically, she knew she wouldn't receive one. Under any other set of circumstances she would have felt deeply hurt at having been so unceremoniously dumped, but their relationship had been discovered at the worst possible moment. Sasha was doubtless coming under enormous pressure from her father, and Kerry felt sick that the photographs had caused the royal family further distress during an already terrible time. But she refused to apologize for what she and Sasha had shared. If she said so much as one word to the media, she knew they would find a way to twist it to suit their agendas. And so she kept her mouth shut, no matter what tawdry remarks they hurled her way.

She was also feeling quite a lot of guilt for how the situation had affected her own family and friends back home. As soon as her identity had been confirmed, the American press had flocked to Pearl River to dig up every bit of information they could about "Sassy Sasha's Latest Conquest," as one headline had read. Her sister had been positively mortified by what she had done. Upon calling home, she'd heard a tirade from Mary about offending God and sullying the family name, and how much the entire "situation" was adding untold amounts of stress to her already busy life. Fortunately, her parents had adopted a much gentler attitude, promising that the community was rallying around her to keep her privacy as intact as they could. Aidan and Declan remained thoroughly supportive, as they had always been. "If anyone could deserve you, Ker," Declan had said during their brief phone conversation, "it would be a princess."

The professor stepped to the podium, jarring her out of her reverie. For the first few minutes, Kerry managed to retain the thread of his talk and even jotted down a few notes. But as the room grew stuffy and his voice droned on, her fatigued mind began to drift to thoughts of Sasha. Resolutely, she stayed away from the sad or stressful memories—picturing Sasha's smile, hearing her laughter, feeling the ghost of her touch. Despite the ever-present ache in her chest, the thoughts brought her a small measure of comfort.

But as her professor began to conclude his remarks, her anxiety resurfaced. The paparazzi would be waiting at the building's entrance. The police had arranged two guards to escort her everywhere, but they could only protect her physically. She still had to endure the mockery and the jeers and the endless, completely inappropriate questions.

When she left the lecture hall, she found Harris waiting outside, holding two coffees. He handed her one and wrapped an arm around her shoulders. "How are you holding up, champ?"

He had been her rock for the last few days—running interference, keeping her supplied with food, and even filtering information when she didn't feel up to wading through all the muck on the Internet.

"Better now," she said. "Thanks for this. Ready to face the horde?"

"Whenever you are. There's no rush."

She took a tentative sip of coffee. "You know you don't have to keep doing this, right? The police said they'd provide me with an escort as long as I needed one."

"It's not that I don't trust Oxford's finest," he said, "but they're doing a job. I'm your friend. It's different, and I want to be there."

"And trust me, I appreciate it." She patted his shoulder. "When you next find yourself embroiled in an international scandal, I promise you'll be able to count on me right back."

He laughed and linked his free arm through hers. "Let's do this."

At the door, they met up with the same two policemen who had walked Kerry to the hall earlier.

"Good afternoon," she said. "And thanks, as always."

Guilt over having forced the Oxford Police Department to attach personnel to her had made Kerry err on the side of being overly polite. She thought she detected the flicker of a smile on the taller one's face before he pushed open the door. But when she stepped outside, the mob was waiting.

A cry of, "There she is!" was soon swallowed by her name being shouted, over and over. Looking straight ahead, determined not to meet the eyes of a single reporter, she slowly descended the steps behind the first officer who gestured for the crowd to make way. Harris followed at her heels, and the second officer brought up the rear. As they reached street level, the questions poured in fast and furious.

"Have you heard from Sasha?"

"How does it feel to have been rejected by Princess Alexandra?"

"Was Sasha a good roll in the sack?"

"How much did the princess pay you, Kerry?"

That was a new one, and she couldn't stop herself from wincing. Suddenly, Harris was darting past her in an impressive burst of speed to loom over the unfortunate soul who had dared imply she was a whore. She couldn't see much of the man from behind Harris's broad back, but he seemed short and rather skinny—certainly no match for an Olympian rower.

"You piece of scum. Apologize to her. Now."

The police crowded close, warning both men away from each other. The crowd surged in behind them, and Kerry felt a rush of claustrophobia as bulbs flashed and someone cursed and the threatened paparazzo vehemently protested Harris's menacing attitude.

Kerry had once thought of Harris as a gentle bear, but there was no trace of gentleness in the tendons that stuck out from his neck like cords and the mottled skin of his face. His hands were clenched into fists. Feeling dizzy, she rested one hand on his back as much for support as to calm him.

"Let it go, Harris," she said, pitching her voice beneath the angry shouts. "Let's get out of here."

But he was on the warpath. "That goes for all of you! Bullies, every one! Can't you see she's a human being? An intelligent woman who—"

"Sod off, faggot!" The shout came from nearby. When Harris turned his head to seek the source of the insult, the skinny man wound up and punched him in the jaw.

Harris's head snapped back only a few inches, but a line of red opened along his jawline where the man's ring had caught the taut skin there. A roar went up from the crowd as people shoved and clamored for a fight.

The first officer leapt forward to subdue the antagonist, and Kerry tugged hard at Harris's raised arm. His eyes were dark and furious.

"Enough! You're hurt! Damn it, Harris, let's just get out of here. Please!"

As he finally let her pull him away, the other officer beckoned to them, a baton raised in his free hand. He shoved forward through the crowd in the direction of a nearby side street.

"Backup," he explained, pointing to a waiting squad car. At that moment, a siren wailed nearby. "And more coming. Go!"

They piled into the car, which promptly roared away. Harris had his shirt pressed to his jaw, and he still looked like he wanted to commit murder. Kerry could think of nothing else to do but rub the back of his neck in small, hopefully soothing circles.

"Where are we going?" she asked the policemen.

"To the station. There's a clinic nearby if you need stitches, sir."

Harris pulled away the shirt briefly and turned to Kerry. "What do you think?"

"Just Steri-Strips, probably. But get another opinion. Harris, I—"

"Damn it, Ker." He smacked his fist on his knee. "I'm sorry."

"Why are you sorry? You didn't throw a punch." She leaned her head against his shoulder. "You stood up for me. Thank you."

"They just made me so angry. How can they say those things about you? You're a Rhodes scholar!"

"Not to them, I'm not. To them, I'm some opportunistic trollop who had an affair with their princess."

When the car pulled into the police station, they were taken to a small, windowless room where they delivered their statements about the incident to the police chief—a graying, stocky man named Watkins—and a detective. When an officer arrived to take Harris to the clinic, Kerry was left alone with the battered, steel-topped table. As the door swung shut, she was swamped by a wave of fatigue. The adrenaline had abandoned her, and she leaned back in her chair and closed her eyes, mind churning sluggishly. Left alone for the first time since the incident, she finally had the chance to reflect on how quickly the mob had disintegrated from mean and nasty to downright violent.

Her very presence here was a menace—and not just to orderly society. She was a danger to herself, to her friends, to innocent bystanders.

The door opened a few minutes later to admit Mary Spencer with Brent in tow. Their presence made the room feel even more cramped. When Kerry caught Brent's eye and tried out a smile, he looked away. A premonition fell over her, but she forced herself not to betray the sudden surge of anxiety.

"Hello, Ms. Spencer. Brent."

Brent kept his eyes trained on the floor while Spencer sat in the seat the chief had vacated and rested her hands palm down on the table. Her face was expressionless save for a subtle tightening around her thin lips that, if Kerry had to guess, probably signaled suppressed fury. Mary Spencer had not come to bail her out, but to ream her out.

"Ms. Donovan, do you know why you were selected for this program?"

Kerry blinked, nonplussed by the unexpected question. The word hung in the air between them, before her brain suddenly kicked into overdrive, recalling the language of the Rhodes Trust's mission. "I…I would hope because of the caliber of my character, commitment to the common good, and leadership qualities."

"Character, commitment, leadership." Spencer cocked her head. Her hair had been pulled back into a bun so tight that the corners of her dark eyes slanted ever so slightly. She suddenly reminded Kerry of the ravens in the Tower of London. "Do you believe you have, thus far, fulfilled the expectations of a Rhodes scholar?"

"I do." Kerry could see where this was going. Clearly, Spencer thought she was behaving abominably. But Kerry refused to give her the satisfaction of saying what Spencer wanted to hear. She had done nothing wrong. Her professors respected the caliber of her work. Her teammates turned to her for guidance on the pitch. But none of that, she suddenly realized, had turned out to be as important as Sasha. Being there when Sasha needed her, making her laugh, proving her loyalty—these were the accomplishments she was most proud of.

"You do?" Spencer leaned forward, her body language menacing. "You have precipitated an international crisis. How is that in keeping with the mission of this Trust? The Rhodes is not a matchmaking agency!"

The obedient schoolgirl in Kerry wanted to vomit, but the rest of her bristled. "My academic work has been exemplary thus far," she said, trying hard to modulate her voice despite the rising anger. "I am in good standing at Balliol. My personal relationships are none of the Trust's concern."

"Surely you can't be this naïve." Spencer's tone was icy. "You cannot have a *personal relationship* with Alexandra Carlisle. She does not exist. She is always Her Royal Highness Princess Alexandra—an office and a title, in addition to a citizen. Quite literally, she belongs to the United Kingdom."

Beneath the table, Kerry dug her fingernails into her jeans in a vain attempt to anchor herself. "You describe her as though she's a slave."

"In some ways, she is." Spencer shook her head. "I saw so much potential in you, Kerry. I blame myself for not anticipating how someone of your background would react to moving in these sorts of circles."

Kerry's mouth wanted to fall open, but instead she clenched her teeth. She couldn't believe this. "Someone of my background? What exactly are you saying?"

Spencer held out one hand. "Brent?" He stepped forward and placed an envelope into her palm, which she slid across the pockmarked table to Kerry. "I am saying that you are going back to the States. Immediately."

"What?" Kerry was on her feet before she realized she'd moved, her gaze flickering from the envelope to Spencer's impassive face. The wrinkles around her eyes and mouth seemed deeper than they had at the beginning of the term. "But—"

"If this ruckus has blown over by next spring, you may petition to return for the following year."

Kerry blinked hard as her vision blurred. No. She would not lose it. Not here, not now. "Petition to return?"

"Submit a written request to the Trust to be reinstated as a Rhodes scholar."

Reinstated. At a rush of dizziness, Kerry grabbed hold of the edge of the table. She was being…what? Suspended? Expelled?

"Your tutors have already been informed," Spencer said as she stood. "That envelope contains your travel information. Your flight leaves very early tomorrow morning. I suggest you return to your room to pack. Immediately."

She exited the room without a backward glance, Brent trailing in her wake like a puppy. Kerry watched the door slowly close behind them, and when it finally clicked shut, she felt it in every cell. Gone. Just like that. The goals and dreams that had been dangling within her reach…gone. Stripped of her fellowship, vilified by the media, unable to reach the woman she loved—all she had now was the plane ticket in that envelope.

Suddenly unable to catch her breath, she sank back into the chair and rested her head in her palms. Her head spun, thoughts and memories scattering like autumn leaves before the brisk wind outside. As she tried to gather her composure, one question finally emerged like a refrain. What was she going to do now?

The door opened to readmit Chief Watkins. He didn't smile, but his gaze was sympathetic. She wondered if he had watched the entire showdown between her and Spencer on the surveillance equipment.

"We have a car to drive you back to your residence, Ms. Donovan," he said.

Kerry tried to speak, failed, and swallowed hard. "Thank you."

They walked down the hallway in silence. Around them, the station was a beehive of activity. Guilt joined her despair. How many resources had she personally caused to be diverted? The price tag of all this turmoil had to be immense. But was Spencer right? Should she really feel culpable? Had she actually done something wrong, or was the public to blame?

The thoughts were a barrage against the wall of her brain. Blinking hard against tears that threatened to fall, she focused on her feet. She had to hold it together until she was in the privacy of her own room. Where she would have to start packing. Immediately.

Kerry swallowed hard against the sharp flare of grief in her chest. When Watkins finally led her out into a small parking lot where a nondescript black car was idling, its back door ajar, she turned toward him.

"I'm sorry. For all the trouble." It wasn't enough, but she had to say something.

Not waiting for a reply, she ducked into the vehicle to begin the first leg of her journey into exile.

CHAPTER NINETEEN

I can't believe you're not fighting this." Harris sat in Kerry's desk chair, gesticulating with the ice pack that was supposed to be pressed to his jaw. "They can't just…just banish you!"

"Yes, they can." Kerry's suitcase was open on the floor. As soon as she had entered her room, she had thrown every piece of clothing she owned onto the bed, mostly to stop herself from collapsing on top of the covers and venting the tears of frustration still building behind her eyes. A few had escaped while she neatly folded her sweaters and slacks, but she had stubbornly let them fall without acknowledging their presence.

Harris had arrived a few minutes ago bearing a bottle of Jack Daniels. He hadn't needed stitches, thankfully, but the skin around the bandage on his face was already showing signs of discoloration. He had waved off her concern with a lame joke about how she should see the other guy.

"But—"

"Harris." Kerry paused in the act of picking up one of her collared shirts. "What do you want me to do? Bring a lawsuit against the Rhodes Trust? With what money?" The thought suddenly occurred to her that this suspension would mean she couldn't claim student status any longer. Would she have to begin paying back her college loans? With just over two thousand dollars in her savings account, how on earth was she supposed to do that?

"I have to find a job," she said, hearing the anxiety in her own voice. "Like, now."

"Ker. Relax. If you can't somehow resolve this, the jobs will come knocking on your door. You're a Rhodes scholar."

"Am I?"

He swore, set down his ice, and reached for the bottle. They'd already had two shots each, but the liquor had yet to dull Kerry's panic. As soon as he handed her the glass, emblazoned with Balliol's crest, she knocked the whiskey back.

"Besides," she said a moment later, "even if I had the money and inclination to sue, that would be the quickest way never to be invited back here. Don't you think?"

Harris looked away to stare gloomily out her window. "Probably. Fuck. I can't fucking believe this!"

A knock came at the door before Kerry could reply. Frowning, she went to the peephole, wondering if the paparazzi had somehow made it past security. When she saw Brent waiting on the other side, a spike of anger trumped her surprise. But that wasn't fair, was it? Brent was just Mary Spencer's aide. He hadn't made the decision to send her home. Taking a deep breath, she turned the doorknob.

"Kerry. Hi." Before today, she had never seen Brent look nervous. He shifted his weight back and forth, and couldn't seem to look her directly in the eyes. "May I come in?"

"Sure."

"Brent?" Harris's voice carried a clear note of distrust, and Kerry felt warmed by his loyalty. When she had told him of Brent's presence at the station, Harris had immediately called him a turncoat.

"Hi. I sent you a few texts..."

"All of which I ignored." Harris's bandaged face was grim. He looked to be spoiling for another fight.

Brent raised both hands in a gesture of placation as he looked between them. "I feel awful about what happened today. Kerry, I hope you don't think I agree with that decision. Because I don't."

"Thank you." It felt oddly relieving to hear of his support. If he didn't think she deserved Spencer's sanctions, then perhaps there were others out there who didn't believe all the negative press.

"I could probably lose my job by telling you this, but I think you deserve to know." Brent leaned against the wall near the desk, as though he needed the physical support. "Shortly after the...incident on campus this afternoon, the Secretary received a call. From King Andrew."

Kerry felt her jaw drop. "What—what did he want?" she asked, though she suspected the answer already.

"He wants you gone. Plain and simple."

"I take it Spencer didn't even try to change his mind?" Harris's tone was still belligerent.

"Of course she didn't," Kerry said. "He's the King of England. His son is in a coma, and the next in line to the throne is embroiled in controversy. Would you argue with him right now?"

"I sure as hell would."

Kerry rolled her eyes. "No, you wouldn't." The news made her feel better. Spencer had been put under enormous pressure, and she had done what she had to do to keep the peace. The last thing Kerry wanted was for a disagreement about her to spark any kind of political tension that could potentially affect her peers. "It helps to hear this, Brent. Thanks."

"What are you going to do?"

"What can I do?" Kerry moved back to the side of the bed and resumed her folding. "I'll go back to New York and stay with my brother Declan until I figure out a next step. Apply to some architecture firms in the city, maybe."

"And then petition for next fall?"

"Maybe." Kerry had been thinking about this ever since climbing into the unmarked police car a few hours ago. Given everything that had happened, would she really want to come back? Even if they let her?

"Maybe?" Harris was looking at her as though she had grown two heads. "What are you saying?"

"I'm saying that against my better judgment, I fell in love with Sasha. And it didn't work out. I mean, of course it didn't, right? How could it have?" She forced her lips into an approximation of a smile. "But the thing about Sasha is that she's a British princess. She's always going to be here. Maybe it would be easier if I stayed away."

"You can't mean that." As he spoke, Harris poured another shot. "God damn it, Kerry, you belong here!"

"I don't know where I belong anymore." She plunked her empty glass down next to the bottle. Mercifully, the haze was finally starting to encroach on her fevered brain. "But I do know I want another."

He poured; they clinked; the whiskey burned. After downing the shot, Harris looked to Brent. "You need one?" When he nodded, Harris glanced around the room before refilling his own glass. "Here. Share mine."

Brent's answering smile was tinged with relief. "Thanks."

Kerry barely stopped herself from telling them to get a room. They would eventually, she suspected—one of the perks of a normal relationship untainted by the spotlight of celebrity. For now, though, she wanted them to stay and distract her from her own thoughts until she was intoxicated enough that her demons would never be able to find their way into her dreams.

As the sky outside her window began to brighten, Sasha finally gave up on sleep. She sat up slowly so as not to aggravate the dull ache in her temples that had been her constant companion for days. Ever since hearing the news that Kerry had returned to the States, she'd been plagued by insomnia. Her eyes felt like sandpaper, gritty and rough. Her stomach churned sluggishly, perhaps in protest that she'd barely eaten anything the night before.

She slid out of bed and walked slowly into the bathroom. If she was going to be awake, she might as well get herself to the hospital. Tomorrow would mark a week since Arthur's accident, and despite the assurances of his physicians that he could still make a full recovery, everyone was growing increasingly desperate.

Traffic was light at such an early hour, and she and Ian arrived at the hospital just as the shift was changing. The crowd outside had dissipated after the first few days, but the hospital staff had roped off a small area of the courtyard where well-wishers could leave flowers and other tokens of support. Every morning, royal guards collected the items, but by nightfall the space had filled again.

Inside, the halls were mostly deserted. The doctors and nurses whom they passed all greeted her with sympathetic murmurs of "Your

Royal Highness." Here, at least, she wasn't a disgrace. Not only did the specter of death make all humans level; it also had no patience for trivial matters.

As she approached the nursing station, she recognized the head nurse as the one who had charge of the morning shift. She knew all their names by now.

"Hello, Robert."

"Good morning, Your Royal Highness."

"May I see him?"

He made a few clicks on the computer, probably consulting Arthur's chart. "Your brother is scheduled for another CT scan at nine o'clock, but until then, certainly."

Sasha reached for the desk as alarm skittered along her already frayed nerves. "Another?"

But Robert smiled gently at her. "Not to worry, ma'am. It's routine. I'll take you to him."

Near the end of the corridor, he ushered her into Arthur's room. It was dimly lit and very quiet, save for the soft whoosh of the ventilator and the rhythmic beep of the heart monitor. Almost immediately, she felt her breathing align with Arthur's heartbeats.

As the door shut, leaving her alone with him, she pulled up one of the nearby chairs to his bedside and reached for his left hand. It was warm to the touch, but entirely limp. She pressed it between both of hers and cleared her throat. His head was swathed in bandages, but most of his face was clear, and she focused on the prominent cheekbones he had inherited from their mother. Despite how frightened it made her to see him helpless like this, she had to be strong. He might be able to hear her.

"Hi, Artie. I know—you hate when I call you that." Her laugh was strangled. "I couldn't sleep, again. I'm so worried about you. All of us are. Practically the whole world is praying for you. How does that feel?"

She kissed one of his knuckles, still slightly bruised from the accident. "But there's something else on my mind, too. Something I can't talk to anyone about, except you. It's something rather selfish, and since everyone already thinks the worst of me, I'd rather not have this getting out. You'll keep my secrets, won't you? You always have."

The memories came rushing back, then: Arthur conspiring with her on pranks of their childhood nanny, Arthur taking the blame for the window she'd broken at Kensington playing cricket, Arthur refusing to tattle when she had drawn some rather inappropriate cartoons in permanent ink all over the fine Easter linen tablecloth. He had been the first person she told about her sexual preference—even before Lizzie or Miranda—and she couldn't imagine making this confession to anyone else.

"I've met someone. A woman. Her name is Kerry, and she's a Rhodes scholar. She's extraordinary, Arthur." Sasha felt herself smile as Kerry's handsome face crossed her mind's eye. "You'd like her. She's a footballer—quite brilliant at it, actually. And even smarter than you. She's kind and generous and passionate. She told me she loves me, and I think…"

She took a deep breath. This was the hardest part. "I think I'm falling in love with her, too."

Arthur remained still and silent, and Sasha furiously blinked back a sudden rush of tears. What had she expected—that her announcement would jolt him out of his coma?

"That should be happy news, right?" She reached for a tissue on the nightstand and dabbed at her eyes. "But I've made such a mess of things. For years, really, so many messes. I've been so angry. About Mother, and how Father changed, and my miswired brain. But Kerry makes me want to stop being angry. I feel at peace when I'm with her. I've never felt that before."

She leaned closer, resting her elbows on the railing of his bed. "The paparazzi caught us in a kiss, and now the photographs are everywhere and it's all a complete shit storm. Father is irate and has forbidden me to communicate with her. Kerry went back to America—or at least, that's what the papers are saying. I know what I want to do; I want to tell the media to sod off and then fly across the Atlantic and apologize for trying to hide her in my closet. But would that really fix anything? Even if we could have a relationship, it would be scrutinized at every turn. No one knows that better than you."

Sasha squeezed his fingers. "You've always been so brilliant at playing the public figure. You make it look so effortless. Ashleigh, too. But what if that's not what I want? Or worse, what if it's getting in the way of the very thing I want most of all?" Gently, she laid his hand back on his chest. "I feel torn up inside—like polo turf after a match. Maybe that's what happens when a person doesn't allow themselves to be authentic."

As she looked past Arthur's motionless body to the generic paintings on the wall, the heart of her problem leapt into focus. "The fact of the matter is that I've been living two lives for a while now. I thought it would be easier than choosing just one. Perhaps I was wrong, but how am I supposed to choose between my duty and my deepest self? What would you do?"

It was a question for which she truly had no answer. As heir to the throne, Arthur's duty had always been crystal clear: when their father died, he would rule. That fact was as much a part of him as his hazel eyes and sandy hair. Part of the reason why Ashleigh was so perfect for him was that she understood his dedication to the Commonwealth. Who he was dovetailed with what he was, and she enabled and supported both aspects of his identity.

But Sasha had never been able to reconcile her royal imperatives with her personal dreams. They were in direct conflict, now more than ever. Her father would say that she was under an obligation to subjugate her own desires for the sake of her countrymen and family. But was that truly the honorable path? Shouldn't a modern monarchy have a different set of priorities? And wasn't there a sense in which she would be creating a terrible example for her subjects if her reign as queen was inflected by a deep and endemic hypocrisy?

At a sound near the door, she turned so quickly that dizziness threatened. Ashleigh stood just inside, regarding Sasha with an expression at once compassionate and pensive.

"How long have you been there?"

"A few minutes."

Ashleigh pulled up a chair and sat close enough for their knees to touch. At first, she said nothing—only stroked the back of Arthur's hand. Sasha was too exhausted to be angry that Ashleigh had eavesdropped. At this point, what did it even matter? She returned her gaze to Arthur's face, silently willing him to wake.

"Kerry sounds special."

"She is. I think I've known that for a while." Sasha smiled ruefully. "Though I fought my instincts hard."

Ashleigh rested her free hand on Sasha's knee. "Why didn't you tell me?"

"I should have. I know you would have listened." She thought of Miranda's suggestions, which had been entirely focused on what the outside world would think and not at all on what might actually be best for Sasha. By taking that mentality to heart, she had only succeeded in further distancing herself from Kerry. "You would have given me good advice."

"That's where you're wrong. I wouldn't have given you any advice at all." Ashleigh squeezed her knee gently. "The questions you're asking right now can't be decided by anyone but you."

As they sat together in silence, Sasha felt the beginnings of a radical idea tugging at her weary brain. It was a decision that never would have occurred to Arthur, but with a little bit of research, a great deal of personal fortitude, and some luck, it might work for her. And if it did, she realized, she would not only make herself happy, but also silence her critics.

"You should have some time alone with him," she said, leaning in to kiss Ashleigh on the cheek. "Thank you for the chat. And for all your support over the years."

Ashleigh rested one hand on Sasha's shoulder. "We'll get through this, Sash. All of us."

When Sasha pulled back to nod in agreement, she made sure a smile was plastered to her face. But as soon as she turned around, she let it fall. Ashleigh was being brave, but they both knew there were no guarantees that Arthur would ever reawaken. As much as she wanted to, she couldn't control his fate. She could only control her own.

Ian rejoined her as she returned to the hallway. "How shall I instruct the driver, ma'am? Will you remain here, or return to Clarence House?"

"Neither." Striding toward the elevator, she prepared to make the opening salvo in what, if she played it properly, would be the last of her power struggles with her father. "I need to consult with someone in Oxford. In person. Immediately."

CHAPTER TWENTY

Three hours later, she had gained entry into Magdalen College using the alias and fake identification card she had employed so often as a student of the university. With her wig and hoodie firmly in place, she felt reasonably confident that she would resist detection. Obtaining Harrison Whistler's contact information had been a simple matter for Ian, and she had phoned ahead to ensure he would be home when she called. His confusion during their brief conversation had been palpable, but she had refused to say anything more until they could speak in person. Now, as she followed the directions he had given to his room, she hoped her instincts about him were correct. If not, her plan would be derailed before it could gain any momentum.

When she rapped lightly on the door, it opened within seconds. Dressed in a gray sweater and jeans, Harris towered over her, frowning. "Excuse me? Can I help—" Suddenly, his eyes widened. "Oh. I beg your pardon, Your Royal Highness. I didn't recognize you."

"That's entirely the point. May I come in?"

"Of course." Harris held the door while they ducked inside. Ian had insisted on following her into the room, arguing that the other students might be tipped off to her visit if he waited in the hall. Reluctantly, she had agreed that he was right. Her only fear was that he, too, would take exception to her plan.

"Would you like some coffee, ma'am? And please, sit."

"Let's dispense with the formalities. It's Sasha. And coffee sounds wonderful. Just a hint of milk, please."

Harris fetched two cups from a cabinet above his desk as she took one of the chairs flanking a small table near the sole window that looked out onto the college's quadrangle. His room was small but tidy, and Sasha felt a sudden pang that she had never made an effort to see Kerry's living space.

"Have you heard from Kerry?"

"A few times," he said cautiously. It was disconcerting, though not altogether surprising, that he clearly felt the need to protect her. Sasha would be the first to admit that she had let her own complex situation stand in the way of treating Kerry properly. Perhaps now, that could change.

"How is she?"

"The media attention has been intrusive, but her family has reacted better than expected. And she's praised the law enforcement in her town for doing the best they can. Apparently, they've rallied around her." After carefully handing a steaming cup to Sasha, Harris sat down, clutching his own. "She's living with her brother Declan at the moment, to keep the reporters away from her parents."

Sasha's heart ached at the thought of Kerry under siege. Her escape from the turmoil in Britain had only landed her in a nearly identical situation at home. "When will she return?"

Harris looked startled. "You don't know?"

"Know?"

"She isn't coming back. Not this year, anyway. Your father instructed the Secretary of the Rhodes Trust to suspend her from the program."

"Excuse me?" Sasha felt her blood pressure skyrocket. The edges of her vision were tinged with crimson. Her father had banished Kerry, jeopardizing her entire future in the process, just because of a few photographs? She had known he could be ruthless, but this...this was beyond all sense of justice or proportion.

"I heard this from an aide to the secretary. It's the truth."

"I believe you." Squeezing her eyes shut, she tried to get her riotous brain to focus. "Will Kerry...what will she do now?"

"She said she would try to find a job. She has the option of reapplying for the Rhodes next year, but last I heard, she didn't know if she would."

Sasha gripped the arm of her chair tightly and stared down at the swirling liquid in her cup. Everything had spiraled out of her control. This latest revelation only strengthened her resolve to find a way to finally gain independence from the monarchy's dispassionate machine. Feeling Harris's gaze on her, she sipped gingerly at the coffee, willing the haze to clear from her mind.

"I wish I could say that I can't believe my father would do such a thing. I feel awful. Kerry must be devastated."

"What do you intend to do about it?"

The bluntness of his question was refreshing. "Can I trust that this conversation will be held in the strictest secrecy? Even from her?"

"Yes." His answer was firm and immediate. It inspired a confidence she hoped was not misplaced.

"When we first met, you mentioned that you're studying history. I came here today not only because I wanted news about Kerry, but also because I require your expertise."

"With what, exactly?"

Sasha took a deep breath. "I need you to help me write an Act of Renunciation."

Harris's eyes went as round as the saucers they had forgone. Carefully, he set his coffee cup on the table, clearly trying to buy time as he formulated his response. "Your Royal Highness—"

"No. Sasha."

"Right." He swallowed audibly. "Are you sure you want to do this? I've gotten to know Kerry well over the past few months, and she wouldn't want you to give everything up."

"I won't be giving everything up. I'll merely be relinquishing my place in the line of succession."

"Merely?"

"My place in that line, and the expectations accompanying it, are only holding me back." She leaned forward, willing him to see her sincerity. "I've made my decision. I'm not doing this for Kerry. I'm doing it for me. I need to be free, and this is the only way."

"You do understand that an Act of Renunciation isn't enough on its own, right? It has to be approved by every country in the Commonwealth."

Sasha felt a grim smile curve her lips. "Have you been reading the papers recently? Do you really think anyone would oppose cutting me out of the line of succession?"

"I would."

She touched his arm lightly. "You're sweet. But I need to do this. And I'll bungle it if I try to write it on my own."

Harris stared into his cup for a long moment before finally putting it aside. "All right." He walked over to his desk and brought back his laptop. "You dictate. I'll type. Then we'll compare what we come up with to some historical examples. Okay?"

At his agreement, Sasha exhaled slowly, feeling a piece of her anxiety fall away. "Yes. Thank you."

"I have one condition," Harris said, hands poised above the keyboard like a bird of prey. "That you never, ever link my name to this document. As far as the world is concerned, you wrote it yourself."

Puzzled, Sasha felt herself frown. "Of course. If that's what you wish."

"What I wish is that you could find another way." His expression was serious. "The monarchy needs you."

"It really doesn't." Sasha felt her hand tremble and quickly set down her own mug. "And there is no other way."

❖

Unlike the last time she had visited her father in his Buckingham office, Sasha wasn't obliged to wait even for a moment. As soon as she entered the anteroom to her father's office, his secretary, looking visibly exhausted, greeted her with a desultory, "Your Royal Highness," and waved her through.

"Thank you," she said, tightening the grip on the leather portfolio beneath her arm. Inside it lay a single sheet of heavy, bone-colored paper bearing her personal seal and letterhead. She had printed it out at Clarence House not half an hour before. This was the moment of truth. She knocked once and then entered at King Andrew's muffled summons.

"Hello, Alexandra." He sat stiffly behind his desk, expression wary. Dark bags hung beneath his narrowed eyes. As Sasha approached, she realized with a flash of surprise that for the first time, she didn't feel nervous in his presence.

"Thank you for taking this meeting," she said formally. "Over the past two weeks, I've done quite a lot of thinking and soul searching. This is the result." Before she could change her mind, she passed the folder across the desk and took her seat in one of his low, uncomfortable chairs. He flipped the folder open quickly and perused the document inside. Her breaths came shallowly as she traced over the words in her mind.

I, Alexandra Victoria Jane, do hereby declare my irrevocable determination to renounce my place in the royal succession of the House of Carlisle...

The more he read, the more the frown lines across his forehead deepened. "What is this?"

"It's exactly what it looks like." For once, Sasha found it easy to speak with her father without getting angry.

He looked up from the paper, his bloodshot eyes dazed. "I don't understand."

"I wish to be removed from the line of succession." Even as she spoke the words, she also heard them—as though she were floating above her own body.

"That's preposterous."

"It isn't."

He stared at the paper for a long time, whether rereading it or mulling it over, she couldn't guess. "This is about that American, isn't it? The woman?"

She had expected this question, and was prepared. "Her name is Kerry Donovan. She's a Rhodes Scholar studying sustainable architecture. And no. This is not about her. This about me, and who I am. Something you've never bothered to find out for yourself."

"I know exactly who you are, better than anyone else." Frustration seeped into his voice, making his syllables more clipped than usual. "I was there when you took your first breath, Alexandra. You are my daughter, second in line to the throne."

Instead of the frustration that would have once made her lash out, Sasha only felt sadness. "That's true. But I'm so much more. Before Kerry, I didn't realize how much. But I do now."

His jaw stiffened. "Why would you want to give up your birthright precisely when your country needs you most?"

"The country doesn't need me. It needs Arthur."

"And if he dies?" The words were spoken roughly, but Sasha forced herself not to react.

"Lizzie will make everyone much happier."

He looked away, out the window facing the spire of Westminster Abbey. "Have you spoken to Elizabeth about this?"

"Not yet."

"Then how do you know she would be willing?"

The question confused her. Lizzie was intelligent, socially conscious, and discrete. She had never felt the need to make waves. "We both know that she would make the perfect queen. Why wouldn't she be willing?"

He spread his hands, signaling his ignorance. "Potentially, many reasons. But do you wish to force her into a role she might not want?"

Sasha folded her hands tightly in her lap, feeling as though the world had just tilted slightly. "No, of course not. But surely you recognize that she is much better suited for the monarchy than I am. Be honest, Father. Do you truly want me to be next in line to the throne?"

His brow creased in a frown. "With some dedicated study and time, you would make a strong queen."

"Excuse me?" The words shattered her equilibrium. "Why would you dissemble about something like this?"

"You believe I'm lying to you, Alexandra?"

"Of course!" Her knee began to bounce in agitation. "When have you ever given any indication that you believe I would be a 'strong queen'?"

He leaned back in his chair, seeming truly surprised by the accusation. "Yes, I have always pushed you hard, but that was for your own good. You have so much wasted potential, and—"

Sasha was on her feet before she realized she had stood. "There! Don't you see? 'Wasted potential'? How could you possibly expect me to believe in my own abilities when you constantly speak of me that way?"

For once, he didn't have a tailor-made response. "I did not intend to—"

"I don't care what you intended, Father. Your constant criticism has made me feel like utter *shit* for years. And now I'm finished." She gestured to the paper on his desk. "Sign it, for the love of God. Let me disappoint you one last time and have done."

He stared at her for a long, fraught moment. Sasha could hear her own racing pulse in her ears, but she struggled not to betray any more of her internal strife. She didn't want to do anything that might be interpreted as doubt or weakness.

"You do realize, do you not," he said finally, "that even if I were to sign this, it would not be legal until ratified by our Parliament and that of every nation in the Commonwealth?"

"I can't exactly see them putting up much of a fight, Father." A sudden wave of fatigue washed over her, but she forced herself to attempt a smile. "They might even declare an international holiday."

Again, he was silent. Sasha could practically see the gears spinning inside his powerful brain, churning out questions from every angle. If she renounced her claim on the throne, she would fall outside of his jurisdiction. Did he want to allow that to happen? But even more importantly, what did the British public want? Would they be relieved or upset? Would pruning this particular branch from the royal tree be a move toward undercutting the monarchy, or strengthening it? Always the intellectual, her father would want to examine this idea from all sides.

"I can't make a decision of this magnitude so quickly," he said, settling back into his chair. "I need at least a few days to consider the implications."

"And consult with your advisors. I understand." Sasha had expected he would say as much, but she wasn't about to let him table the matter indefinitely. Straightening her spine, she played what she hoped would be her trump card. "My advice is that you not wait too long. I've scheduled a press conference for Friday, where I will inform the media of my intentions and release this document to them."

His cheeks grew mottled, anger and surprise warring on his face as he sat momentarily speechless. Wanting to have the final word, she turned to leave. "I'll see you at hospital, Father."

As the door closed behind her, she listened for his hurried footsteps across the floor, certain he would pursue her once he had gotten over his shock. But the only sounds in the anteroom were the rhythmic tocks of the grandfather clock and the quiet patter of her father's secretary's fingers flying across the keyboard. Perhaps the King was rethinking his objections.

Sasha exhaled slowly and walked toward the elevator, Ian trailing behind. The exhilaration was somehow more hollow than she had anticipated. She had announced her intentions, and she'd managed, for the most part, to remain poised and articulate. But she had also hurt him through her request. That much had been plain, and the guilt weighed on her. This was a deeper wound than the ones inflicted by her frequent jabs.

Then again, wasn't she always hurting him? Didn't her very existence cause him pain? She couldn't be what he wanted. Wouldn't it be better for everyone if she renounced her birthright? Lizzie was intelligent, gracious, and beautiful. She was also unequivocally straight. She would do much better in the spotlight than her dyslexic, hot-tempered, queer older sister. Surely, she would be able to recognize that herself.

CHAPTER TWENTY-ONE

S asha found Lizzie at Arthur's bedside, reading. As she crossed the threshold, Lizzie glanced up and her face brightened. She looked so much like their mother, especially when she smiled, and Sasha felt the familiar pang of longing all the more acutely for being in the hospital.

"How is he?" she asked as she took the spare seat and focused on the pale, still form of her brother.

"No change." Lizzie patted the cover of her thick book. "I read aloud to him for a little while. I just…I want him to know we're here."

Sasha's heart twinged again at the memory of Kerry reading out loud to her on that morning after her disastrous speech. That had been such a watershed moment for them. "I'm sure he does," she said, despite not having any such certainty. "What book?"

"*Ulysses.* For my literature course."

"Are you reading any T.S. Eliot?"

Lizzie seemed rather surprised to be discussing literature. "We just did. What made you think of him?"

"Kerry introduced me to his work." She hadn't told Lizzie much about Kerry. It had seemed selfish to prattle on about her with their brother in the hospital.

"Really." Lizzie's eyes narrowed. "Since when do you read modernist poetry with your flings?"

"I don't." Sasha took a deep breath. "She isn't a fling."

"You care for her?"

"Very much."

Lizzie immediately pulled her into a hug. "I know it's been difficult this past week, but I'm very happy for you, Sash."

That simple act of kindness made tears well up in Sasha's eyes. If only the rest of the world could be so accepting. She held the embrace for a long moment, gathering her strength for the question she was about to ask.

"I want to be with her. Openly."

Lizzie's expression was somber. "That won't be easy, but you have my support. Of course."

"I might need something even more than that. I'm intending to renounce my position in the succession."

Lizzie pulled back, looked thunderstruck.

"This isn't only about Kerry. No one thinks I'm fit to rule, including me. I don't want to be the wayward princess anymore." She searched Lizzie's eyes, hoping to find understanding. "I just want to be myself."

"Have you told Father?"

"I just did. And then I needed to tell you. Because this could change your position in a radical way." She glanced back at Arthur.

"I understand." Lizzie reached for his hand, and for a while, they sat in silence. Finally, she turned back to Sasha. "It must be so strange, mustn't it? To be the heir? It's something I've never even considered. Most people probably wouldn't believe that."

"I know exactly what you mean." Sasha squeezed her shoulder. "Arthur carried that burden for all of us, and we didn't even realize it. Until—"

"Sasha!" Lizzie suddenly gripped her arm hard, nails digging into her skin beneath the fabric of her sweater. "His left hand. I swear it moved."

"What?"

She leaned forward, focusing every ounce of her attention on Arthur's hand. The ventilator whooshed. The heart monitor beeped. Sasha frowned. Was the interval decreasing? Had his heart rate sped up, just a little? She could hear her own blood roaring in her ears. Beside her, Lizzie's breaths came fast and shallow.

And then she saw it—the faintest twitch of his index finger.

"There!"

"I saw!" Sasha stood, but too quickly. Vertigo washed over her, and she grabbed for the back of her chair. "We have to call the—"

"Arthur," Lizzie breathed. "Oh Arthur, thank God…"

When Sasha's vision snapped back into focus, she gasped. Lizzie was leaning forward, holding the hand that had moved, staring into the open eyes of their brother as tears of relief trickled down her cheeks.

❖

The remainder of the day passed in a blur. The doctors had needed to run a battery of tests that had taken several hours, leaving Sasha and Lizzie to repeat their story over and over as other family members arrived. Once the tests were complete, they had been allowed to see Arthur only briefly. He had recognized each of them, but then almost immediately lapsed into confusion about why he was at the hospital, why he was in London rather than Scotland, and what day of the month it was. Despite having been prepared by the doctors, Sasha couldn't help but be jarred by his obvious disorientation. Dr. Herren had indicated that it might take weeks, or perhaps even longer, for his brain to fully recover.

That somber note notwithstanding, she felt as though a massive burden had been lifted from her shoulders. Lizzie had decided to return to Cambridge to begin catching up on the work she had missed, and so Sasha found herself having an impromptu celebration with Ashleigh at Clarence House over an insanely expensive bottle of wine and a very fine steak. After toasting Arthur's health several times, Sasha found herself quickly headed toward tipsiness. Judging from the glaze over Ashleigh's eyes, she wasn't alone.

"Did you decide what to do about Kerry?" Ashleigh asked suddenly, glass poised to her lips.

"No. I wish I could see her. That she could be here with us, celebrating."

"Why don't you phone her?"

The rush of adrenaline that greeted Ashleigh's advice was somewhat sobering. "Now?"

"There's no time like the present," Ashleigh said, beginning to rise. "I can finish this in the sitting room."

"Don't be silly. Stay. I might need you."

Heart pounding in her ears, Sasha scrolled down to select Kerry's number. She smiled at the accompanying photograph, which she had snapped during one of their breaks for water on the climb up Torc Mountain. Kerry was sitting on a large rock, hair tousled by the wind, grinning broadly. She seemed so happy.

"You certainly have the look of someone in love," Ashleigh said, curiosity compelling her to get up and stand behind Sasha. "And so does she."

"Let's hope she hasn't changed her mind."

But instead of ringing, the call was answered by an electronic voice that announced the number had been disconnected. Her first, panicked thought was that Kerry was trying to cut her out entirely.

"Don't look so stricken," Ashleigh said, squeezing her shoulders. "Likely, the American media got her number and pestered her to the point of purchasing a new phone."

Sasha exhaled slowly. That was a logical explanation. "I'm sure you're right."

"Regardless, perhaps it's time to make a grand gesture."

"A grand gesture." Sasha thought back to the wish she had verbalized this morning. Now that Arthur was awake, did she dare defy her father and go haring off across the ocean to make things right with Kerry? Did she dare return with Kerry at her side, in plain view of the paparazzi? Or, to put it differently: did she dare to do nothing and be plagued forever by doubt?

"You're right," she said, picking up her phone again. "I do believe it's time to take a hop across the Pond."

When Ashleigh left an hour later, Sasha took the opportunity to call Ian inside her apartment. As much as she wanted to act like the ordinary woman she would soon become, she couldn't simply book a flight and take the Tube to the airport. His presence at her side would be necessary, and she hoped he was willing. Once she sat down at the table in her kitchen, he followed suit.

"Tomorrow morning, we'll be going to Heathrow. I've already made the arrangements."

His expression never changed. "Will we be flying to New York, ma'am?"

"Yes." She stared at him intently. "I won't have to contend with you trying to stop me, will I?"

"No, ma'am."

"Your superiors might take exception to your permissiveness. Are you willing to risk dismissal?"

"I am." His voice, as always, was calm.

"Thank you." Quite unexpectedly, Sasha found herself on the verge of tears. "Your loyalty and dedication are inspiring. Should you be dismissed, I promise to hire you back once I am a private citizen. So long, of course, as you are willing."

For a few seconds, Ian was silent. "May I speak plainly, ma'am?"

It was the first time he had made such a request. "Always."

"I am willing. But forgive me when I tell you that I hope you're able to avoid relinquishing your claim to the throne."

"You do? Why?"

"The succession needs you."

"It needs me? A barely literate playgirl who cares more for her nightclubs than for her charity work?"

"That is a front, Your Royal Highness. The succession needs you to be who you really are." His gaze flickered to the doorway behind her. "If I may be excused, I will call for a replacement in order to make preparations."

"Of course."

His words echoed in her brain as she watched him go. Each person she had told about her plan had urged her not to go through with it. Was that simply because they were close to her, and could see what the general public did not? Were they deluding themselves? Did the institution of the monarchy truly need her to be open and honest, as well as a princess?

Or would it crumble under the weight of the truth?

CHAPTER TWENTY-TWO

S asha spent most of the seven-hour flight to New York City tossing and turning in her roomy, first class seat. All around her, passengers slept or watched their in-flight films, but she couldn't escape the doubts that plagued her every thought. She had treated Kerry so poorly in those final weeks of their relationship. What if, upon reflection, Kerry wanted nothing to do with her anymore? What if she didn't believe that Sasha would welcome the opportunity to free herself from the shackles of her birthright? What if she wasn't willing to stand in the spotlight beside her and bear the inquisition of the press? What if Sasha couldn't successfully engineer Kerry's reinstatement as a Rhodes scholar?

When those questions sent her spiraling into a panic thirty thousand feet above the Atlantic, Sasha forced herself to think of happier things. Assuming that everything went according to plan, they could embark on a shared private life shortly after returning to the United Kingdom. Sasha's personal inheritance was sizeable and would allow them to live quite comfortably, though in a manner worlds apart from the palaces in which she had grown up. That didn't bother her one bit. They could pick out a small flat in Oxford to rent, and she could run her party-planning company from there, traveling to London as necessary. During holidays, they could visit the architectural marvels of Western Europe, or lie out on the pristine beaches of Mustique, or go on safari in South Africa.

Of course, it wouldn't be perfect. The media would still hound them, even when Sasha was no longer in line for the throne. But after a while, she had to imagine, their interest would die down. Most importantly, she and Kerry would be able to be together, without royal imperatives or traditions getting in the way.

But by the time the jet touched down at JFK Airport, her anxiety had returned. Once she and Ian were firmly ensconced in one of those quintessential yellow cabs, she could barely sit still and tried to distract herself by gazing out the window. Kerry's hometown of Pearl River was twenty miles north of the metropolis, just off the Hudson River. Once they were out of the city, the countryside rapidly became pastoral. A few orange and yellow leaves still clung stubbornly to some trees, and Sasha could imagine how beautiful the drive would have been just a few weeks earlier.

The taxi driver had looked at her incredulously when she had informed him of their destination, but after she paid half his quoted fare up front and promised a generous tip, he'd been more than happy to oblige. She had found Declan Donovan's address quite easily online and managed to direct the cabbie there thanks to the map in her smart phone. Situated two miles outside of the town center, his house was situated just off a country road, in the shelter of a small copse of trees. The taxi turned into the driveway and pulled up next to a pickup truck with "Donovan & Sons Roofing Corp" stenciled on its door. Just the sight of Kerry's last name made Sasha smile, and she shook her head slightly as she carefully counted out the foreign money. If only the rest of her family could see her now.

"Would you mind waiting, please?" she asked.

"Sure, sure," the cabbie muttered as he counted the large stack of bills.

Ian opened her door and she stepped out onto the asphalt. She had agonized over her wardrobe before finally settling on a monochromatic look: black cashmere leggings, turtleneck, and cardigan, all by Donna Karan. Jimmy Choo pumps completed the outfit. She had a very stylish parka packed in her bags as well, but the day was mild enough that she didn't need it.

Sasha was not laboring under any misapprehensions. It would be her words and actions, not her appearance, that would matter most to Kerry. But fashion was her armor, and today she needed to feel strong.

"Your Royal Highness," Ian said as he walked beside her toward the front door. It was painted a deep red, and an autumnal wreath hung below the knocker. "Forgive me if I'm overstepping my bounds, but I just want you to know that I admire your courage."

Sasha smiled tightly but kept her eyes on the door. "I haven't done anything truly courageous just yet, Ian. Let's put your vote of confidence to the test."

Despite the flutter of nerves in her throat, she pressed the doorbell firmly. And waited. No sounds or movement came from within. Was no one home, despite the vehicle in the front?

"Are you from the press?"

Sasha let out a small shriek at the unexpected voice. To her right, a man stood near the corner of the house, a tool belt hanging from his waist and his curly red hair matted with sweat. Even through her surprise, Sasha could see the family resemblance immediately.

"We most certainly are not." Ian sounded affronted. "May I present to you Her Royal Highness the Princess—"

"You must be Declan." Sasha cut him off. "Hello. I'm Sasha."

Declan's mouth opened soundlessly, then closed. He looked at his feet, cleared his throat, and then managed to meet her eyes. His face was flaming in clear embarrassment. "M-my apologies, Your Majesty."

"It's just 'Sasha.' Really." She extended her hand as she walked toward him. "And it's a pleasure to meet you. Is Kerry here?"

"She's working on the barn." He jerked his thumb over his shoulder in the direction of the back garden. The distant sound of hammering punctuated his words.

"I'd like to speak with her, if I may."

"Of course." He couldn't seem to stop nodding his head. "It's just around the corner. You can't miss it."

Sasha nodded, suddenly frozen to the spot. Her heart throbbed beneath her rib cage, and she licked her lips in a vain effort to restore some moisture to her mouth. She had raced here from across the ocean, and now she couldn't make herself move? Her brain swirled in panic, the speech she had mentally composed in a shambles. She needed to pull herself together.

"Would you mind if I use your facilities, first?"

"Of course not. Please come in."

Sasha trailed Declan inside, praying for eloquence.

❖

Kerry glanced over toward the front of the house, wondering about the fate of whatever member of the press corps had been foolish enough to drive up to Declan's front door in a city cab. After so much intrusion over the past week, he was not in a generous mood and had insisted on kicking them out himself while Kerry stayed safely on top of the barn roof.

With a grimace, she bent back to her work. Each time she ripped up another sheet of rot, she felt a small burst of satisfaction. There was nothing quite like demolition work to clear the frustrated mind. When Declan had casually mentioned that he was thinking of turning his barn into a studio, she had leapt at the chance to begin the project—to do something constructive and physical and real. The day was unseasonably warm, and she had stripped down to her black tank top. Both her shirt and her tan Carhartts were streaked with grime. She probably looked completely unlike a woman who had recently been hobnobbing with royalty.

"You don't belong in that world," she muttered as she pried up another decayed board. "You never did."

Her first day back home had been the worst. While the citizens of Pearl River—many of whom were law enforcement officers or first responders in New York City—had banded together to frustrate the media's attempts to get close to Kerry's family, the sensationalist press had found other ways to intrude into her life. Declan had temporarily disconnected his land line, and Kerry had been obliged to buy a new cell phone. Her e-mail inbox had also completely exploded. At least she could take comfort in the knowledge that the media would soon forget all about her—especially now that Arthur had regained consciousness.

The thought almost made her smile. Sasha must be so happy. So relieved. Despite knowing it was impossible, Kerry wished she could be sharing her joy right now. She had even caught herself wondering whether Arthur's recovery might free Sasha to reach out. But that line of thinking would only lead to disappointment. She had to toughen up and face the facts. Even before Arthur's injury, Sasha had never been planning to go public with their relationship. The sooner she accepted that, grieved for it, and tried to move on, the better.

After replacing the warped metal with a new tin sheet, Kerry focused on the placement of her nail and then carefully raised her hammer. Maybe in some ways, this whole debacle had been a blessing in disguise. She hadn't felt this close to her immediate family—or to her community—since coming out. She owed everyone a debt of gratitude for the way in which they had embraced and protected her, despite her notoriety. Giving back by helping Declan with his barn was only the first step. The elementary school had a leaky roof, the firehouse needed to replace several of its windows, and the library was sorely overdue for a fresh coat of paint. While she was looking for jobs, she could easily lend a hand around town.

With swift and efficient strokes, she pounded the nail into the joist. Once she was finished, she looked up again, wondering whether she should go lend Declan a hand. And then her heart stopped as Sasha walked out the back door of the house, skirting the edge of the deck and stepping onto the brick path leading to the barn.

The hammer slipped through nerveless fingers, and she barely managed to grab hold again before it could fall on her foot. She couldn't breathe. She couldn't blink. Her head buzzed and her thoughts were slippery, sliding away before she could grasp them.

Sasha somehow looked more beautiful than ever. Her dark, glossy hair curled down around her shoulders, several strands fluttering in the gentle breeze as she drew steadily closer. Dressed entirely in black, she looked both elegant and alluring. Never once did her eyes leave Kerry's face. When she reached the corner of the barn, she stopped. Only twenty feet of vertical space separated them, and Kerry was suddenly possessed of the insane urge to jump.

For a long moment, the silence hung heavily between them.

"Hi," Sasha finally said, sounding more uncertain in that one syllable than Kerry had ever heard her.

"Hi." Tamping down the surge of hope that had accompanied her arrival, Kerry reminded herself to remain logical. That Sasha was standing in her brother's backyard was nothing short of a miracle, but nothing had truly changed between them. "How…how is Arthur?"

"Still in the hospital, but he's healing well. Thanks."

She looked so nervous, and Kerry wanted nothing more than to comfort her. Even though that wasn't her place, and never would be. "Why are you here, Sasha?" she asked instead.

"To apologize to you." When Sasha ducked her head, her long, lustrous hair shimmered in the sunlight. "I'm sorry, Kerry. I treated you so poorly."

"You didn't. You don't have anything to apologize for."

"I do. I was too focused on maintaining my own image to think about how it must have felt for you to be ignored and marginalized every time we were together in public."

Kerry's chest ached at the note of self-loathing in Sasha's voice. "Please, stop. You're being too hard on yourself. I knew the stakes. I walked into our relationship with open eyes."

"I don't accept those stakes any longer." Chin jutting out defiantly, Sasha crossed her arms beneath her breasts. "Yesterday, I renounced my place in the succession."

Kerry couldn't believe what she'd just heard. As her legs wobbled, she sank onto her knees to maintain her balance. "Excuse me?"

"It has to be ratified by Parliament and approved by the nations in the Commonwealth. But I can't imagine they'll object."

"But..." Feeling dizzy, Kerry gripped the edge of the roof with both hands. This was more than just about the throne. Sasha was talking about giving up her place in her family. "I object! Why are you doing this?"

"Because being in that line makes it impossible to be myself. I'm so tired of pretending."

The current of fatigue in her voice was palpable. "Why do you have to pretend? Don't you think your people would accept you for who you are, and accept you as their princess?"

"I don't know. My father certainly doesn't think so." After a moment's reflection, Sasha offered up a wan smile. "I'll be making an announcement about my renunciation in a press conference at Clarence House tomorrow. Will you stand next to me?"

"Will I..." Kerry's voice trailed off as she blinked in utter disbelief. "What are you saying, exactly?"

"What I'm saying, exactly, is that I love you." Her smile grew wider. "Which felt really quite wonderful to say out loud, actually."

"You love me." Kerry's ears were ringing, and much to her mortification, tears blurred her vision. Swiping her wrist across her eyes, she desperately tried to focus. "Are you sure?"

"Am I *sure*?" Sasha belted out that hearty laugh that Kerry had found so endearing all those months ago. "Oh, yes. I'm certain. In fact, right now, it's about the only thing I'm sure of. I love you, and I want you to come back to the UK with me."

Like the sun going behind a cloud, dismay suddenly crowded out Kerry's joy. "But my scholarship. I don't have it anymore."

"I know." Sasha's hands clenched into fists. "I'm so sorry for what my father did. I want to force the Rhodes Trust to see reason and reinstate you. But I don't know whether I have that kind of influence."

"I suppose it's worth a try." Kerry wondered what Mary Spencer would do if Sasha approached her. Would she be persuaded, despite the King's displeasure?

"Does that mean that you'll return with me?"

"Yes." The simple syllable had never tasted so good. "Yes. I'll come back with you. Scholarship or not, I refuse to give you up."

When Sasha twirled in a celebratory pirouette, Kerry laughed out loud. "Give me a second, and I'll come down."

"You'd better. Our flight leaves in just under six hours."

"Sure of yourself, were you?" Kerry picked up the hammer and crossbar and tucked them into her tool belt before reaching for the nails. "Just let me clean up and I'll be right there. Don't disappear."

"I most certainly won't."

As she worked quickly to gather her supplies, Kerry felt as though she was in shock. Sasha Carlisle was standing in her brother's backyard and had just proclaimed that she loved her. Surreptitiously, she pinched herself. Amazing. This was no dream.

"O, Romeo, Romeo," Sasha quipped from below. "Wherefore art thou, Romeo?"

Kerry laughed again. She simply couldn't believe it. Sasha had come for her—all the way across the Atlantic—and was quoting *Romeo and Juliet* in her backyard. Warmth spread through her chest. "To be honest, I don't think the situation is quite that dire. Our families aren't trying to kill each other."

Sasha appeared to mull this over. "Not yet, anyway."

"It wouldn't be much of a contest. Yours has access to much more firepower."

She huffed a sigh and put her hands on her hips. "Here you've gone and taken my words literally, when all I wanted to do was to impress you with my knowledge of Shakespeare."

"You don't have to try to impress me," Kerry said, hoping Sasha could hear the earnestness in her words. "I find you completely irresistible."

"You have no idea how grateful I am for that. Now will you please come down from there? Carefully? If you break your neck now, you will absolutely spoil my plans."

Not trusting the steadiness of her own legs, Kerry took extra care in descending the ladder. Once her feet were back on solid ground, she turned to face Sasha and swallowed hard. Only two feet separated them. So close, Kerry ached with the need to touch her. But she was a grimy mess.

"What plans would those be?"

Sasha stepped forward, slipped two fingers through the hammer loop at Kerry's waist, and gently pulled their bodies together. The fragrance of her scent and the promise in her eyes threatened to completely overwhelm Kerry's reason.

"But I'm filth—"

Just as she had on the first night they met, Sasha pressed two fingertips to Kerry's mouth. Sliding her hand around to the back of Kerry's neck, Sasha pulled her down. Instantly, Kerry was lost in the incomparable softness of lips that moved tenderly against hers in a kiss equal parts worship and reclamation. When it finally ended, Kerry brought her fingertips to Sasha's face, tracing the arc of her delicate cheekbones with both thumbs.

"I love you."

Sasha's smile was as brilliant as the sunlight. "And I love you." Her eyes dropped, and she began to trace Kerry's waistband with one finger—back and forth, back and forth. The movement was utterly distracting, but Kerry didn't think she meant it that way. Just as she was about to ask what was wrong, Sasha met her eyes again.

"Are you absolutely certain you want to join me? The media will have a field day with all this. I have to live in the spotlight, but you actually have a choice."

"I do." Kerry leaned down to brush a quick kiss across her lips, feeling the rightness of her decision in every cell of her body. "And I choose this. Us. Wherever you are, however bright or dark, I want to be standing next to you."

CHAPTER TWENTY-THREE

Sasha pillowed her head on Kerry's shoulder as the Bentley pulled away from the curb. It was just past ten o'clock in the morning, and she had asked the driver to take them directly to Clarence House. When Kerry began to trace gentle patterns just above her knee, Sasha cuddled closer.

"You must be so tired," Kerry murmured, "after two transatlantic flights in the space of twenty-four hours."

She had managed to sleep for much of their return trip, but she was still bone weary. Her body's internal rhythm had been completely derailed—first by her insomnia over the past several days, and then by the quick changes in time zones.

"I'm exhausted," she admitted. "Once you left England, I barely slept."

Kerry kissed the top of her head. "May I hold you while you sleep tonight?"

The solicitous question sent a shiver down Sasha's spine. Such a simple request, and yet so powerful. For as long as she had been aware of her position in the world, Sasha had felt wanted. But Kerry was the first person to make her feel truly cherished.

"Please do."

Sasha stared out the window as the cityscape flashed by. The contours of London were so familiar, but today she was seeing them through new eyes. She rested her hand on Kerry's thigh and felt the flicker of powerful muscles beneath her palm. For the first time, she had a future to look forward to that was entirely her choice—entirely of her making. A future in which she would no longer be fighting herself. She had always thought of commitment as a set of chains, but now she knew the truth. By committing herself to Kerry, she would finally be free.

"You know, I told Arthur about you. Before he woke."

"You did?"

She nodded. "He's always been my closest confidante, and I finally poured my heart out to him, even though I knew he couldn't respond. That's when I realized what I needed to do—that I had to find you and apologize. And then find the strength to show the world who I really am."

Kerry brought their lips together. "You are beautiful. Inside and out."

"You make me feel that way. I want everyone to know that I'm not ashamed of any part of me."

As the car was waved through the front gates of Clarence House, Sasha sat up and examined her reflection in the mirror on the seatback in front of her. After touching up her lipstick and combing her fingers through her hair she squared her shoulders. "I'm ready."

"You look fantastic." Kerry paused to squeeze her hand. "You're sure this is what you want?"

"I am."

As the car slowed to a stop, she saw Darryl waiting beneath the awning over the side entrance. When she stepped out onto the gravel drive, he approached. "Your Royal Highness, your father the King has requested a word with you before the press conference begins. He's asked me to take you to him."

Sasha exchanged a glance with Kerry. She looked concerned. "Shall I wait?"

"No more hiding. I want to introduce you." Clasping their hands together, she turned back to Darryl. "Lead on."

But the further they proceeded into the winding corridors of Clarence House, the more anxious Sasha became. What did her father have up his sleeve? Had he found some way to bully her into abandoning her plan? Silently vowing to hold firm, she focused on taking slow, steady breaths. Kerry must have been able to sense her nerves, because she stroked her thumb over Sasha's knuckles in a soothing rhythm.

Just before they reached the designated press conference chamber, Darryl paused at a small door that opened onto a greenroom of sorts, where final preparations were often made to wardrobe or makeup before the beginning of a media event. "Here you are, ma'am."

Sasha took a deep breath, squeezed Kerry's hand, and led her inside. Her father was the sole occupant of the room, and he looked up from his phone when they entered. His expression was inscrutable as he slid it back inside his jacket pocket.

"Hello, Father." Sasha didn't wait for him to speak. This was her press conference, and she wanted to take the initiative. In every way. "Please allow me to introduce Rhodes scholar Kerry Donovan. The woman I love."

To his credit, he didn't flinch. But neither did he extend his hand. "Hello, Ms. Donovan."

"Good morning, Your Majesty." Kerry's voice was hoarse but didn't tremble. "I'm honored to meet you."

"Alexandra, I need to speak with you in private."

When Kerry began to move away, Sasha held her firmly in place. "Anything you'd like to say to me right now can be said in front of Kerry."

At first, it seemed he might argue. His eyes narrowed and his mouth tightened and he drew himself up to his full, formidable height. But then, apparently, he thought the better of it. "Very well. Alexandra, I don't want you to give this press conference."

"Why not?"

"Because it is unnecessary. You don't need to remove yourself from the line of succession. Your entire reason for doing so is moot. Arthur is healing well."

Sasha tried to hold back her irritation. For such an intelligent man, her father could be uncommonly dense. "I don't know how to convince you that my decision has nothing to do with anyone but myself. I fully intend to live in an open relationship with Kerry for…" She turned to meet Kerry's eyes and was warmed by the love and affection she could plainly see there. "As long as she'll have me, quite frankly. And it has been made very clear to me that I will not be free to do so unless I am no longer a princess."

His jaw clenched, but he refrained from snapping at her as he had always been so wont to do. "Over the past few days, I have had ample time for reflection while sitting at your brother's bedside. And I do not want to lose another of my children."

Taken aback, Sasha had no ready response or retort. Never, not once in her entire life, had she heard him speak in such emotional terms. "But you haven't lost Arthur. And you won't lose me, either."

"I will if I continue to push you away." He pinched the bridge of his nose before refocusing his tired eyes on her. "My advisors have encouraged me not to be myopic. Our country has new laws—laws that allow for you to create a civil union with another woman, should you so choose. In light of this provision, I would be the worst kind of hypocrite if I forced you out of the succession over your choice in... life partner."

Sasha couldn't believe what she was hearing. "I can't tell you how much that means."

He waved her words aside. "You and I have had an adversarial relationship for so long. I want that to change. I also realize change will not be easy. We are very different people, and each difficult in our own right. Although..." And here he offered a small smile. "I daresay our stubbornness makes us especially formidable."

For the first time since they had left the car, Sasha let go of Kerry's hand to embrace her father. He smelled the way he always had—of Trumper cologne and pipe smoke. "Thank you," she whispered fiercely. "I'll meet you half way, Father. I promise."

When she pulled away, he turned to Kerry. "Ms. Donovan, I owe you an apology for prematurely ending your tenure as a Rhodes scholar. I will ask the secretary of the trust to return your scholarship to you promptly."

"Thank you, Your Majesty." Kerry's tone radiated relief.

Sasha nearly embraced him again, but the stiffness of his body language seemed to indicate that another such a display would be unwelcome. He began to move toward the door.

"I will instruct Bloom to cancel the press conference, and—"

"Wait, please." Sasha hoped this wouldn't be a major disagreement now that they had finally reached détente. "I still intend to speak today, Father."

"About what, exactly?" he asked, clearly suspicious.

"The country has seen photographs of me with Kerry. I believe they deserve to know where we stand and that they should respect her rights as a private citizen."

For a moment, it seemed he might protest. And then, to Sasha's amazement, he inclined his head. "Very well."

She turned to Kerry. "Ready?"

"Whenever you are."

After bidding her father good-bye, Sasha briefly stroked Kerry's cheek. "Time to disturb the universe."

Her answering smile was brilliant. "I love you."

"And I love you. It's time they all knew it." She double-checked the alignment of her necklace. "Stay close to me," she murmured, before preceding her through the side door connected to the press room. It was filled with photographers and reporters who immediately quieted at her entrance. As she approached the mahogany podium set against the backdrop of Commonwealth flags, she felt nervous but not afraid. This was her moment—her chance to say everything in her heart. Everything that none of her father's speechwriters had ever put down on paper. When she faced the crowd, Sasha held up one hand and the hubbub subsided. A forest of microphones surrounded her, punctuated by telephoto lenses.

"Good morning, everyone. Thank you for being here." She looked at each camera in turn, imagining her audience. The majority of them thought her a spoiled brat. A few probably felt sorry for her. She didn't need to change their minds, but she did need them to see her for who she really was.

"Now that my brother is on the road to recovery, I am turning my attention to my own personal affairs, which, for some reason, you all seem to think are your business." She paused to let the dig sink in. "My primary purpose in speaking today is to introduce someone to you who has become a very important part of my life. Many of you may believe you already know her, but I can assure you that you do not." Sasha moved closer to Kerry, allowing their shoulders to brush. She felt so good. That incredible chemistry was just as strong as it had been at their first meeting, but now it was undergirded by love and respect and shared purpose.

"Kerry Donovan is not only the most intelligent person I know—she is also one of the most generous and compassionate individuals I've ever met. I love her. I am *in* love with her. And since she has forgiven me for abandoning her to your invasive and inappropriate scrutiny last week, I would venture to say that you'll be seeing much more of her in the future. I am not going to ask you to afford her the same courtesy you do me. I'm going to demand you do much better."

She paused for a moment to let the words sink in. "In addition to loving and supporting me, over the past several months, Kerry has helped me understand what it means to be honest. I don't need to tell you all that I have made quite a few mistakes. But the most significant of them all has been dishonesty. I haven't been forthright with you, and you deserve that from me, especially because of who I am. Honesty isn't always comfortable, and it isn't always pleasant. But it always sheds light—often on subjects that have languished too long in the dark.

"The honest truth is that I am a woman who loves another woman. I am also a British princess. Our great nation provides civil unions to citizens like me, for which I am very thankful. But there is still much progress to be made in a world in which hate crimes, school bullying, and discrimination in the workplace persist. These and other related issues must be resolved. And so I pledge to every gay, lesbian, bisexual, transgender, and intersex member of this Commonwealth that I shall be your champion in the years to come."

Camera shutters clicked and microphones rustled, but otherwise, the room was silent. Sasha spared a brief moment for exultation. Even the seasoned reporters were eating out of her hand.

"But Kerry's gentle lesson in honesty has extended far past the closet of my sexual orientation. She has also taught me not to be ashamed of my learning disability." A low murmur rose up from the throng, and she waited for it to die down before carrying on. "When I was seven, doctors diagnosed me with moderate dyslexia. I have tried to keep it hidden for years, because I was ashamed that a task as basic as reading was so difficult for me. But Kerry has helped me understand that I have nothing to be ashamed of. My brain simply works differently. By covering up my dyslexia, I have only helped to reinforce its stigma, and I won't be party to that any longer. Instead, you will see me ardently campaigning on behalf of the British Dyslexia Association in an effort to help children manage their condition within traditional education environments."

Sasha brought Kerry's hand to her lips and pressed a lingering kiss to her fingertips. "Speaking of education, Kerry is a Rhodes scholar. She is here to study and learn from one of the greatest institutions of higher education in this country. In the days to come, allow her to do her work. Respect her. Respect us. And please continue to pray for Arthur as he recovers." With a gentle tug at Kerry's hand, Sasha turned and walked toward the door. As soon as she found herself inside the greenroom, she slumped in exhaustion. Kerry shepherded her around a corner until they were out of the line of sight of the front door, then pulled her into an embrace.

"That was a very brave thing you just did," she said quietly. "Are you all right?"

Sasha allowed herself to be held. She rested her cheek on the lapel of Kerry's suit jacket and breathed her in, taking comfort in that knowledge that she would never have to hide their embrace again.

"I'm fine. Just a few nerves."

"You were so poised. So eloquent. Every word was perfect." Kerry's grip tightened momentarily. "I just fell in love with you all over again."

Sasha looked up to find Kerry's eyes bright with unshed tears. "Do you know what I enjoyed the most? Holding your hand in public."

Kerry laced their fingers together again. "Believe me when I say you can do that anytime you like."

"Why don't you plan to hold my hand as we walk back to the car, then?"

"Oh? We're not staying here?"

Sasha shook her head and began to move toward the door. "Now that you've been introduced to my father, I want you to meet the rest of my family."

❖

Less than an hour later, Sasha led Kerry down the pristine corridor toward her brother's room, eager to show each off to the other. Arthur had improved in leaps and bounds since regaining consciousness, and there was even talk that he would be discharged within a matter of days.

"May I see him, Robert?" she asked the nurse before he could so much as greet her.

"Certainly, Your Highness. Ms. Dunning is in with him at the moment."

"Oh, perfect." Aside from her siblings, there was no other person to whom she wanted to introduce Kerry more.

Despite her excitement, she opened the door to Arthur's room slowly, not wanting to startle him. She entered to the sight of him sitting up in bed, Ashleigh holding his hand. A broad smile lit up his face as soon as he saw her, and she felt relief at his ability to recognize her instantly.

"Hello, Artie," she said, unable to keep herself from mirroring his expression. "You're looking well today."

"I thought I told you—"

"Never to call you that. I know." She winked at him. "I'm sorry I didn't get to see you yesterday, but I had to run a quick errand to retrieve something I had very foolishly allowed to go missing." Looking over her shoulder, she beckoned Kerry into the room. "Arthur and Ashleigh, this is Kerry Donovan. My girlfriend."

As Ashleigh crossed the room, Kerry put out her hand, but Ashleigh ignored it and embraced her instead. "It's such a pleasure to meet you," she said.

"Likewise, Ashleigh. Sasha's told me so much about what a wonderful friend you've been to her."

Ashleigh released her and reached for Sasha's hands. "We just want her to be happy."

"I am," Sasha said, her voice suddenly quavering with emotion. "So happy."

Meanwhile, Kerry was regarding her brother. "You're looking very well, Your Royal Highness. Congratulations."

"Thank you," he said, his voice still hoarse from so many days on the ventilator. "And thank you for putting that smile on my sister's face."

Sasha began to move toward him, intending to give him a very careful hug, but he immediately waved her aside.

"Just a moment." He narrowed his eyes as he looked at Kerry. "Come closer, please."

Clearly puzzled by the request, Kerry moved a few feet nearer to the bed and stopped, but he continued to beckon.

"Closer still."

"Arthur—" Sasha began, but he shushed her.

"I'm trying to see it. Give me a moment."

She and Ashleigh shared a suddenly concerned glance. What was he referring to? Was he having some sort of relapse?

Only when Kerry was standing just a few feet away did he finally allow her to stop. After scrutinizing her carefully from head to foot and back, he squinted again. "I just don't see it."

"Arthur?" Sasha asked, trying not to betray her growing alarm. "See what?"

"You don't look like a bloke to me, Kerry."

At the jest, Sasha's trepidation faded and she exchanged an exasperated glance with Ashleigh. Even from his sickbed, Arthur was determined to keep them on their toes. When Kerry laughed, Sasha froze the moment in her head. Her brother and her lover, sharing a joke. Had she even dared to dream of such a moment?

"I don't think you were really expecting one, were you?" Kerry said, smiling as she looked between them.

"No, indeed." Arthur stretched out his hand toward her and grinned. "It's a pleasure and an honor. Welcome to the family."

EPILOGUE

S asha reclined on the lawn chair next to Ashleigh's, sipping a vodka tonic and enjoying the warm July afternoon from beneath the umbrella that sheltered them from the sun. It simply wouldn't do to get too much color on the day before her brother's wedding.

A family football match had sprung up on the adjacent lawn, which they were watching with quite a bit of interest seeing as Arthur and Kerry had found themselves on opposing sides. Various cousins rounded out the teams, and the King himself had seen fit to officiate the match. Sometimes, when Sasha reflected on how much had changed since the previous year, she could hardly believe she was living in the same reality.

It hadn't taken nearly as long for her father to warm to Kerry as Sasha had feared. After a few rather strained meetings, he had happened to overhear her chatting with Raymond Fletcher about some obscure architectural movement during the Victorian era. And just like that, the ice had thawed. "I like her intellectual rigor," he had later told Sasha gruffly.

The sound of Arthur calling for the ball turned her attention back to the lawn. When he received it, he moved quickly down the left flank of the makeshift pitch, toward the opposition's empty goal. It looked as though he might be unopposed until Sasha saw Kerry on a mad tear across the field, determined to intercept him. At the last moment, she slid for the ball and knocked it cleanly out of bounds. Arthur somersaulted dramatically forward onto the ground and lay there, clutching his ankle.

Ashleigh sat up with a start and pulled down her sunglasses to glare at Sasha. "If your girlfriend has injured him on the day before his wedding—"

"Are you mad? That was a clean tackle!" Sasha cut her off. "He's a dirty diver!"

"Well." Ashleigh crossed her arms. "Your father will sort it out properly. Look."

King Andrew had joined both players as Kerry offered her hand to Arthur. He made a big show of limping as she helped him to his feet and Sasha stood too, rolling her eyes.

"Quit those theatrics, you cheat!" she hollered, hands cupped around her mouth.

"What happened?" the King asked them.

"I'll tell him what happened," Sasha muttered beneath her breath.

"She took me out," Arthur panted.

"Kerry?"

"You saw it, Your Majesty." No matter how many times he had told her to call him Andrew at private gatherings, she had never managed to do so. "You be the judge."

He looked between them, then smiled and shook his head at Arthur. "Your sister is right, son. That was a flop if ever I saw one. Free kick to Kerry."

Sasha turned to regard Ashleigh with a triumphant grin. "See?"

As Ashleigh huffed out a sigh and settled back into her chair, Kerry beckoned her teammates down the field. Her kick was beautiful—a long, arcing ball that was easy pickings for one of the cousins, who headed it down between the cones.

"Nicely played," her father called as the team huddled in congratulations. "Now, we'd best get cleaned up. It's nearly time for tea."

As Kerry and Arthur approached them, Sasha pushed her sunglasses to the top of her head.

"Admit it, Arthur. You dove."

Arthur grinned and clapped Kerry on the back. "All right. I confess. I tried to get one past the old man, but apparently, he's still too sharp."

Kerry perched on the edge of Sasha's chair, smiling broadly. "Hi."

"Hi." Even after many months, Sasha's heart fluttered whenever they were close. "You were brilliant."

Kerry shrugged. "I was all right."

Suddenly, Ashleigh squealed. "Arthur! You're dripping sweat on me!"

Sasha reached up to pull Kerry close, lips caressing the shell of her ear. "They must not have very good sex," she whispered. "I never mind when you drip sweat on me."

Kerry's shoulders shook as she tried not to betray her laughter. "Hush! That's your brother you're talking about—the future King of England!"

"I'm just saying."

"Just saying what?" Ashleigh looked over at them suspiciously.

"She was just saying how much she loves me," Kerry said impishly. "Right, Sash?"

"I do." Arching one eyebrow, she looked up into the bright blue eyes of her beloved. "How do you like the sound of that?"

About the Author

Nell Stark is the Chair of English, Philosophy, and Religious Studies at a college in the SUNY system. She and her partner live, write, and parent a rambunctious toddler just a stone's throw from the historic Stonewall Inn in New York City. For more information, visit www.nellstark.com.

Books Available from Bold Strokes Books

The Princess Affair by Nell Stark. Rhodes Scholar Kerry Donovan arrives at Oxford ready to focus on her studies, but her life and her priorities are thrown into chaos when she catches the eye of Her Royal Highness Princess Sasha. (978-1-60282-858-2)

The Chase by Jesse J. Thoma. When Isabelle Rochat's life is threatened, she receives the unwelcome protection and attention of bounty hunter Holt Lasher who vows to keep Isabelle safe at all costs. (978-1-60282-859-9)

The Lone Hunt by L.L. Raand. In a world where humans and praeterns conspire for the ultimate power, violence is a way of life... and death. A Midnight Hunters novel. (978-1-60282-860-5)

The Supernatural Detective by Crin Claxton. Tony Carson sees dead people. With a drag queen for a spirit guide and a devastatingly attractive herbalist for a client, she's about to discover the spirit world can be a very dangerous world indeed. (978-1-60282-861-2)

Beloved Gomorrah by Justine Saracen. Undersea artists creating their own City on the Plain uncover the truth about Sodom and Gomorrah, whose "one righteous man" is a murderer, rapist, and conspirator in genocide. (978-1-60282-862-9)

Cut to the Chase by Lisa Girolami. Careful and methodical author Paige Randolph falls for brash and wild Hollywood actress, Avalon Randolph, but can these opposites find a happy middle ground in a town that never lives in the middle? (978-1-60282-783-7)

More Than Friends by Erin Dutton. Evelyn Fisher thinks she has the perfect role model for a long-term relationship, until her best friends, Kendall and Melanie, split up and all three women must reevaluate their lives and their relationships. (978-1-60282-784-4)

Every Second Counts by D. Jackson Leigh. Every second counts in Bridgette LeRoy's desperate mission to protect her heart and stop Marc Ryder's suicidal return to riding rodeo bulls. (978-1-60282-785-1)

Dirty Money by Ashley Bartlett. Vivian Cooper and Reese DiGiovanni just found out that falling in love is hard. It's even harder when you're running for your life. (978-1-60282-786-8)

Sea Glass Inn by Karis Walsh. When Melinda Andrews commissions a series of mosaics by Pamela Whitford for her new inn, she doesn't expect to be more captivated by the artist than by the paintings. (978-1-60282-771-4)

The Awakening: A Sisters of Spirits novel by Yvonne Heidt. Sunny Skye has interacted with spirits her entire life, but when she runs into Officer Jordan Lawson during a ghost investigation, she discovers more than just facts in a missing girl's cold case file. (978-1-60282-772-1)

Murphy's Law by Yolanda Wallace. No matter how high you climb, you can't escape your past. (978-1-60282-773-8)

Blacker Than Blue by Rebekah Weatherspoon. Threatened with losing her first love to a powerful demon, vampire Cleo Jones is willing to break the ultimate law of the undead to rebuild the family she has lost. (978-1-60282-774-5)

Another 365 Days by KE Payne. Clemmie Atkins is back, and her life is more complicated than ever! Still madly in love with her girlfriend, Clemmie suddenly finds her life turned upside down with distractions, confessions, and the return of a familiar face... (978-1-60282-775-2)

Silver Collar by Gill McKnight. Werewolf Luc Garoul is outlawed and out of control, but can her family track her down before a sinister predator gets there first? Fourth in the Garoul series. (978-1-60282-764-6)

The Dragon Tree Legacy by Ali Vali. For Aubrey Tarver time hasn't dulled the pain of losing her first love Wiley Gremillion, but she has to set that aside when her choices put her life and her family's lives in real danger. (978-1-60282-765-3)

The Midnight Room by Ronica Black. After a chance encounter with the mysterious and brooding Lillian Gray in the "midnight room" of The Griffin, a local lesbian bar, confident and gorgeous Audrey McCarthy learns that her bad-girl behavior isn't bulletproof. (978-1-60282-766-0)

Dirty Sex by Ashley Bartlett. Vivian Cooper and twins Reese and Ryan DiGiovanni stole a lot of money and the guy they took it from wants it back. Like now. (978-1-60282-767-7)

The Storm by Shelley Thrasher. Rural East Texas. 1918. War-weary Jaq Bergeron and marriage-scarred musician Molly Russell try to salvage love from the devastation of the war abroad and natural disasters at home. (978-1-60282-780-6)

Crossroads by Radclyffe. Dr. Hollis Monroe specializes in short-term relationships but when she meets pregnant mother-to-be Annie Colfax, fate brings them together at a crossroads that will change their lives forever. (978-1-60282-756-1)

Beyond Innocence by Carsen Taite. When a life is on the line, love has to wait. Doesn't it? (978-1-60282-757-8)

Heart Block by Melissa Brayden. Socialite Emory Owen and struggling single mom Sarah Matamoros are perfectly suited for each other but face a difficult time when trying to merge their contrasting worlds and the people in them. If love truly exists, can it find a way? (978-1-60282-758-5)

Pride and Joy by M.L. Rice. Perfect Bryce Montgomery is her parents' pride and joy, but when they discover that their daughter is a lesbian, her world changes forever. (978-1-60282-759-2)

Ladyfish by Andrea Bramhall. Finn's escape to the Florida Keys leads her straight into the arms of scuba diving instructor Oz as she fights for her freedom, their blossoming love…and her life! (978-1-60282-747-9)

Spanish Heart by Rachel Spangler. While on a mission to find herself in Spain, Ren Molson runs the risk of losing her heart to her tour guide, Lina Montero. (978-1-60282-748-6)

Love Match by Ali Vali. When Parker "Kong" King, the number one tennis player in the world, meets commercial pilot Captain Sydney Parish, sparks fly—but not from attraction. They have the summer to see if they have a love match. (978-1-60282-749-3)

One Touch by L.T. Marie. A romance writer and a travel agent come together at their high school reunion, only to find out that the memory of that one touch never fades. (978-1-60282-750-9)

The Raid by Lee Lynch. Before Stonewall, having a drink with friends or your girl could mean jail. Would these women and men still have family, a job, a place to live after…The Raid? (978-1-60282-753-0)

The You Know Who Girls: Freshman Year by Annameekee Hesik. As they begin freshman year, Abbey Brooks and her best friend, Kate, pinkie swear they'll keep away from the lesbians in Gila High, but Abbey already suspects she's one of those you-know-who girls herself and slowly learns who her true friends really are. (978-1-60282-754-7)

Month of Sundays by Yolanda Wallace. Love doesn't always happen overnight; sometimes it takes a month of Sundays. (978-1-60282-739-4)

Jacob's War by C.P. Rowlands. ATF Special Agent Allison Jacob's task force is in the middle of an all-out war, from the streets to the boardrooms of America. Small business owner Katie Blackburn is the latest victim who accidentally breaks it wide open, but she may break AJ's heart at the same time. (978-1-60282-740-0)

The Pyramid Waltz by Barbara Ann Wright. Princess Katya Nar Umbriel wants a perfect romance, but her Fiendish nature and duties to the crown mean she can never tell the truth—until she meets Starbride, a woman who gets to the heart of every secret, even if it will be the death of her. (978-1-60282-741-7)

The Secret of Othello by Sam Cameron. Florida teen detectives Steven and Denny risk their lives to search for a sunken NASA satellite—but under the waves, no one can hear you scream... (978-1-60282-742-4)

Finding Bluefield by Elan Barnehama. Set in the backdrop of Virginia and New York and spanning the years 1960–1982, *Finding Bluefield* chronicles the lives of Nicky Stewart, Barbara Philips, and their son, Paul, as they struggle to define themselves as a family. (978-1-60282-744-8)